It Ends
with Revelations

D0339282

Also available

The New Moon with the Old
The Town in Bloom

It Ends with Revelations

Dodie Smith

corsair

CORSAIR

This edition published in Great Britain in 2012 by Corsair

3 5 7 9 10 8 6 4 2

A CIP catalogue record for this book
is available from the British Library.

ISBN 978-1-78033-302-1

Printed and bound in Great Britain by
CPI Group (UK) Ltd, Croydon CR0 4YY

Papers used by Corsair are from well-managed forests
and other responsible sources

MIX
Paper from
responsible sources
FSC® C104740

Corsair
is an imprint of
Little, Brown Book Group
Carmelite House
50 Victoria Embankment
London EC4Y 0DZ

An Hachette UK Company
www.hachette.co.uk

www.littlebrown.co.uk

LORD ILLINGWORTH: The book of life begins with a man and a woman in a garden .

MRS ALLONBY: It ends with Revelations.

– Oscar Wilde, *A Woman of No Importance*

Contents

⚜ 1 ⚜

A Double Row of Shaving Brushes

After she had unpacked in the old hotel bedroom Jill leaned out of one of its two tall windows and came face to face with a lion. It was a gilded lion, presumably made of plaster, and she had seen it on entering the hotel less than an hour ago. Still, its sudden proximity startled her. Then she smiled, both at her own absurdity and in response to its ferocious grin, looked past it, and located the pillared portico of the theatre. It stood, as she had dimly remembered, on the opposite side of the gracefully curving street, only a short walk away. Soon she would stroll along and call for Miles. He had gone straight there from the station, ostensibly just to look at his dressing room; but with a new play about to open he was liable to hang around indefinitely – a habit which, she suspected, must have annoyed some directors, though none of them had felt they could ask their star performer to get out from under foot. He

1

would undoubtedly want to spend the evening watching the scenery going up and being lit, so she was determined to get him back in time for an early dinner. But there was no hurry; it wasn't yet six. She continued to look out on Spa Street basking in the August sunshine.

It must be twelve years since she had last seen it. She and the least important members of the company had then stayed at a cheap boarding house in the new, ugly part of the beautiful old town, quite a long walk from the theatre. Had it rained every day of that dreary week? Certainly her last memory of Spa Street was of seeing it in a downpour, looking utterly gloomy. And not only the rain had been responsible for the gloom. The chestnuts, then, had been as high as the houses, their branches touching the upper storeys. The shop windows were so shadowed that most of them had their lights on even in the morning. She had appreciated the beauty of the street but found the total effect infinitely sad.

Now the chestnuts had been pollarded; some years ago, she guessed, as the new shoots were already tall enough to make a good balance with the sturdy trunks – not that one could see the shoots, because the foliage was so thick. The trees were now of uniform height and almost uniform shape; fat trunks were surmounted by fat, rounded foliage. They were charming and also somehow comic, reminding her of Miles's shaving brush, with its bulbous ivory handle and domed brush of badger hair. She glanced through the open bathroom door – yes, the proportions were just the same. A whole street with a double row of shaving brushes,

2

absurd perhaps but undoubtedly cheerful. And one could now see the houses clearly; they were, she judged, almost uniformly eighteenth century.

She would call for Miles now, but first she would get out of her town suit; the day was much warmer than when she had left London. She changed into a grey linen dress and then went downstairs by way of a corridor, subduedly resplendent with dark red carpet, and a handsome oak staircase. Nothing in this solid old hotel seemed to have been spoilt. She was glad she had remembered it and brought Miles here, instead of going to the new station hotel with most of the company.

Spa Street seemed almost deserted, surprisingly so, with a Festival Week approaching. But she had gathered it was to be only a small festival, mainly of local interest, its *raison d'être* the opening of the rejuvenated old theatre; remembering its dressing rooms, she trusted the rejuvenation had extended back-stage. The shops certainly looked festival-minded and their displays were attractive but there was nothing she wanted; a pity, rather, as spending money here would be like making a present to that ill-dressed girl under a dripping umbrella who, when window-gazing here, had wanted almost everything. Poor wretch, with those two quite awful years ahead of her before she married Miles. But one could, it seemed, while basking in one's happy present, be a little wistful for one's unhappy past . . . and not merely wistful for one's youth. Young Jill Morrison, with all her miseries, would not have found Mrs Miles Quentin's particular brand of contentment enviable. Well, young Jill,

3

as always, would have been wrong. Having decided this, her successor continued to stroll along . . . contentedly.

She had almost reached the theatre when she saw, opposite to it, a café that she instantly remembered. Here she had several times drunk that solace of life on tour, morning coffee, and once bought a quarter of a pound of superb chocolates which had done duty as lunch. It occurred to her now that a box of chocolates would make a good first-night present for the little boy in the play. On Monday morning she would have to cope with telegrams for all the company and flowers for all the women, so it would be as well to buy the chocolates now; the café was still open. She went in.

Through an archway she could see the white-alcoved tea room, almost empty by now though the smell of toast lingered. The only customer besides herself in the front shop was a slight, dark-haired man who was talking across the counter to the elderly assistant. He broke off the conversation as Jill entered, as if releasing the assistant to serve her. Jill smiled her thanks and approached the counter, on which were several boxes of chocolates, one of which had a view of Spa Street, including the theatre, on its lid. She picked the box up.

'I'm sorry, madam,' said the assistant, 'but this gentleman's just bespoken that for his little daughter's birthday tomorrow.'

Jill hastily put the box down. 'And you haven't another like it, or anything which has the theatre on it? I need a present for a little boy who'll be playing there.'

4

'Then of course he must have this box,' said the man, smiling. 'It wouldn't mean a thing to my daughter; she's known Spa Street all her life. In fact, she might prefer a plain box; her taste is sometimes austere. But I think I'll take this one.' He chose a box with a black cat on the lid. 'The cat has a distinct look of her.'

'Well, if you're sure you don't mind,' said Jill.

'Absolutely. I only need a token present, really. She likes money for her real present, to spend on books. You're Mrs Miles Quentin, aren't you? I was introduced to you once, in a theatre foyer, but you wouldn't remember. I'm Geoffrey Thornton.'

'Why, of course.' She didn't recall meeting him but she could, now, place him. 'This is your constituency, isn't it? I saw you on television, the night of your victory.'

'Hardly a victory. This is one of the safest seats in England.'

'But he did increase the majority,' said the assistant, beaming.

'A case of local boy makes good. My grandmother lived for seventy years up in Queen's Crescent and I was a regular visitor.'

'Used to come in here for ice creams when he was a schoolboy,' said the assistant.

'And we had a nice little arrangement about credit.'

'They ended up on his grandmother's account.'

Waiting while the chocolates were packed, Jill and Thornton talked casually. He, too, was staying at the Lion – 'Not as many bathrooms as at the station hotel but the

5

food's better.' He spoke of the Festival – 'I shouldn't think there'll ever be another. It's going to cost the town a packet.' He enquired about the play, to which he and his daughters would be coming on the first night – 'And I hope you and your husband will be at the Civic Reception afterwards. The Assembly Rooms are worth seeing.' Jill said they were looking forward to it. (Miles would groan but Miles would go – and end by enjoying himself.) She mentioned having played at the theatre – 'That is, I was an overworked assistant-stage manager – I never acted except as an understudy. I was only too glad to retire when I married Miles.'

'I admire his work very much,' said Thornton, and spoke of performances he had seen Miles give. While she listened with pleasure, she decided that Thornton looked rather older than he had seemed on television; perhaps excitement at winning the by-election had then lent him a touch of boyishness. She now assessed him as being perhaps forty. He had clean-cut, regular features and was quite good-looking but in a most unspectacular way. His eyes, even when smiling, were somehow shadowy; indeed, his whole personality seemed to her a little muted, veiled. Being slim, he looked tall, but she guessed him to be not more than five foot ten; his eyes were only an inch or so above her own eye level.

The chocolates, packed and paid for, were handed across the counter. Thornton, taking both boxes, asked if she was going back to the hotel. She decided she was. It was still, perhaps, rather early to rout Miles out of the

6

theatre, and she quite liked talking to this courteous, under-stated man who was the first Member of Parliament she had ever met. For that matter, how seldom did she meet *anyone* unconnected with the theatre.

As they strolled back along Spa Street she told him that the pollarded chestnuts had reminded her of shaving brushes. He laughed and said it was a perfect comparison – 'But, believe me, the pollarding was no laughing matter. My grandmother said it would kill her – and then lived on five years, to reach the age of ninety. I'll admit the poor trees did look wretched for a year or two.'

'I love them now,' said Jill. 'What a charming town this is.'

'To me, it's the most delightful of all English spa towns; not as fine as Bath but so much more intimate. Everything here is on such a delicate scale.'

She commented on the quietness of the street.

'That's because all through traffic has to use the bypass and no parking's allowed here. Cars have to set people down at shops and then go to the car park – which exists by courtesy of a Blitz that knocked some houses down but obligingly left the screening chestnuts. Our shops are doing the Festival proud, aren't they?'

'They certainly are.' She glanced at a window full of very floral hats. 'Will people here buy those – and wear them?'

'They will indeed. Mainly old ladies, but they'll look prettier in them than without them, old ladies being apt to have thinning hair. Do you ever wear a hat?'

'Only when occasion positively demands it. Then I wear one with a brim wide enough to balance my height. I strive for something with what's known as "a good line". The young eye it with derision and old gentlemen go into ecstasies over it. Such hats are hard to find now.'

'You can find them here. Shall I show you where? It's only just across the road.'

She went willingly, faintly surprised that he should be interested in hats. He took her into a narrow, glass-roofed arcade of very small two-storeyed shops. They walked on old flagstones to the far end and as they approached it he said, 'Perhaps they'll let me down today, but they usually have one superb hat in the window. This was where my grandmother bought her hats. She was a beautiful woman who dressed beautifully until the end of her life. I came here with her to choose a hat when she was eighty-nine.'

'They haven't let you down,' said Jill.

The hat, alone in its grandeur, was poised on an old-fashioned hat-stand against grey velvet curtains. It was of black straw, trimmed only by a black velvet ribbon. What constituted its elegance? The relation of the large brim to the small crown? (How she loathed large, top-heavy crowns.) The slight droop of the brim, which looked so casual but wasn't? The exact placing of the ribbon?

She asked, 'Is *that* doomed to be worn by an old lady?'

'Almost certainly, unless you buy it.'

'I'm not sure I have the arrogance. Unless one *is* an old lady – oh, I can see her so clearly: tall but rather bent, in

8

such a *graceful* dress – unless one's old enough, well, not to compete, that's a beauty's hat.'

'I'll only say I think you could wear it.'

'Well, thank you. But I wasn't fishing. It's just that I was so excessively plain as a girl that I've never got used to being just a little less plain. I seemed to improve when my hair turned grey.'

'Not exactly grey, is it? More like dark hair lightly powdered. I've seen the same effect in eighteenth-century portraits.'

'No doubt it'll soon get on with its job of turning white, but it's been this peculiar dust-colour for years now. I must bring Miles to look at that hat.'

They walked back along the arcade, their footsteps sounding on the flagstones, and out into Spa Street. They were now only two chestnuts from the Lion. They recrossed the road and went in.

Thornton, glancing into the lounge, said, 'My daughters are there. Have you time to meet them?'

'Yes, I'd like to.'

He left the chocolates at the desk and escorted her in. Two girls rose with an alacrity which suggested extreme courtesy. The elder – Jill guessed her to be about seventeen – was unusually pretty, with wide-apart blue eyes and straight fair hair falling to her shoulders. The younger girl was small and dark, and obviously the daughter of whom Thornton had said the cat on the chocolate box had a look. The line of her mouth and the slant of her eyes were cat-like, even two little quirks in her short hair were suggestive

9

of cats' ears. There was no resemblance to a starry-eyed kitten, only to a small, thin, and highly alert young cat. The girls were dressed with fashionable teenage casualness and yet managed to look both tidy and scrupulously clean.

Thornton was introducing them as Robinetta, known as Robin, and Katherine, known as Kit – 'And this, my dears, is Mrs Miles Quentin, with whom I've cleverly scraped an acquaintance.'

'Marvellous,' said Kit. 'Will you introduce us to your husband, Mrs Quentin?'

'I will, indeed. Do you collect autographs?'

'Well, I don't – but I could,' said Kit, politely. 'Oh, *yes*. If Mr Quentin will start me off I'll rush round the Civic Reception and collect the local worthies. They'll like that, won't they, Father?'

'More than probably,' said Thornton, placing a chair for Jill. 'These two are my very determined helpers; in fact I rather think they got me nominated. Selection committees now expect to see the wives of would-be candidates. I'm a widower so my dear daughters wrote and asked if they could be seen instead of a wife. I gather they covered themselves with glory.'

'It was even suggested we should make speeches,' said Robin. 'We thought that would be a bit too much, but we canvassed terrifically. Mainly preaching to the converted except in the New Town – but even there they sort of bore with us.'

'You said "sort of", Robin.' Kit turned to Jill. 'We're trying to oust "sort of", "I mean" and "you know" from

10

our vocabularies. "You know" is the worst – people never *stop* saying it in television interviews.'

'It's a sort of – there I go – plea for understanding,' said Thornton. 'An effort to get people onto one's side. The absurd thing is that foreigners, trying to speak English, use it all the time. They think it's idiomatic – as by now, it is.'

Robin said, 'Actually – another word we should oust – I'm more worried about our accents than our vocabularies. We heard ourselves on a tape recorder and we *mince* deplorably. I was shocked to hear myself say "noe" for no.

'You should talk to my husband about that. He has a hatred of what he calls pinched vowels.'

'Can we meet him very soon, please?' said Kit.

'Of course. But he may be rather busy until the play gets going.'

'Ah, yes. And he won't care to be worried by pushing children.'

'Speak for yourself,' said Robin. 'I'm no pushing child.'

'Well, I shan't be, after tomorrow – that is, not a child. I consider fifteen maturity. Anyway, I've left school,' she informed Jill, 'and with deep thankfulness. There were compulsory games. Still, they did teach one to read and write.'

Thornton said, 'Your great-grandmother taught you to read when you were three.'

'Four. It was she who could read at three; she said lots of Victorian children could. I proved something of a laggard.'

Jill said to Thornton, 'Don't you mind her leaving school so early?'

'Frankly, no. She'll have private tuition at subjects that interest her. Anyway, when these girls decide on a course of action I seldom oppose them. You might not think it on a first meeting but they're outstandingly sensible.'

'Sounds stodgy,' said Kit. 'Couldn't you call us brilliant?'

'Well, not when you're there. But I'll admit you're not dimwits.'

'He's a mite besotted about us,' said Robin, 'but as we're besotted about him too, it works out quite well. Have you any children, Mrs Quentin?'

'No, alas.' The 'alas' was a tribute to the Thornton girls. She did not usually hanker for children, but it had flashed through her mind that she would have liked them as daughters.

Kit, looking through to the hall, said, 'Oh, there's Mr Quentin. Goodness, he's even larger than I'd remembered.'

'But not fat,' said Jill, a shade defensively.

'Oh, not a bit fat. Just wonderfully tall – and wide. Could we meet him now, do you think – just for a moment? Oh, he's getting his key. Could we catch him before he goes up?'

'Certainly not,' said Thornton. 'He must be given the chance *not* to meet us.'

'There's no fear of that. But he just may want me to hear him in his part before dinner.' Jill could think of few things less likely as he had been word perfect for ten days. But it seemed a tactful excuse.

12

'I quite understand,' said Kit. 'Sorry that pushing child got loose again.'

'I'll see how he feels. But don't count on his coming down now.'

Still, he might be willing to. He liked meeting people. And he would, almost certainly, like the Thorntons, especially the little black cat. Jill followed him upstairs.

⚓ 2 ⚓

The Involving Misfortunes of
Cyril (Doug) Digby

She found him leaning out of the open window. He turned as she opened the door.

'Have you seen this preposterous lion?'

'Yes, just before I went out. I meant to call for you but I got involved with . . .' She told him about the Thorntons, concluding by saying, 'They're in the lounge now, if you happen to feel like coming down.'

He said they sounded nice but he didn't want to meet them at the moment. 'I rather need to talk to you.'

'Something wrong at the theatre?'

'Peter's being difficult. I'd like you to know about it before you see him tonight. Then you can support me.'

'All right. Lie down and rest while we talk.'

He took his jacket off and lay on his bed – so weightily that she wondered if he *was* getting fat. But after sneaking

14

a glance at him, before she lay down on her own bed, she decided there was no need to worry. He was merely, as Kit had said, wonderfully tall and wide.

He swept back his thick, fair hair and lay staring at the ceiling, saying, 'Why did I ever do this play?'

'We both know the answer to that one. You did it as a kindness to a new management, a young author and a boy actor.'

'Not entirely. I enjoyed doing the play on television and it really was a great success.'

She refrained from telling him that successful television plays could seldom be turned into successful stage plays; it was a fact he knew quite as well as she did.

'Anyway, it isn't going to prove a kindness to anyone,' he went on gloomily. 'Frank Ashton's going to lose his shirt, the author's going to be torn to pieces by the critics; and as for young Cyril, I'm beginning to wonder if he'll ever even open.'

'Surely you can't change him now, with the London first night next week?'

'There may not *be* a London first night – in fact, I'm not sure Cyril will keep the curtain up here, unless Peter comes to his senses. Just imagine, the boy makes a huge success on television, starts rehearsals in a blaze of glory, is praised, coaxed and directed with exemplary patience by Peter, who's sure he can get a great performance out of him. Well, he can't, because Cyril hasn't an iota of stage technique. So Peter gradually withdraws all approval, then gets irritable, and finally takes a real dislike to the kid.'

'You told me you saw this coming.'

'How right I was. But Peter's only this afternoon admitted his full reason for it. You know the boy was supposed to be fifteen, which means that he's free to act without a licence? Well, he looks so much younger that Peter got suspicious and asked him to bring a birth certificate; and, after some delay, Cyril did. It turns out that he's *eighteen*, and his name's not Cyril, it's Douglas. And just when Peter had assimilated this he noticed that there was a black line at the roots of Cyril's hair.'

'So instead of being an attractive, fair-haired little boy, he's a peroxided midget'?'

'Well, that's what Peter feels. But there was one thing he liked about that birth certificate: the name Douglas. He thinks "Doug Digby" will be a tougher, more with-it name than Cyril Digby. And he thinks Cyril will *look* more with-it if he has his hair dyed black – and I gather Cyril doesn't want to, or to be called Doug. And now Peter's decided to cut a lot of Cyril's lines and change some of his positions so that the focus of interest is more on *me*. And this, God help us, is to be rushed through at tomorrow's dress rehearsal.'

'I must say it sounds tricky.'

'Tricky? It's insane. The child couldn't possibly cope.'

She was silent for a moment. Then she said tentatively, 'He's not a child if he's eighteen. And would a few cuts and changes of position be so very difficult for him?'

'There's more to it than that. He'd lose all confidence. Take the end of the second act, when the boy admits he's an imposter. On television that scene was treated naturalistically, with normal lighting. Peter's planned a stunty bit of direction with most of the stage in darkness, me a hulking figure with my back to the audience, and Cyril up on the stairs brilliantly lit by a shaft of light – presumably coming direct from heaven. Well, now we're to be realistically lit, with me in the best position. Cyril's big speech is to be cut down and he's to make it shame-facedly instead of hurling it defiantly, and the audience is to watch *my* reactions. He'll not only feel his great scene's being taken from him, he'll guess why it's being taken – and just when he needs building up, not smashing down. That scene must be *handed* to him.'

'I wonder how many stars would feel that about the end of a second act.'

He grinned. 'Well, I did think Master Peter's original admiration for Cyril was going a bit far. But his instincts were right. He saw that the television director built up Cyril's importance and that it worked, made the play more unusual. It may not work so well in the theatre but we shan't help Cyril's weakness by making his part weaker – anyway, not in a wild rush of panic. I'm not just being kind-hearted. It's a matter of common sense.'

That might well be true but she felt sure he was mainly thinking of Cyril's feelings. 'Well, what do you want me to do?'

'Just be on my side when Peter talks to you tonight. Act as a tactful go-between. And perhaps hint that if he'll leave things the way they are until we've opened here we'll make the change he wants before we open in London. I don't hold with actors defying directors. And you know how I admire Peter – I persuaded him to do the job. But if he springs this on Cyril at tomorrow's dress rehearsal we shall have a disaster. If changes do have to be made they can be put in gradually, during the week. Anyway, we shall get a much clearer picture after Monday night.'

'What does the author feel about it all?'

'*The author?* In a play directed by Peter? The author either stays away from rehearsals or skulks in the back row of the dress circle. And Frank Ashton's as bad. He's a charming man but as a management he doesn't exist, except to foot the bills. Which makes me feel all the more responsible for coping with Peter. Oh, he may be more reasonable by tonight. This afternoon he was at his most fanatical, with his eyes trying to get together across his nose. Luckily the company was out of the way,'

'How much do they know of all this?'

'Well, they know Cyril's to be Doug on the London programmes. But they don't know he's eighteen. That's to be kept a secret from them, and from the Press.'

'When's his hair to be dyed black?'

'Peter wants to have it done on Monday morning, but that's another thing I won't stand for. Cyril's got rid of the black line and had a nice touch-up and he'd be humiliated if his pretty hair was altered. Incidentally, it is quite pretty. He's really a very nice-looking little boy.'

'You mean a nice-looking midget.'

'I'm not going to think of him as a midget. In the play he's supposed to be only twelve and that's how I'm going to think of him.'

'I must say it's a confusing life for the lad. He's twelve in the play. He claimed to be fifteen in real life but he's actually eighteen. His name's Douglas but he calls himself Cyril, and now he's to be Doug. He has black hair but it's been dyed fair, and now it's to be dyed black again. He won't know if he's coming or going.'

Miles laughed but only for a moment. 'It's really too worrying to be funny. And I'm worried about the show as a whole.'

'You always are, at this stage of a production.'

'It'll be all right on the night, eh?'

'Well, it usually is, with plays you're in. You've carried worse ones than this.' Not that she'd really felt capable of assessing it, from either its television presentation or its padded-out stage script. And she'd been to no rehearsals. Long ago she and Miles had decided that wives of leading men were apt to be resented if too much in evidence.

A pleasantly deep gong boomed from below. Miles said, 'Good lord, I haven't heard a dinner gong since I was a boy. I suppose there are a lot of permanent residents. They'll probably dress.'

'Not even here, surely; anyway, not the men. But I'll change. I've creased this thing, lying down.'

'And wear your stole. That'll be good for our prestige. And you'll need it afterwards. The theatre was chilly.'

'In this weather?' But she was always glad of a reason to wear her grey mink stole. Miles, choosing it for her, had said it looked like an extension of her hair.

As they went downstairs he said, 'I'll meet the

19

Thorntons any time you like, now. They'll probably be at dinner.'

They were, at the far end of the room, which was almost full. Visitors to the Festival looked up at Miles with frank interest. Permanent residents, easily identified, were less frank; but equally interested, Jill noticed by degrees, once she and Miles were settled at the table reserved for them. The Thorntons were too far away for her to do more than respond to Kit's wave. But after the meal, which was unspectacularly good, she and Miles followed them into the lounge and she introduced him. Both girls instantly rose, as when meeting Jill.

'Hey, ladies don't rise to shake hands with mere males,' said Miles.

'They do when their admiration is intense,' said Kit.

She spoke with sincerity but also with a hint of playfulness. Miles responded to the playfulness with a wink, then sat down between the sisters and made himself pleasant to them, while Jill talked to Thornton. Eventually the conversation became general and Kit asked if the Quentins would come to her birthday lunch next day. Miles, after explaining that they would be busy at his dress rehearsal, added, 'If I'd known about your birthday I'd have stood you some champagne at dinner tonight. What can we do about it now? How about some crème de menthe?'

'No!' said Kit, surprisingly loud. 'Thank you, but Robin and I never drink anything intoxicating.'

Miles laughed. 'It's the first time I've known crème de

menthe to be thought intoxicating. Oh, come on!' He looked from one to the other of the girls.

'No, thank you,' said Robin, more quietly than Kit but no less firmly.

'You're obviously not going to be faced with any alcoholic problems in your family,' said Jill to Thornton.

Miles then suggested that Thornton should join him in a brandy but Thornton refused as firmly as his daughters had done, adding, 'Not that I'm teetotal but I do drink very little.'

'Then we really ought to be getting to the theatre,' said Miles – who, Jill knew, would have no desire for brandy on his own account. She thought he had been slightly deflated by the complete dismissal of his attempt at conviviality but, if so, he swiftly recovered. As he got up, he booked the girls to dance with him at the Civic Reception – to which, as Jill had expected, he had agreed to go.

'Such a pity I didn't bring my stilts,' said Kit, smiling up at him.

He smiled down on her. 'Well, we'll sit out, which was really what I meant. I never dance if I can help it.

'Charming family,' he said to Jill, as they went into the hall. 'But Kit might be a bit much in the early morning, I think we'll breakfast upstairs.'

'I'll arrange it, and order the Sunday papers.'

'Do. While I slip into the gents'.'

It was dusk when they went out into Spa Street. The delicate old street lamps cast pools of light between the chestnuts. It was cooler and Jill was glad of her stole.

'I saw a good hat across the road, this afternoon,' she told Miles.

'Shall we go over and look at it?'

'Oh, let's wait until the shop's open.'

When they came to the café Jill said, 'That's where I met Thornton. As Cyril's really eighteen is he too old to be given chocolates?'

'He's not *supposed* to be eighteen, remember. And anyway, he's always eating sweets, and asking one to have what he calls "a toffee". I had to rehearse once with a humbug in my cheek.'

'Perhaps he's mentally arrested as well as physically.'

They crossed the road to the theatre, outside which framed photographs were already displayed. One was of a flaxen-haired boy looking upwards with a heaven-seeking expression. 'Peter's mad if he thinks that calling him Doug and dyeing his hair will turn that cherub into a tough guy.'

'It's really quite a charming little face,' said Miles.

'I see the front of the house is open. Let's go in this way.' They went into the little foyer. 'I can't remember what this used to be like. Probably I always went in through the stage door, which was at the end of a passage smelling of cats and worse. This is pretty now. I like the Wedgwood plaques.'

'The whole theatre strikes me as pastiche rather than the real thing, but I dare say it was too spoilt for a simple restoration. Thank God they've left some lights on. I'm always expecting to break an ankle just before a first night, stumbling down stairs in a pitch-black theatre.'

'I've a torch if we need one.'

22

After a few paces along a passage Miles peered through the glass half of a door and said, 'The set's up. Let's take it in before we're tackled by Peter.'

They tiptoed into the back of the stalls. On the stage, a working light of dazzling brilliance dangled into a roofless composite set, made up of a sitting room and a kitchen separated by a staircase leading to a room which suggested a look-out for forest fires. The whole gave the impression of a giant toy badly put together, rather than a place where human beings could conceivably live.

'Did you know it was to be like that?' Jill whispered.

'Well, I knew it wasn't to be realistic but I didn't expect it not to make sense. And it's hideous, into the bargain.'

'It'll look better when it's furnished.'

'It'll look worse. You can't put normal furniture into rooms shaped like that.'

'Perhaps Peter's found some abnormal furniture.'

'Not he. We've been rehearsing with the furniture and it's perfectly normal. If you ask me, dear Peter's gone stark out of his mind.'

The back of dear Peter could be seen, in silhouette, half way down the stalls. He suddenly shouted towards the stage, in a voice hoarse with tiredness, 'Jack, what the hell's happening – or rather, why isn't something? I swear there hasn't been a sign of life for the last ten minutes.'

Jill repressed a laugh. The evening had reached a stage she remembered well. Jack Anderson, the stage manager, and his two assistants would be working doggedly somewhere, as would, almost certainly, the master carpenter, the property master, the electrician, and anyone else belonging to the 'crew' which had come from London with the company. But nothing could be *seen* to be happening. The only unusual thing was the silence. Such moments were usually accompanied by the sound of hammering.

Getting no answer, Peter Hesper shouted again. 'Come on, for God's sake. I've got to light tonight. Are you there, Jack?'

Jack Anderson stepped from the prompt corner and said grimly, 'Yes, Mr Hesper.' Jill recognized the 'Mr' as a rebuke. Peter liked to be on Christian-name terms with his stage management. An altercation then began about the lighting installation, wrinkles in the backcloth to a small section of garden (Jill hadn't realized it *was* a garden), a missing piece of furniture and the fact that the local staff had just 'stepped out for a bite'.

'I could do with one, too,' said Peter Hesper. 'Send someone for some sandwiches.'

The stage manager shouted, 'Mary!' An untidy girl appeared at the top of the stairs and said, 'Right! I'll get them. Will you have ham or cheese and tomato? That's all they've got at the pub.'

'Both,' said Peter. 'And get plenty for everyone.' Though frequently short-tempered he was always kind to his staff. 'Here, take this.' He went to the front of the stalls. Mary, having come down the stairs, accepted the couple of pounds he handed up and scurried away.

'But for the grace of Miles Quentin, there go I,' said Jill. 'Except that I'd by now be older than Mary is. Come on, let's be nice to Peter. We must pull our punches about the set.'

Peter, turning, saw them and came to meet them, looking more like a tired boy than a man of forty. Jill had always found it astonishing that he was only two years younger than Miles – not that Miles looked old for his age; it was simply that Peter, short, slight, and with a school-boyish mop of red hair, looked abnormally young for his. Subject to swift changes of mood (though Jill was never sure if these were real or assumed), he now smiled affectionately. 'Darling Jill, how nice of you to look so nice. That lovely dress – would you call it off-black or gun-metal? And the world-famous Quentin sables.'

'I wonder if there *is* such a thing as grey sable,' said Jill.

'If so, I'm sure Miles would send to the ends of the earth for it, if you'd let him. Lucky Miles! If only I'd someone like you to brighten my life.'

'How's Gaston?'

'Hardly a life-brightener, these last weeks. I've sent him to spend a few days in his native Paris, which was probably what he was after. Now I want to talk to you – and without Miles, who is being his usual kind-hearted self at a moment when kindness will turn out to be cruelty.'

'I'll leave you to it,' said Miles, 'while I study the set.'

'Ghastly, isn't it?' said Peter, disarmingly. 'I've made every conceivable mistake over this production and I've simply got to correct some of them. Come on, Jill.' He led her away from Miles. Loud hammering started. 'Oh, God, we can't talk through that. Let's get out of earshot.'

They went into the foyer and sat in an alcove which faced the glass doors. Jill listened patiently but she knew from the outset what she was going to say. And the more Peter talked, the more sure was she that, though he was right in wanting to change his direction of the play, Miles was right in thinking the job could only be done by degrees, during the coming week.

Peter was saying, 'How could I have been so fooled by that television performance? But wasn't everybody? Didn't *you* think Cyril – Doug – was brilliant?'

She said, 'The trouble is, dear Peter, that you despise television. You won't direct it and you hardly ever watch it, so when you do see good television you've no idea what makes it tick – or why it won't tick the same way in the theatre.'

'You're telling me. The boy can't even project his voice. He can't be heard unless he shouts.'

'He didn't have to project it on television. He didn't have to *act*, he just had to *be*. Still, he must at least have some imagination to be as good as he was.'

'Go on, tell me he was better directed.'

'He was directed by a television director, for television. The same director couldn't get a stage performance out of him. Peter, darling, you know all this, really.'

He nodded glumly. 'I also know the play stinks. As a rule, when one's involved with a play, one digs deeper and gets to believe in it more and more. But I believe in this less and less.'

'Have you never been wrong about plays you believed in?

He grinned. 'Two of them closed in a week.'

'Well, you may be equally wrong about this one.'

'I doubt it. Have you tried summing the plot up, without trimmings? This is what you get: Into the lives of a childless married couple there erupts a boy who claims to be the illegitimate son of the husband by a dead mistress. He's accepted and pampered – only to disclose that he's an imposter, whose father was some other lover of his mother's. She isn't dead at all but has primed the kid with facts and documents, and she's all set for a big scene in Act III. Could anything be more bogus?'

Jill laughed. 'Well, put like that . . . But it's not without interest, how a man reacts when he finds the son he's come to care for isn't his son. And the women's parts are well written. How *are* the women?'

'Pretty fair but nothing matters but Miles. He's so good that he just might carry the play to success, but only if it's treated as a vehicle for him, with the boy merely a supporting character.'

She said, with truth, that she agreed; and then proceeded to hand on Miles's proposition as if it were her own, concluding by saying, 'Look, I'll make a bargain with you. If you'll leave things the way they are until after Monday night, I'll persuade Miles to let you do what you want before the London opening. I'll point out that you'll be making various changes during the week, so Cyril won't feel so specially insulted. And, honestly, Peter, the boy couldn't cope with vast changes at the dress rehearsal.'

'I only meant to change the end of Act II. He could cope with that on his head if he were a real professional.'

'Well, he isn't. And what he needs at tomorrow's dress rehearsal is to be praised and encouraged and given confidence for Monday night. Anyway, is it a bargain?'

'I suppose so, if you really will persuade Miles.' He looked at her anxiously, his red eyebrows drawn together in a harassed frown.

'I promise. And you'll be specially nice to Cyril tomorrow? Oh, Peter, look!'

Through the glass doors of the foyer, a boy wearing grey flannel trousers and a striped blazer was to be seen. He was standing beyond the pillars of the portico and looking up at the theatre.

'The soul's awakening,' said Peter. 'That's a new outfit – I suppose he thinks he looks like a boy from a good Prep school. Why can't he dress like a normal teenager?'

'Poor love, he isn't a normal anything. I hope he sees his photograph – yes, he's going to it. Come on, Peter, let's start the good work. Encourage him.'

'Oh, not tonight, Jill – please!' But he let himself be steered through the foyer doors and said, pleasantly enough, 'Hello, Doug.'

The boy turned quickly. 'I'm not Doug yet, Mr Hesper – look, it says "Cyril Digby" under my photo and it'll be on the programme here. And we can't have my hair dyed this week, can we? Not with that fair photo here.'

'Maybe not.' Peter had switched on a charming smile. 'We'll see how the audiences here like you fair.'

28

Jill, who had met the boy on the train, always gave herself a dispensation regarding lies spoken to actors in need of encouragement. She said now, 'I know you're going to be splendid.'

'I ought to be, to act with such a wonderful actor as Mr Quentin. And with such a wonderful director. Do *you* think I'll be all right, Mr Hesper?'

'Of course you will.' Peter managed it fairly convincingly.

'Honest, Mr Hesper? You had me worried this last week.'

'Well, we often get worried towards the end of rehearsals. Now cut along and get a good night's sleep. Everything's going to be fine. You'll be as good as you were on television.'

'Came out all right there, didn't I? Thank you for your faith in me, Mr Hesper. You know I'll do just anything to please you, change my name, dye my hair – though I *feel* right, fair.'

'Well, we'll see. Now be in the theatre by one o'clock tomorrow and I'll help you with your make-up.'

'I got all the stuff you told me to.' He turned to Jill. 'You don't have to do your own make-up on television.'

'You'll soon learn how to. Good night, Cyril.'

'Good night, *Doug*,' said Peter, firmly.

'Good night, Mrs Quentin. Good night, Mr Hesper. Thanks ever so for cheering me up.'

Jill, as they went back into the foyer, said, 'Don't tell me that boy's eighteen.'

'He is. I've seen his birth certificate. It's his dwarfishness that's put me off him.'

'But, Peter, his voice is young, too. He's got an ugly accent, hasn't he? Simply choked with glottal stop. But I suppose that's good for the part.'

'It would be, if he'd stick to it. He's now starting to imitate Miles – oh, not all the time; just every now and then, when the fancy strikes him. I haven't the heart to tell him the part's that of a gutter-snipe and he just needs to be himself.'

'I should hope not, poor kid. Come on, your sandwiches will have arrived.'

Back in the stalls, she reported to Miles. He thought she had done well and was particularly pleased that Peter had been kind to Cyril. 'What with that and seeing his photograph displayed, he should be feeling much better.'

'I found him more than a bit pathetic. Is anyone looking after him?'

'No one has to, specially, as he isn't a child, but I did make enquiries,' said Miles. 'He's sharing rooms with his understudy who's got his Mum with him. Cyril's an orphan.'

'Wouldn't you guess it? Tell me he's all alone in the world.'

'No, I gather he lives with a brother. What he needs most is an agent. I was wondering if Tom Albion would take him on.'

'Rather small beer for Tom, isn't he? Look, Peter's beginning to light.'

30

'Let's stay and watch for a bit.'

They stayed until the first act had been lit. Jill knew enough about lighting to enjoy watching it being done but by eleven-thirty she felt they ought to leave; with a dress rehearsal next day, Miles needed a long night. They congratulated Peter warmly, and sincerely, on some highly dramatic effects he had achieved, and then left him, a solitary figure, in the blue and white auditorium which contrasted so oddly with the unrealistic, unrealistically lit, set in front of him.

'Is he going on all night?' said Jill, as they made their way to the foyer.

'If so, he'll ruin the management with overtime. No one could call our Peter economical. But I do admire him.'

Outside there was a full moon. Jill said, 'That's a better effect than Peter will achieve with any amount of overtime. How lovely Spa Street looks. I've just remembered. Twelve years ago I went up to look at Queen's Crescent by moonlight.'

'Who with?'

'No one. That's why I went. I had an idea beauty might be soothing. Like hell it was. But when one's miserable there's something to be said for wallowing in it. And at least I've never forgotten how beautiful the Crescent looked.'

'Is it far? Could we go now?'

'As late as this? But it might be rather fun. It's up at the back of the theatre. There's a short cut up an enormous flight of steps. This way, I think.'

They found the steps a little further along Spa Street.

'Well, they'll help to keep my weight down,' said Miles, looking up them. 'There must be quite a hundred.'

'But they're not steep.'

Still, they were both of them a trifle breathless when they reached the top. Then they only had a little way to walk, mercifully over level ground, to the terrace.

'It's worth the climb,' said Miles.

No light showed in any window. The houses, built of pale grey stone, looked almost white under the moon. In front of them, the expanse of grass that sloped towards the roofs of a lower terrace was bleached of colour. Far below, beyond Spa Street, was the open countryside.

'Lucky the houses have their backs to the New Town,' said Jill. 'What, exactly, constitutes their beauty?'

'I don't know enough about architecture to say. Perhaps it's partly due to their uniformity – and no one's put in a fancy window or added a porch or an attic storey. And the curve of the Crescent is superb. I suppose it's not as imposing as the Royal Crescent at Bath but I find it even more pleasing.'

Jill, peering, said, 'There's a row of bells at every front door. That must mean the houses are divided into flats now. Seems sad.'

'Still, as long as they're well taken care of, as they obviously are . . .'

'I wonder which house Geoffrey Thornton's grandmother lived in. Did you really like the Thorntons or do you want me to protect you from them?'

'Oh, I liked them well enough. We might give the girls some little outing, a picnic or something.'

'Not Thornton?'

'I imagined he might be too busy with constituency work. But by all means give him the chance.'

'We must see how the week works out. You're bound to have a few rehearsals.'

'More than a few, I'd say. Yes, I may not have much time.'

They were leaning, now, on the stone balustrade at the top of the grassy slope. She noticed that he was looking troubled – his face was so expressive that, when playing in films or television, he often had to school it into immobility to avoid giving the impression of overacting. She said, 'Are you still worried about Peter's behaviour to that boy?'

'Not now. We can sort things out once Monday night's over.'

But his expression remained clouded. After a few seconds she said, 'Then what *is* worrying you?'

He smiled. 'Read me like a book, can't you? Jill, things *have* worked out for you, haven't they? I mean . . . well, us.'

'Miles, dear!' She looked at him in blank astonishment. 'Surely you know they have? What made you ask?'

He hesitated for a moment, then said, 'Oh, perhaps it was seeing you in this place, imagining you as a girl here. I just wondered.'

'Well, you can stop wondering. That girl who stood here twelve years ago couldn't have believed such luck would come her way. Funny, I was thinking about that . . . well, something like that, this afternoon, walking along Spa Street.'

'What did you think exactly?'

'It added up to the fact that I'm contented. I am, indeed. And you, Miles?'

'As if you didn't know. I still say prayers every night simply so that I can thank God for you.'

'Do you say prayers? I've never seen you.'

'Well, I *think* them, before I fall asleep.'

'Then you must think them jolly fast, seeing how quickly you can fall asleep. And it's time you set about it. Come on.'

'I can't say I'm looking forward to going down those steps. Almost worse than coming up.'

'We can go by the road. It's longer but one can walk fast as it's all down hill.'

When they were approaching the hotel, Miles said, 'I suppose it's too late to get any food. I could do with some, in spite of that solid dinner.'

'Well, it's five hours since you finished it. There'll be a thermos of soup and some sandwiches in our room. I ordered them when I arranged about breakfast.'

'Marvellous woman.'

When they eventually got to bed, Jill found she could see one of the pollarded chestnuts, silvered by moonlight; both she and Miles liked to sleep with the curtains drawn back. Then she remembered coming face to face with the lion. What colour would moonlight turn his gold? Other brief memories of her day came back to her: strolling along

Spa Street, meeting Geoffrey Thornton – and then the theatre, young Cyril-Doug gazing at his photograph. How kind Miles had been about the boy! But when wasn't Miles kind?

She looked across at his bed. He was already asleep. The room was light enough for her to see his face clearly. She had often thought that he did not really look like himself when asleep, any more than he did in a still photograph. In absolute repose his features were almost too classical to be interesting; it was his constantly changing expression, particularly the liveliness of his eyes, which gave them charm. She wondered if an Impressionist painting could capture some of that charm. But Impressionism, she believed, was out of fashion – and, anyway, Miles disliked the idea of being painted; he was the least vain actor she had ever known. Dear Miles! She remembered his troubled expression when he asked if things had worked out for her. Never before had he seemed in need of such assurance. Why now?

A possible explanation flickered in her mind – and no more than flickered, for she turned her thoughts away from it, both finding herself faintly distressed and knowing she had no right to be. The tiny unease dwindled. She slept.

⚔ 3 ⚔

Night of the Long Gloves

Guessing they would stay late at the theatre she had given instructions that they were not to be disturbed until ten. She woke some little while before that and had time to tidy her hair, put some make-up on, and awake Miles before their breakfasts arrived. He always woke unwillingly but, within seconds, would be smiling – at her and at the prospect of a new day.

This morning he remained relaxed until he had finished breakfast and taken a very cursory glance at a Sunday paper. Then he sprang up with a suddenness which almost brought disaster to his breakfast tray. She knew that from now on he would be mentally at the theatre – and physically, too, as soon as he could get there, and hours before his presence was needed. Nothing but the theatre would now exist for him until after the first night.

When he had gone into their bathroom she decided to

find another, to use herself, partly to save time and also because she liked the idea of wandering about the old hotel. After walking some way along the wide corridor outside their room, she turned into a narrow passage, one wall of which had windows looking onto the hotel's courtyard. Almost at once she came to a door open onto thin air. No steps led up to it and only an iron bar discouraged one from stepping into the courtyard some fifteen feet below. She stood looking down at the cobbles; then turned, on hearing a nearby door open.

Geoffrey Thornton was coming out of his room. He greeted her, then said, 'Excuse me a moment,' went to the next door room, knocked on the door and called, 'Hurry up, girls,' then came back to Jill. She commented on the open door she was standing by and he told her it dated from the days when luggage from the bedrooms would be loaded through it onto the tops of stage coaches.

'Fascinating,' said Jill, gazing round the sunny courtyard.

'If you're looking for a bathroom there's a gem on the next floor, with a huge porcelain bath surrounded by mahogany. Most of the bathrooms are new, or modernized.' Church bells began to ring. 'If my daughters don't get a move on, we shall be late. It's the done thing here to *walk* to church, so as not to litter the Close with cars; one's entitled to park there but it's highly unpopular with the residents.'

'Vote-losing?'

'Oh, not as bad as that. The inhabitants of the Close would vote Conservative even if the candidate was a double murderer.'

Out of their room came Robin and Kit, rather conspicuously holding Prayer Books. They greeted Jill enthusiastically and she remembered to wish Kit many happy returns of the day. Then Robin said, 'Do we look all right? Meek enough for church but smart enough for church parade? I've forgone my white boots.'

'Good,' said Thornton. 'I find those white boots a bit much.'

'But they give Robin such confidence,' said Kit. 'I'm sure white boots have a psychological effect.'

Jill said, 'An elderly actress once told me much the same thing. She was showing me a photograph of herself during the First World War, with white boots up to her knees, and she said, "My dear, when I'd me white boots on I could have kicked God's throne from under him." But perhaps I shouldn't have told you that, especially when you're on your way to church.'

'We only go to church to help Father make a good impression,' said Kit. 'And none of us believe in a God who would have a throne. Anyway, it was a lovely remark. I didn't know white boots had been in before. I must do some research.'

Robin said, 'I think I can risk my white *satin* boots at the Civic Reception, don't you, Mrs Quentin?'

'Valuable as Mrs Quentin's views on boots would be, we must now go,' said Thornton. He steered his daughters along the passage, then called back to Jill, 'Do try that vintage bathroom on the second floor.'

'But make sure the water's really hot,' Kit shouted.

'That bath can be chilly to sit on.'

Jill settled for the first bathroom she came to; she was anxious not to keep Miles waiting. He was fully dressed when she got back to their room, so she told him to go on without her – 'While I organize food to get you through the day. I suppose there's no hope you'll come back for an early lunch?'

'No, thanks, I've a lot to do. And I want to be around to help Cyril with his make-up.'

'Peter said he'd do that.'

'Peter may be a brilliant director but he's never been an actor. He knows practically nothing about make-up. I'm not having him turning the boy into a freak.'

Which wouldn't be too hard, thought Jill. Poor Cyril! If Miles and Peter started arguing about how he was to look, it would be enough to make any boy embarrassed. Well, she'd plenty to do, as she would undoubtedly have to feed others besides Miles. Few members of a company ever organized food for themselves during a dress rehearsal. After seven or eight hours they would be existing on chocolate – if they'd even brought that – and sending out for cups of tea carried in by none too willing dressers.

The hotel, having supplied a hamper of food and drink, provided a car to take it and her to the theatre. She asked the driver where church parade was held and learned that it took place in the gardens surrounding the Pump Room. She felt a slight wistfulness to be there, and a whiff of regret at going out of the bright day into the theatre's semi-darkness. Never had she been stage-struck; in her youth the theatre had merely meant work. Any play Miles was in was of interest to her but mainly on his account; and one did not, merely by attending a dress rehearsal, become part of the little closed world of a play's production.

Miles was not in his dressing room and his dresser did not know where he was. She deposited her supplies of food and then went to the front of the house where she had a long and what she found to be depressing conversation with Frank Ashton, who assured her how honoured he was to be presenting Miles, and in a play which was to re-open this wonderful old theatre. Everything was so splendidly worth-while – 'whatever happens.' She wondered if he knew what *could* happen in the way of monetary loss to himself, poor, pleasant, inexperienced young man; but she loudly agreed with him about the worth-whileness and expressed great optimism – and even more when the play's young author arrived to sit beside Frank Ashton.

Time passed. Long after the rehearsal was due to start the curtain remained down and the silence was only broken by sporadic hammering. Jill returned to Miles's dressing room and found him arguing fairly fiercely with Peter Hesper about Cyril-Doug Digby's make-up, which both of them seemed to have worked on. She persuaded them to eat a few sandwiches and then, on being assured by Peter that the rehearsal would now start, went back to the auditorium. Forty-five minutes later, the rehearsal did start.

The television play, like so many television plays, had begun with a noisy party presumably intended to establish important characters but actually, Jill often thought, establishing nothing but a noisy party. As no stage production could afford the cost of a score of players to be seen for only three minutes, the stage adaptation began at the end of the party when only characters who would pull their weight later were still lingering. After some complicated exposition which Jill, in spite of having read the script, found hard to follow, Cyril-Doug arrived with credentials from his allegedly dead mother and Miles came to believe he had a son. This scene was well written and Jill thought Cyril-Doug was surprisingly good, if difficult to hear. Peter interrupted the rehearsal to tell him to speak up, after which Cyril shouted and was less good. Still, by the time the curtain fell on the short first act Jill felt unexpectedly optimistic. She would go round and tell Miles so.

But as she reached the back of the stalls she was intercepted by a short, bald-headed, rubber-featured man who embraced her warmly.

'Tom, darling! Were you there for the whole act? I thought it held splendidly.' She then whispered, 'Take care. Frank Ashton and the author are in the front row of the dress circle.'

'Admirable first act,' said Tom Albion, loudly and clearly. 'Even better than I thought it was.' He then steered Jill out of the stalls and added, 'Actually, it *is* a little better, but then you know how abysmally bad I thought the script was. Why, why, did we let Miles get involved with this play?'

'I don't attempt to dictate to him,' said Jill.

'*I* do – but I don't have much luck; anyway, not when

your dear husband's notorious kindness of heart is involved. But never mind. As you know, I'm keeping a film offer on ice for him.'

'You're a money-grubbing old ghoul, Tom – just ill-wishing this show because you want him to do the film.'

'I should be a bad agent if I didn't want him to. And not so much of your money-grubbing, my girl. It'll be a worth-while film and this is hardly a worth-while play.'

'Don't say that to Miles, will you?'

'Not again. But I don't tell him lies. I shall just say he's superb and leave it at that. All I hope is that this thing won't limp on too long. My guess is that Ashton will tide it over for three weeks, to entitle him to a share of any film offer for it – not that there'll be one. He'd be well advised to cut his losses and never open in London at all.'

'You could be wrong, Tom. We may get a respectable run.'

'Three weeks,' said Tom firmly.

They went round to Miles and were tactful, then returned to the auditorium and worked hard on tact to Frank Ashton and the author. Then the second act began.

Jill had three categories in which she placed dress rehearsals. There was the truly dreadful rehearsal, in which every conceivable thing, and various inconceivable ones, went wrong. This was often followed by a smooth and triumphant first night. There was the almost faultless rehearsal, often followed by a faulty and/or lifeless first night. And in between these extremes was the thoroughly mixed rehearsal, partly good, partly bad, from which it was

impossible to prognosticate anything. Today's rehearsal
went into the mixed category. Her hopes rose in the second
act – to be shattered by the ending, which Cyril certainly
could not carry. (Peter was right about that.) Act III had a
melodramatic confrontation between Miles's wife and the
mother of the boy which Jill found highly embarrassing,
but the end of the play, when Miles accepted the boy as
his son while knowing that he wasn't, was extremely
moving. Jill could, with sincerity, praise it to the author
and Frank Ashton.

'Let's get a breath of fresh air before we go round to
Miles,' said Tom Albion.

They went out through the foyer and stood blinking in
the late afternoon sunshine.

'Well, at least it's over earlier than I expected,' said Jill.
'What did you think of the boy?'

'I think all child actors are ghastly – on the stage, that is;
on television they can be marvellous, as this kid was. He's
got a certain amount of appeal. I suppose he just might
make a hit. But even so, I only give it three weeks.'

'You *want* only to give it three weeks.'

They found Miles cheerful. He had already asked Peter
to dine with them at the Lion, and Tom of course joined
them. The whole of the evening was spent discussing the
rehearsal and the play in general. Tom praised Miles's
acting and Peter's direction but otherwise was non-
committal. Jill voiced her optimism and kept her pessimism
to herself. But neither she nor Tom really needed to say
very much. Peter and Miles did most of the talking and

seemed oblivious of the fact that they were covering the same ground over and over again. It was after midnight before Tom was able to coerce Peter back to the station hotel with him, and Jill got Miles to bed.

Most of her Monday morning was spent in sending wires to the company and ordering flowers; and at the last moment she remembered to buy chocolates' for Cyril's understudy – he, anyway, was a real child and would welcome them. Miles had dug himself in at the theatre by eleven o'clock, ostensibly to 'be around if needed' but really to continue his conversation with Peter. Jill considered their shared capacity for practically non-stop discussions was the main reason they so much liked working together. And she was thankful that, while still disagreeing about Cyril, they were on their usual good terms with each other. After coaxing them out to lunch she left them on their own.

She had tea with the Thornton girls, Geoffrey Thornton being absent, and was impressed on hearing that Kit had already done some research about boots – 'There's a good library here with a pet of a librarian. White boots *were* worn during the First World War but they were laced, and often only the tops were white, with patent leather toes and heels.' Jill was then shown the sisters' dresses for the first night and the Civic Reception which was obviously going to be a grand occasion; she rather wished she had brought a grander dress for it. But the sisters admired her grey chiffon and mink stole. She found the gals' gossip atmosphere pleasant; the girls somehow managed to treat her with deference and yet almost to co-opt her into their own age group.

She would quite have liked to join them at dinner, as they suggested when they found she would be on her own. But she felt she should get to the theatre earlier than dinner at the hotel would permit; also, once she thought about getting to the theatre her appetite deserted her. She was always nervous for Miles on first nights, and the fact that she had scarcely given him a thought while chattering to the girls added a sense of guilt to the nervousness which now took possession of her. She dressed quickly and hurried to the theatre – and then found herself at a loose end for well over an hour. True, Miles talked to her avidly for a few minutes but his dressing room was then invaded by a stream of people – the cast, the stage management and, of course, Peter Hesper, to all of whom he talked with equal avidity. She wondered if he would ever get his make-up on. But it was not her job to clear his dressing room. She lovingly wished him good luck, and then made a goodwill tour of all the dressing rooms. Cyril-Doug thanked her 'ever so for the chocs'. Already made up (by Miles, she learned) he looked not a day over eleven. His understudy, a genuine fifteen, looked years older than Cyril did.

Waiting for Tom Albion in the foyer she felt her spirits rising. The incoming audience was dressed with an elegance she had never before seen in a provincial theatre. It was, on the whole, an elderly elegance and few of the long, graceful dresses were on bowing terms with fashions of the moment; but it seemed to Jill that the Spa Town ladies achieved a distinction that was timeless, and they were certainly doing their best to honour the re-opening of their old theatre.

Tom, as they went into the stalls together, said, 'The Night of the Long Gloves – haven't seen so many since I was a boy. God, this place is a backwater.'

'But a charming backwater, surely?'

He shook his head with faint disapproval. 'Backwaters get stagnant. But I'll admit this looks a well-disposed audience. And let's hope they take those gloves off to clap.'

'Much you care if they clap or not. You want the show to fail.'

'I don't want to *watch* it fail. I suffer agonies for the actors when things go badly, even when one of them isn't one of my top clients. But don't worry. There's bound to be at least a polite reception tonight because of the occasion and also because of Miles. They can't have had an actor of his standing here for well over ten years.'

Jill's nervousness dwindled even as the curtain rose and the very peculiar set got a round of applause. It was wonderful what audiences could take when in the mood to enjoy themselves, as this audience most obviously was. And it had, she decided as the act got fully into its stride, quite a lot to enjoy. The play certainly had a dramatic story line and a star actor was giving a first-rate performance – though in the stalls bar, during the first interval, she and Tom overheard almost as much praise for 'that marvellous little boy' as for Miles. Young Cyril might alternately shout

46

and choke himself with glottal stop but the audience loved him.

Only at the end of the second act did Jill's nervousness return. Surely even this audience could not but realize how Cyril failed to carry it? But Cyril did not fail. He yelled his little head off and brought the curtain down to tumultuous applause – during which Tom whispered to Jill, 'If Peter doesn't re-direct that before you open in London, there'll be a huge roar of laughter.'

The third act went even better. The audience lapped up the melodrama and were then deeply moved by the last scene, which Miles played superbly. Jill counted six handkerchiefs (most of them lace-edged) being taken out of evening bags (some of them gold mesh). If powder compacts were taken out of bags near the end of a play, it was a sign of boredom; but handkerchiefs used for eye-mopping augured well. The reception was rapturous. Miles made a speech, paying special tribute to Cyril and putting his arm round him. The author bowed his thanks from a box, looking dazzled by the spotlight suddenly focussed on him. Jill whispered to Tom, 'Have you ever seen a reception like this in London?'

'Oh, they used to be fairly common before the war – not that they always meant anything. I remember one show that got nineteen curtains – and came off at the end of the week.'

They took their time getting out of the theatre, listening to comments. But there were seldom many of these. In London, audiences switched their thoughts to plans for supper, or the journey home. Here people asked people if they were going to the Civic Reception. 'Oh, God, we've got that ahead of us,' said Jill.

'Not me,' said Tom. 'I've got to drive back to London. Will you tell Miles I'll be along in a few minutes? I want to catch Peter first and try to make him see sense about that ludicrous second act curtain.'

Jill found Miles so cheerful that even the thought of the Civic Reception was not damping his spirits – 'Think how much worse we'd feel if we had to face it knowing we'd been a flop. And I was right about the end of the second act, wasn't I? The kid carried it splendidly.'

'Tom doesn't think so – not for London. He's now engaged in telling Peter so.'

'Then he'll be out of luck. Peter's as pleased as I am. We both now think that Cyril's got what it takes.'

Well, perhaps he had. Perhaps she had been too much influenced by Tom. All the same, in the argument that was still continuing when, before leaving for London, he drove them and Peter to the Civic Reception, she still found herself on his side. She feared that Miles and Peter were suffering from applause-intoxication.

The Assembly Rooms, with their tall pillars and high, domed windows, looked classically beautiful. Lights streamed out into Spa Street with its pollarded chestnuts. In the entrance hall marble goddesses in marble draperies, standing in niches, were thigh-high in non-marble flowers. Considered separately, the goddesses and the flowers were delightful; combined, they were slightly funny as the goddesses appeared to be legless. But nothing interfered with the admirable curves of the double staircase.

Jill, leaving her stole in the cloakroom, ran into the Thornton girls. They had been far away from her in the stalls and she had not met them in the intervals as Tom had felt the need of visiting the bar. She could now see them in the full glory of their party frocks. Kit was in a muslin Kate Greenaway dress reaching to her ankles. Robin's white satin shift ended a couple of inches above her knees.

'Perhaps I ought to have lengthened it for this highly conservative occasion, but I always feel my knees are my best feature. And one needs a good space between the bottom of one's hem and the top of one's boots.'

Jill paid due respect to the white satin boots.

Kit, pulling a cat-like face at herself in the glass, said, 'If *I* wore them, people would call me Puss-in-Boots. I wonder if I should wear cat whiskers and start a vogue – false whiskers instead of false eyelashes. May we hang on to you, Mrs Quentin, so that Mr Quentin won't forget he's asked us to sit out with him?'

In the entrance hall Jill found that Miles and Peter had been joined by Geoffrey Thornton. They all went to shake hands with the resplendent Mayor and Mayoress at the top of the stairs, then went on into the gallery to look down at the dancers in the ballroom. Peter, introduced to Kit, asked her if she had enjoyed the play. Jill thought there was a shade of talking down to a child in his tone and, presumably, Kit did too, for she gave him her most

49

cat-like smile and said, 'Oh, loved it. The touch of Henry Arthur Jones was so refreshing.'

Peter, startled, said, 'Good God, child, what can you possibly know about Henry Arthur Jones?'

'Oh, I've no first-hand knowledge but I've read Shaw's *Our Theatres in the Nineties*, though it was some years ago, when I read all through Shaw. Anyway, am I right – or could I be mixing Jones up with Sardou? How would Sardou revive, Mr Hesper? I mean, of course, treated seriously – as you treated the play tonight.'

'It's a fascinating idea,' said Peter. 'Not that I've read a line of Sardou. Are you, by any chance, making fun of me?'

Kit denied it charmingly, but Jill had her doubts.

Miles remembered having seen Sardou's *Diplomacy* when he was a boy and obliged with vivid impressions of it, to Kit's delight. A dance began below and a young man approached Robin. She whispered to her father, 'Don't forget your dance with the Mayoress,' then tossed back her long, fair hair and went off with the young man. Geoffrey Thornton said to Jill, 'I booked the Mayoress for the next waltz but this certainly isn't it, so shall we?' She looked at Miles, saw that he and Peter were happily talking to Kit, and said, 'Yes, I'd like to – though I'm terribly out of practice.'

How long was it since she had danced? Miles never did, if he could get out of it. (As a dancer, he was unusually awkward and held women as if he disliked them – surprising for an actor whose stage movements were so easy and who was particularly good at love scenes. It had once occurred to her that he might dance better on the stage, *acting* dancing, than in a ballroom.) On the way downstairs she wished she had simply said that she didn't dance. However, she got on quite well: Thornton was easy to follow. And though she was particularly conscious of his slightness of build she also noted that he held her firmly, imparting confidence. When the dance ended, he said, 'That was delightful. It reminded me of how fond I once was of dancing. Now I'd better take you back to the others in case a waltz calls me to my civic duties.'

Up in the gallery, Peter was no longer talking down to Kit. If anything, Jill noticed with amusement, Kit was talking down to him, and to Miles, and she certainly seemed better informed than they were about the subject under discussion. This was the evolution of the nineteenth-century theatre after the production of Tom Robertson's *Caste*. Kit was pointing out that it was a forerunner not only as regards naturalism but also as regards disapproval of class distinctions. Jill, after listening for a few moments, said to Thornton, 'I hadn't realized Kit was so specially interested in the theatre.'

'She isn't. Oh, she may be, this particular week, because of your husband; but I'd say she's equally interested in all the arts. Indeed, she can get herself interested in almost any subject. She has an astonishing all-round intelligence.'

'Any particular talents?'

'Not outstanding. She can write a bit, paint a bit, play the piano fairly well, but it's her *general* intelligence that impresses me. I sometimes worry about her. She seems to

51

me a sort of *prodigy* of general intelligence. And prodigies, one knows, sometimes fizzle out.'

'I doubt if Kit will.'

'So do I, really. There's nothing freakish about her. I daresay she's just the result of my grandmother's theory that children, from the moment they can understand the spoken word, should begin their education. Kit's probably just a few years ahead of her age. Still, Robin had the same upbringing and, though she's bright enough, she's not, at seventeen, as bright as Kit is at fifteen.'

'Anyway, they're both of them darlings. There's a waltz beginning. You must fly to the arms of the Mayoress.'

While discussing Kit, they had drawn a little apart from the others. Now momentarily on her own, Jill leaned on the gallery rail and looked down, interested to compare the dresses here with those of the theatre. She decided that those occupants of the stalls who had come on here weren't dancing. There were indications of wealth among the dancers but not much elegance. Bright colours abounded and seemed to be specially favoured by women who filled their dresses rather too well. Most of the young girls were wisps and most of the middle-aged women were overweight. It was hard to believe that the wisps would eventually become overweight but probably matrimony, babies and too much bread would do the trick. Presumably the inelegant ladies came from the prosperous New Town and were likely to be better off than the ladies of the Spa Town. She found herself resenting the New Town, on behalf of the Spa Town, and then accused herself of snobbishness. But she knew she had been too poor, and was too conscious of her very mediocre background, ever to be really snobbish. She just liked elegance for its own sake. Still, all these people looked kind and jolly. And if there were no lovely long suede gloves, the Mayoress had handsome white kid ones, which somehow managed to suggest that they could creak. Dancing with her, Geoffrey Thornton looked even slighter than he had felt.

Kit, suddenly at Jill's elbow, said, 'Won't you come and join us, please?'

'I was admiring the Mayoress's gloves,' said Jill.

'They're what our great-grandmother called twenty-button length. They only had six buttons so I suppose it meant that there would have been room for twenty. Well, if she trips Father up I do hope he manages to fall on top. Oh, look!'

For an instant, Jill feared that Thornton and the Mayoress had met with catastrophe, but it turned out that Kit had merely spotted Cyril-Doug Digby sitting all by himself watching the dancers.

'I think something should be done about him,' said Kit. 'Would he like it if I asked him to dance?'

'It just might embarrass him,' said Jill. 'Let's see what my husband and Peter Hesper think.'

Peter, consulted, said, 'Nothing would embarrass that lad.' Miles was slightly dubious but decided that Kit would cope all right. She flitted off and they watched her approach Cyril, who shortly took the floor with her.

'Good God, he's wearing a miniature dress suit,' said

Peter. 'He must have swiped it from a ventriloquist's dummy.'

Miles said, 'Do you still dislike him, now you've seen his effect on an audience?'

Peter, after consideration, said, 'I'm afraid I do still dislike him. It's odd, that – because, usually, if an audience accepts an actor I dislike, I get over my dislike out of sheer relief. Well, I'm relieved all right about that midget but I can't like him. I suppose the truth is that I find him unattractive; quite a bit repulsive, really.'

'I don't feel that at all,' said Miles. 'I'll admit he looks distinctly comic in that suit but that strikes me as touching.'

Jill, looking down, said, 'Seeing them together, you'd say he looked younger than Kit – and she looks young for her age.'

For a moment they all watched the little couple; then Miles and Peter fell to discussing the play, covering almost exactly the same ground they had covered after yesterday's dress rehearsal but from a more optimistic standpoint. Jill listened, or watched the dancers. And later, she danced again with Geoffrey Thornton. They all had supper together and then walked home along moonlit Spa Street. Miles, deprived of Peter, who had gone back to the station hotel, squired Robin and Kit. Before leaving the Assembly Rooms he had put Cyril in a taxi and paid the driver in advance. Cyril's last words were, 'Smashing evening, wasn't it, Mr Quentin? Let's hope we all get gorgeous write-ups in the papers tomorrow.'

⊰ 4 ⊱

Distant View of the Lion

She had arranged for the two morning papers to be left outside the bedroom door. Bringing them in, with a quietness that was unnecessary considering the depths of Miles's sleep, she felt apprehensive. Some provincial critics, anxious to demonstrate that their reactions were not provincial, were apt to do so by writing tough reviews. And bad notices, even in the provinces, would depress Miles as much as the first-night success had cheered him. But the notices in the Spa Town and the New Town dailies were both excellent – for the play, the acting, the scenery, the theatre and the audience. Possibly the glamour of the occasion had disarmed the critics. Anyway, all was more than well.

Of the players, naturally Miles came in for the most praise, but Cyril had made a very real success. And Jill was particularly enchanted to read, in the Spa Town paper, about 'the brilliant directorial touch whereby the underprivileged boy gradually attempts to imitate Mr Quentin's beautiful English.' Peter, having an unfailing sense of humour, would laugh about that – but later, very possibly, come to think it *was* a directorial touch. Well, with these notices in hand she could happily awake Miles. He read them with delight, then reminded her that they did not, of course, 'count' as regards London. This was merely a form of touching wood. She knew that he would let himself believe that they 'counted'.

He had arranged to be at the theatre at ten-thirty to discuss the notices with Peter. Jill did not offer to accompany him as it was one of her rules, as a non-interfering wife, never to join in back-stage discussions unless invited; also, though more than glad about the notices, she had no particular desire to put in a couple of hours talking about them. But sitting alone in the lounge she felt at a loss for something to do, and was glad to be joined by the Thornton sisters.

'We're on our own for the day,' said Kit. 'Father has constituency work that doesn't call for our presence. Anyway, *he* thought not.'

Robin said, 'Our principle is always to be available but never to push ourselves.'

'Like me with Miles,' said Jill.

On hearing that she, too, was on her own they eagerly invited her to accompany them to a concert of chamber music in the Pump Room. She liked the idea of visiting the Pump Room but said she knew nothing about chamber music and rather feared it might be beyond her.

'It's the loveliest music in the world,' said Kit. 'The only drawback to it is that it can put one off symphonic music, which now seems to me rather a noisy blur. Anyway, if you know nothing about chamber music, you can't know if you dislike it. You've just *heard* that it's difficult.'

Robin said, 'I'm not as up in chamber music as Kit is – all the late Beethoven quartets simply eat out of her hand. But I do think you'd like the Schubert Octet, which they're playing this morning. It's full of wonderful tunes.'

'You can invent stories to fit them,' said Kit. 'That's frowned on by purists but it does help beginners. Dear me, how abominably patronizing that sounds. I do apologize.'

'You needn't. No one could be more of a beginner than I am. Anyway, I'll come.'

'Oh, marvellous! Let's start now and then we can walk round the gardens before the concert begins.'

When they were on their way along sunny Spa Street, Jill said, 'This will be the first concert I've ever been to.'

Both sisters looked astonished. Then Robin said politely, 'I expect that's because you're so much occupied with the theatre. Do you go every evening?'

'Only during provincial try-out weeks like this. Once the play opens in London I shall hardly ever go. And I don't much care to go to other theatres when Miles isn't free to come.'

'Then what do you do with your evenings?' Kit enquired.

'I expect Mrs Quentin has lots of friends,' said Robin.

'Not very many, really. As a rule, I just look at television or read, and then I call for Miles and we go out to supper. That's easier than having it at home.'

Kit said, 'The evenings would be a wonderful time for you to get interested in serious music. Have you a record player?'

'No, but I could get one, I suppose. But I must see how I react this morning.'

The Pump Room, a circular building, its many windows separated by fluted columns, was surrounded by lawns, flower beds and gravel paths. Kit, sniffing, said, 'They've been cutting the grass. How that takes me back to child-hood.'

Jill asked if anyone still drank the waters.

'Visitors do, sometimes,' said Robin, 'but seldom more than once. Hello, there's an attendant at the spring.'

A young woman in vaguely eighteenth-century costume could be seen in the entrance hall, doling out glasses of water. A few visitors to the Festival obliged her by accepting one; there was no charge.

'They'll be sorry,' said Kit. 'It tastes of nothing, gone slightly bad.'

They took a turn round the gardens and then went in; the Pump Room was filling up.

Jill, looking at the flowery toques and gracefully droop-ing brims of elderly Spa Town ladies, punctuated by the wild hair of some of the Festival visitors (both sexes), found the occasion pleasant. The atmosphere was different from that in a theatre; indeed, as the light buzz of conversation died down when the instruments had finished tuning up, there was a moment of almost religious awe. She felt as if at a church service not one word of which she would be able to believe in, but which she must sit through with deep respect.

But only a few minutes after the music began she found she could enjoy it. If this was chamber music, where had it been all her life? For a time she listened carefully, following the melodies, watching the players and trying to note which instrument was playing what. She had no desire to accept Kit's suggestion that she should invent stories to fit the music, but she did fairly soon allow it to become a background for memories, mainly of herself in this town twelve years earlier. These lasted through the gentle, reflective second movement. Then the scherzo began and she had an instant, involuntary vision of a small town band composed of fat, jolly, little men, marching along Spa Street. She had an idea that such bands still existed on the Continent but doubted if there were any in England. And anyway, the band in her mind's eye was a *toy* band, with a drummer who was almost as round as his drum; she saw him so vividly that, on taking a swift look at the platform, she was surprised not to see him there. She returned to her mental picture. The toy band was funny as well as charming. She found herself smiling broadly.

Kit whispered, 'You're enjoying it, aren't you?'

'Oh, madly,' Jill whispered back.

She thought the variations and the minuet went on rather too long – she located them by consulting her programme – but she liked the last movement most of all.

This, like the scherzo, presented her with a mental picture – or rather, a mental adventure; a confused and confusing one and, though she enjoyed it almost deliriously, it left her with a slight feeling of guilt. Why? She must investigate this later, or would it be better to forget it? Certainly it ended with the music and, not for the life of her, could she have found words to describe it.

But she was able, on the walk back to the hotel, to describe the comic little town band she had seen during the scherzo. Kit was fascinated by this – 'Perhaps there was a town band here in the old days. Perhaps you're psychic.'

'Oh, it wasn't in the old days, because the chestnuts were pollarded. They were in bloom, by the way, and their candles were pink.'

'Their candles *are* pink – and you couldn't know that, could you? So you still may be psychic.'

'Anyway, I'm sure you're very musical,' said Robin, 'because you didn't fidget. You sat still as a statue.'

'But your face changed a lot. First it was sad and then it was gay. And in the last movement it was radiant. Oh, there's Mr Quentin – just going into the hotel.'

Jill considered asking the girls to join them at lunch but decided against it. She knew Miles would be charming to them but their presence would prevent his talking exclusively about the play, should he want to – as, in fact, he did. His latest news was that it was rather too long for London, and Peter and the author were now working on cuts – 'Also they're considering a new slant for the ending.

You'll remember the New Town critic wondered if the boy, after all, *isn't* an imposter; he only believes he is. And that's the final twist of the mother's revenge.'

'You mean, first she says he's your son, and then she says he isn't, but all the time he is, only you and he never find out? Sounds very confusing.'

'Peter thought it might add to the play's stature.'

'Has it got any?'

'I suppose not,' said Miles, looking crestfallen. 'It's just that one tries to admire what one's acting in.'

She regretted her momentary impatience. 'Anyway, it's a highly effective play. And who am I to judge its stature? The critics here were impressed with it. Perhaps this new slant will work well.'

But she feared her impatience had been noted for he stopped talking about the play and suggested they should spend the afternoon exploring the town – 'and you can show me that hat you mentioned.'

'Fancy your remembering!'

'Don't I always like helping you to choose clothes?'

'It's one of your nicest traits. All right, then, and I'll change my dress and do you proud. Anyway, that hat will need a bit of dressing up for.'

She was upstairs, changing, when she heard a very odd noise through her open window. Robin and Kit were below, giving an impression of a town band playing the scherzo from the Schubert Octet.

'We're serenading you,' said Kit, as Jill looked out. 'Come shopping in the New Town with us.'

Jill explained why she couldn't, adding, 'And are there any good shops in the New Town?'

'Oh, you can often find skittish little dresses,' said Robin, 'and at bargain prices. Anyway, the New Town's worth seeing.'

'Is it? I hated it when I stayed in it, years ago.'

'It takes a bit of knowing,' said Kit. 'Some of it's far older than the Spa Town. There are queer little back alleys. Very romantic, really.' She offered the last words as if they would be a good come-on.

'Could you show me tomorrow?'

'We're spending the day with Father, visiting old friends,' said Robin. 'But may we book you for Thursday morning?'

Jill said she would consider herself booked – 'that is, unless Miles needs me.'

'We quite understand,' said Robin. 'Well, we hope you and Mr Quentin have a pleasant afternoon.'

Kit, after offering advice as to what they should see, added, 'Of course, we *could* show you.'

'There's that pushing child again,' said Robin, marching her sister away.

Jill, setting out with Miles, felt particularly happy. Snatches of the Octet drifted through her head. She had a retentive ear and could often remember a popular song after a single hearing. Schubert was very different; one's ear could not retain the shimmer. She must certainly get a record player.

As they turned into the arcade, she explained how the

62

hat had been brought to her notice by Geoffrey Thornton. 'But that was on Saturday, after I met him at the chocolate counter. They may not have the same hat in the window now.'

But it was there all right. And to her surprise it made Miles laugh. 'Surely that's just a display hat, a sort of shop sign? You couldn't possibly wear it, even at a Buckingham Palace garden party.'

Slightly deflated, she said, 'I expect you're right – anyway, about me. But I think it's intended to be worn. Don't you admire it in its own right?'

He studied it critically. 'Yes, the line's beautiful and it's very well made. Shall we go in and look at some others? Though I don't really like you in hats; your hair's too decorative to cover. And I wouldn't say Geoffrey Thornton's grandmother's milliner would be *ideal* for you.'

She laughed. 'And if I go in, I shall feel I have to buy something. So let's just leave it.'

'Perhaps we shall see something else.'

As they walked along Spa Street he suggested various purchases but there was nothing she wanted; and when he lingered by a jeweller's window she very firmly led him on. She then showed him the Pump Room and they wandered round various squares and crescents, but none of them seemed as impressive as Queen's Crescent. 'That had the advantage of moonlight,' said Miles, 'which reminds me, Peter's thinking of changing the lighting for the end of Act II.'

His mind had swung back to the play and Jill soon saw

that he was no longer interested in exploring. And it would be more comfortable to talk if not walking. She said, 'Let's get back to the hotel. They're going to give us a sort of high tea. We can have supper after the show.'

The theatre was so full that night that she and Peter Hesper had to stand at the back of the dress circle. She found this tiring but nevertheless enjoyed the play more than on the first night. She was less anxious and could now take a more technical, professional interest, noting slightly different audience reactions to various scenes. Sometimes she rested, by sitting in an alcove from which she could hear, but not see the stage. This was, she knew, the acid test for dialogue and she didn't think the dialogue stood up to it; but the audience was held.

So it was when she saw the show again next day. It seemed more and more a pity that cuts and changes were to be made.

These were to be rehearsed on Thursday morning. After seeing Miles off to the theatre she joined Robin and Kit in the hotel lounge, prepared to be taken to see the New Town.

'We're all taking you,' said Robin. 'Father's gone to get the car.'

'It's our great-grandmother's 1937 Rolls-Royce,' said Kit. 'Father keeps it here at the hotel. We think of it rather like a retired race horse. Old horses like to be visited and old cars like to be driven.'

'Not that it's old enough to be funny,' said Robin. 'In fact, we think it's beautiful.'

Jill, when she went out to the car, thought it the most beautiful she had ever seen. It was a silver-grey Sedanca de Ville, the lines of its elegant, clean-cut coachwork surprisingly modern in spite of the car's height. Paint, chromium and upholstery seemed still to be in perfect condition.

Geoffrey Thornton, helping Jill in to the front, said, 'My grandmother had the body specially built for her, and travelled up to London twice to see how the work was going on. I remember going with her when I was about twelve.' He went round to get in beside Jill. The girls, at the back, drew her attention to the small glass-topped tables that could be pulled down for picnic meals, and to the little cupboards with mirrors inside, where lights went on when the doors were opened.

'And the glass screen between the front and the back goes up and down when you press the button,' said Kit. She demonstrated this, then added, 'I must say it's a terribly class-conscious car. Before the war, I understand, our great-grandmother sat in the back, here, with her pekinese, completely protected from the weather, while her chauffeur and maid sat in front, utterly exposed.'

'They could shut the top if they wanted to,' said Thornton, 'but they seldom did unless it poured with rain. The chauffeur, who adored the car, thought it looked smarter with the front open – as it does. But please say, if you find it too draughty. It closes easily, and then both looks and feels like a completely closed car.

'It's lovely as it is,' said Jill, looking up at the sky.

Thornton asked her if she drove.

'No, and we haven't a car. It wouldn't be very much use in London. And Miles has never driven since he was involved in an accident ten years ago.'

'Was he hurt?'

'No, but a friend of his was killed.' Why had she mentioned that? She quickly spoke of something else.

They were proceeding – it seemed the suitable word – along Spa Street at a snail's pace, so that the girls could point out various shops and buildings. And after only a couple of minutes she noticed that people looked towards the car with smiling recognition.

'I'd never dare drive a modern Rolls here,' said Thornton, 'even if I could afford one. The Spa Town would think it ostentatious, though there'd be no resentment of the money spent on it. The New Town wouldn't give a damn about the ostentation but would strongly resent my being able to afford it. But my grandmother's Rolls is popular in both towns. I even think it won me quite a lot of votes.'

Soon they turned into a street which, Jill remembered, led into the New Town; she had walked it often enough during that long-ago week. The eighteenth-century terraces here showed signs of having come down in the world, and soon the car was passing semi-detached Victorian villas and then rows of small houses with bay windows and stained glass in their front doors.

'I stayed somewhere near here,' said Jill.

'Can you remember the address?' asked Kit. 'We could make a pilgrimage.'

'No, thank you. It was a horrid place.' She had a sudden memory of a linoleumed bedroom with a cold, sagging bed . . . though perhaps it was a composite memory. Life, in those days, had achieved a general average of discomfort.

Already they were entering one of the busy streets of the New Town. Jill gazed with dislike at the gaudy shops.

'Now you must look about you carefully,' said Kit, 'or you'll miss interesting bits. Ignore the shops – these are some of the worst – and look up at the roofs. Lots of these buildings are Queen Anne or older.'

Jill did as she was told and was surprised to note the jumble of tiled roofs and little attic windows, some of these cobwebbed and indicating unused rooms.

'My grandmother told me that shop assistants used to live in, up there,' said Thornton. 'Now very few of the attics are used even for storage; too many stairs and rickety at that. From a hard-headed point of view, all this property should come down. And will, eventually.'

Jill said, 'I suppose, when buildings are so badly spoilt . . .'

'But I like them spoilt,' said Robin. 'I mean, I like the mixture of old and new. Anyway, I like it better than having the old buildings pulled down.'

Kit said, 'You don't think keeping them like this is a bit like keeping old people alive when they've got one foot in the grave?'

'No, I don't. And neither do you,' said Robin.

'True enough. I was just airing the idea.'

'And anyway, we do keep old people alive as long as we can. And when you're old, I bet you won't think you've got one foot in the grave, even when you're dangling both feet into it. And you'll want to go on and on. Most people do.'

The sisters continued to bicker amicably until the car reached the large market square which was in the middle of the New Town.

Robin said, 'Now you see what happens when the old buildings *are* tidily pulled down and replaced.'

There were chain stores, cut-price supermarkets plastered with advertisements, two gaudy cinemas, a particularly hideous town hall. Buses painted blue, green, orange and even striped, were bringing people in from the surrounding countryside.

'I'll admit this is awful,' said Kit.

'But the market itself is rather fun,' said Jill. 'Somehow the crude colours look all right there.'

Racks of bright dresses, rolls of materials, blankets, towels, nylon nightgowns and negligées swinging in the breeze, inflated plastic toys, hardware . . . even the food looked brighter than food normally looks.

'I sometimes buy things here,' said Robin. 'Shall we go and explore?'

'No, you don't,' said Thornton. 'If I park the Rolls here it'll get mobbed. Oh, affectionately mobbed, but I don't want the market boys climbing all over it. When you girls go market shopping, you go on your own.'

They drove on, slowly because there was much traffic. Interest in the Rolls was as lively as in the Spa Town but there it had been greeted with smiles, and occasional bows from acquaintances of the Thorntons; here, the populace waved. Robin and Kit waved back and, presently, Jill waved too; it seemed discourteous not to. She said, 'Really, we might be royalty.'

'Well, it's a queen of cars,' said Kit. 'And you look exactly right for it, with your grey suit and your lovely not-quite-grey hair.'

'You must have a wonderfully clever cut,' said Robin. 'It doesn't at all mind an open car.'

'I wouldn't care if it did; I'm enjoying myself too much.' The day, the car, the interest of seeing the town from a different point of view, the companionship of the three Thorntons, all were giving her pleasure – though she found Thornton quieter than on their earlier meetings; perhaps he was letting his chattering daughters have the floor. It occurred to Jill that he must be unusually lacking in egoism; he seldom spoke of himself unless in answer to some question. She felt she ought to show interest in his political career but was dubious about plunging into a subject about which she knew so little. She had no political views beyond a vague sympathy with the underdog – and these days, who *were* the underdogs and which party their champion? Here, certainly, the prosperous New Town might house more top dogs than the Spa Town. Anyway, judging by Thornton's majority, both towns had accepted him as their champion. She would have liked to say this, making it a compliment, but felt it safer to keep off politics altogether. Also she found his quietness a little inhibiting. She remembered her first impression of him as veiled. The veil was still there.

After they had driven through a number of ancient alleys which linked the main shopping streets (the latter pretty hideous, Jill thought, though she gave due recognition to all the survivals that were pointed out to her) Kit said, 'Let's show her a bird's-eye view from above. It's fascinating, like those old prints called "A Prospect of . . . ."'

They left the town behind and headed for the hills. 'I always enjoy doing this,' said Thornton. 'The car likes to pretend we're merely ambling up a gradual rise, but you'll be surprised, looking down, to see how steep this hill is.'

She was. In only a few minutes they had risen high enough to see the town spread out beneath them. Thornton drew up at a grassy plateau obviously intended for a lookout. A modern pay-telescope was mounted there.

'Oh, good, we've got the place to ourselves,' said Robin. 'So we can hog the telescope. You look first, Mrs Quentin. But it's best to get your bearings in advance, with the naked eye.'

Jill saw that the New Town began at the foot of the hill, its modern suburb of detached houses merging into streets leading to the town centre. Then came the streets leading to the Spa Town, with its squares, terraces and crescents. The hill on which Queen's Crescent was built seemed only a little hill when viewed from here. The whole length of Spa Street was visible.

Thornton, after pointing out various landmarks, said, 'One's apt to forget that for nearly a hundred years after the Spa Town was built, *it* was called the New Town. Still was, when my grandmother was a child. I suppose one day it'll be as spoilt as what used to be the old town has become.'

'Come and look through the telescope now,' said Robin. 'It's a wonderfully clear day.'

Jill, who had never before looked through a telescope, was startled by the way Spa Street seemed to leap towards her. She could see each shaving-brush chestnut, distinguish individual shops. She spotted the café where she had met Thornton; then, swinging the telescope slightly, found herself looking at the golden lion outside the hotel. Just beyond it was her bedroom window and there was someone standing there. Miles? He had not expected to come back for lunch. The figure moved – and before she had even made out for certain if it was a man or a woman; but it had seemed too tall for a maid. She handed the telescope over to Robin and looked at her watch.

Thornton said, 'Are you anxious to get back? We were hoping we might take you out to lunch. There's a good country hotel, just a few miles further on.'

Why not? If Miles *was* back he wouldn't in the least mind her staying out to lunch; he had known she was spending the morning with the Thorntons. All the same, she said, 'I think, perhaps . . . you see, they've been making cuts and that can be tricky. Miles may want me to run through them with him.'

'We could get you back by, say, three o'clock,' said Thornton. 'Still, if you'd rather not . . .'

'It's just that I suddenly felt guilty, out here enjoying myself when they're all working so hard at the theatre.

71

By the way, would any of you like to come with me tonight? I've got tired of standing so they're keeping me a box.'

'Alas, we're all going out to dinner,' said Thornton. 'But we were wondering if we could buy seats for the first night in London – or is it too late?'

She said she could arrange it – 'And now, if we're to get back in time for lunch . . . Oh, I have enjoyed myself.'

The Thorntons, too, expressed their pleasure in the morning. Jill, taking a last look round at the rolling hills and the town below, found that going back when she didn't really want to took the edge off her guilt. But some not quite identifiable sense of guilt remained.

❧ 5 ❧

Shocking Disclosure in a Cosy-Corner

It *had* been Miles at the window and he had been on the look-out for her. The rehearsal had been trying and he wanted to talk about it. Peter's cuts had irritated the whole company – 'I don't mind clean cuts but small, niggling cuts are so difficult to learn.' He described them fully, and niggling they certainly were, but they would shorten the play by some minutes without taking anything of value out of it. In Jill's opinion, that was the right way to cut; but she did not say so, nor did she remind Miles that 'clean' cuts usually removed whole speeches which actors did not care to lose.

She worked with him after lunch, got him to eat an early tea, and then went to the theatre with him for a last-minute run-through with the company – which gave the impression that the evening performance would be disastrous. But it wasn't; the cuts went in smoothly except for Cyril's; and

Miles was able to cover up for him. The play went well. Jill, after arranging with Frank Ashton about the Thorntons' first-night seats, asked how he felt about London and found he was wildly optimistic – 'We just can't fail, judging by the reactions here.'

'Yes, they've been splendid,' she said heartily.

'Our young author's walking round in a daze of bliss. Such luck to get your husband in his first play.'

'And to get such a kind management.' She did not think Frank Ashton knew anything about the theatre but he had been unfailingly pleasant, also generous.

At supper Miles was his usual cheerful self and freely admitted he had been wrong about the cuts. 'They're really very skilful. Naturally they upset the boy, but I can do a little private rehearsing with him during the photo-call tomorrow. He'll be steady as a rock by the evening.'

The photo-call meant that Miles would be in the theatre most of the day. Jill decided to take sandwiches down to him. She ordered these as soon as she had seen him off and then went to the bedroom intending to spend the morning typing thank-you letters for Miles's first-night telegrams; she was often glad that she had learned to type during her days as an assistant stage manager.

She had just settled down at her portable typewriter when the hall porter brought up a note. He handed it to her, saying, 'The young ladies are waiting in the lounge.'

The note read:

Dear Mrs Quentin,

We should like it very much if you would come out and have coffee with us this morning. We rather particularly want to talk to you privately.

ROBIN AND KIT

Robin had written the note. Kit had merely signed her name – Jill marvelled that anyone could get so much individuality into three letters: they were large, angular, and faintly suggestive of Egyptian hieroglyphics.

Well, one could hardly ignore 'particularly' and 'privately'. Jill got her handbag and went downstairs.

The sisters rose to meet her and, on hearing that she would be happy to come out with them, thanked her with a touch of gravity. She had been about to say, 'Well, this sounds exciting,' but it seemed too flippant for the occasion.

'If you don't mind the little walk we'll go to the Spa Street café,' said Robin. 'We have a specially private table there.'

Gravity, Jill decided as they walked along Spa Street, made both the girls seem younger, not older. But they retained sufficient social sense to maintain what could only be described as polite conversation, on their way to the café. Jill found herself both touched and amused – not to mention curious.

As they entered the café Robin said, 'This is where you met Father, isn't it?' to which Kit added, 'We feel grateful to it.' Jill smilingly said, 'So do I!' It was merely the called-for, conventional reply and she wished she had managed something better. The formality of the outing was having a paralyzing effect on her spontaneity.

The sisters conducted her through the shop into the tea room, and on into a small, circular alcove which was the cosy-corner to end cosy-corners. It reminded Jill of a miniature bandstand, but a bandstand with curtains. Once inside it the tea room could only be seen through a heavily draped arch.

'We always come in here unless we're with Father,' said Robin. 'He says it gives him claustrophobia. I'll admit it's a trifle airless.'

'Pure imagination,' said Kit. 'Enough air comes through that arch to supply a regiment.'

A waitress appeared who obviously knew the girls well.

'We usually have hot chocolate,' Robin said to Jill, 'with lots of cream. But I expect you prefer coffee.'

'No, indeed; chocolate would be marvellous,' said Jill, wondering how long it was since she had drunk any.

The order was given. The waitress departed. A silence fell.

'Well,' said Jill, at last, looking hopefully at the sisters.

'Let's wait until the chocolate arrives,' said Kit and then proceeded to chat about the Edwardian decoration of the café . . . 'Once people thought it was hideous and now it's coming into fashion again. By the way, are you interested in Art Nouveau, Mrs Quentin?'

Jill, disclaiming all knowledge of Art Nouveau, thought that the 'private' talk the girls wanted to have with her was likely to be something of an anti-climax after the long build-up it was getting. What *could* they have in mind?

At last the waitress brought the chocolate. Robin, obviously guarding against interruption, said, 'And we'll pay for it now. Then you won't have to come back again.' This transaction finished, she poured the chocolate carefully, spooning whipped cream onto each cupful. Jill thought, 'I will *not* prod them again.'

But at last they prodded themselves, though Robin made only a tentative start by saying, 'I don't quite know how to begin.'

'I do,' said Kit, favouring Jill with a sweet, if cat-like smile. 'And what I want to say first is how very, very much we like you, dear Mrs Quentin, and how earnestly we hope you'll go on being friends with us when we all get back to London.'

'Well, of course I will,' said Jill.

'There's no "of course" about it,' said Kit. 'You might well not have any time to spare for us. But will you, please? I mean quite a lot of time, enough to see us often?'

Jill, aware of the gravity of Kit's tone, stopped herself from answering with another rather perfunctory-sounding 'of course.' Instead, she said with great seriousness, 'I will, indeed. And not just because you've asked me to. I shall want to.' Then, as she noticed the intense gaze of Kit's greenish eyes, it flashed through her mind that these were motherless girls. She found herself adding, 'Perhaps I can even be a bit motherly.'

'No!' said Kit, loudly.

Jill was reminded of the tone in which Miles's offer of a crème de menthe had been refused.

'You really mustn't bark at people like that, Kit,' said Robin, then turned to Jill. 'But I think we both feel –'

Jill put in hastily, 'Of course I know I couldn't really be like your own mother.'

'We devoutly hope not,' said Robin, 'which brings us to what we wanted to talk to you about. If you really are willing to be friends with us, you need to know more about us than you do now or it will make for awkwardness later. You see, our mother had an unfortunate weakness.'

'Let's not beat about the bush,' said Kit. 'Our mother was a dipsomaniac.'

Jill murmured a protesting 'Kit, dear!' then looked at Robin for reassurance. But none was forthcoming.

'I'm afraid it's absolutely true,' said Robin. 'She drank and drank for years and years and finally – about eighteen months ago – she drank herself to death, that is, into one of the illnesses which come from prolonged alcoholism. I suppose she couldn't help it; we believe she inherited it. But whether she could help it or not, it made life hell for Father.'

'Please don't worry about it, Mrs Quentin,' said Kit. 'It's over now and we're all trying to forget it. But you need just to know, otherwise you'll find out later and feel embarrassed in case you've asked Father awkward questions or said the wrong thing or something.'

'As I did, that first day we met. How awful.'

'You mean when you said Father would never be faced with any alcoholic problem in his family,' said Robin. 'None of us minded a scrap, but *you* mind, now. And that's

78

the sort of thing we want to avoid for you. Besides, we'd like you to understand why our whole lives are dedicated to helping Father. You can't imagine what he went through.'

'It almost wrecked his career at the Bar,' said Kit. 'Though he did just manage to carry on. Of course we didn't know about that at the time; I was only two when the trouble with Mother began.'

'We knew about that all right, because we were with her. Though we didn't quite understand what being drunk was.'

'Julian did. He was six,' Kit explained to Jill.

'Is Julian a brother?'

'Oh, haven't we mentioned him? He's two years older than Robin. We heard from him this morning. He's staying in a Scottish castle with some rather fancy friends. Yes, Julian always knew the truth about Mother. But Father asked him not to talk to us about it. We came to believe that she was ill, which was what we were told when we were hurriedly brought here to our great-grandmother.'

'How long were you with her?'

'Until she died, a little over two years ago. There was nowhere else for us to go as Father's parents were dead. Later we went to boarding school, but we came here for the holidays.'

Robin said, 'And all those years Father had to cope with our mother. She'd inherited an old country house and nothing would get her away from it.'

'Did you never see her?'

'Oh, yes, we were taken several times, when she was supposed to be better. But she never stayed better very long.'

'She threw a log at me once,' said Kit. 'Just pulled it out of the log basket and hurled it at me.'

'It was only a very thin log or she couldn't have hurled it. Anyway, it missed you.' Robin turned to Jill. 'Kit picked it up and fetched Mother a fierce blow across the shins. They had to be separated. We weren't taken to see Mother again for a very long time. Indeed, I don't think you ever went again, did you, Kit?'

'No. I refused.'

'After the log-throwing incident Father told us the truth about Mother. He discussed it with me first and we wondered if we should still keep it from Kit – she was only ten. But though she's two years younger than I am she's more than two years cleverer, so it seems best to treat us as if we're the same age, though that's flattering me a bit.'

'Nonsense,' said Kit. 'I'm merely a bit precocious. Robin is a highly talented dress-designer, Mrs Quentin, *and* she has a very fine character. You know, the queer thing is that, once I knew the truth about Mother's so-called illness, all sorts of things came back to me, and even more so when we compared memories with Julian. I've always counted it against myself that I was fobbed off with that illness story.'

'But didn't you say you were only two, Kit, darling?'

'Still, even at two . . .' Kit shook her head disapprovingly.

Jill said, 'My dear, dear children, what a terrible time you must have had.'

'Oh, we've been all right,' said Kit. 'It was Father who had the terrible time. He's never told us very much about it but we do know some things he doesn't know we know. For instance, our dear mother wasn't only a dipsomaniac; she was also a nymphomaniac.'

'Now there I think you exaggerate,' said Robin, judicially. 'In my view a woman doesn't qualify as a nymphomaniac unless she rushes at almost every man she meets, even visiting tradesmen.'

'Well, Mother rushed at the postman.'

'It was the post*master*, Kit.'

'What a very snobbish distinction.'

'Not at all. I was merely being exact. It was just the village postmaster, Mrs Quentin, not the Postmaster General or somebody. He'd called about a lost parcel. Mother certainly twined herself round him. We were watching from the stairs.'

'Anyway, she had lots of men, Robin. And you know you believe she did. That's why you're so scared even to –'

'Shut up,' said Robin, blushing violently.

'Nonsense. Mrs Quentin, as a woman of the world, will you please tell my sister that, though dipsomania may be inherited – which is why we won't touch one drop of alcohol – she's *not* likely to turn into a nymphomaniac if she so much as lets a young man hold her hand?'

Robin, tossing back her wings of hair, looked at Jill with anxious eyes. 'Of course I don't think that but, since we're onto the subject, I *am a* little scared of getting carried away by my lower instincts, particularly as I'm determined not to marry for ages. Father must be able to count on me.'

'He'll always be able to count on *me*, because I shall never marry. It's rather sad, Mrs Quentin, but it begins to look as if I shall be frigid. Of course it's early days yet, but when Robin was my age she'd felt sexual stirrings, hadn't you, Robin?'

'Well, yes. But I knew about Mother by then, so I repressed them. And now I'm always nervous in case they dash at me all the worse for being repressed. Oh, dear, you haven't drunk any of your chocolate, Mrs Quentin. Has it gone cold?'

'No, no.' Jill took a hasty drink. 'It's just right.' She drank some more, gratefully, feeling slightly battered by the conversation.

The girls had punctuated their disclosures by chocolate drinking and were now refilling their cups.

'We haven't meant to harrow you, Mrs Quentin,' said Kit. 'Everything's set fair now. Already Father's a new man, and doing very well at the Bar though he's really more interested in his political career.'

Robin said, 'What we'd like most is for him to marry again, if we could find just the right person.'

'Someone like you,' said Kit. 'Really, from our point of view, it's a great pity you're married. And very happily married, I'm sure.'

It had been a statement, not a question. All the same Jill thought there was a hint of a question in the slowly raised smiling eyes. She answered, with great firmness, 'Very, very happily married.'

'Naturally – to such a wonderful husband,' said Kit. 'One knows at once that Mr Quentin is a good person, as well as a great actor.'

'He is, indeed,' said Jill. 'But reverting to your father, I do advise you not to go wife-hunting for him.'

'No doubt it is a job he should do for himself,' Kit conceded. 'Though he did slip up over Mother. And we *are* a bit scared of getting a step-mother we dislike.'

'Still, what really matters is that Father should be happy. Now we've talked far too much about ourselves. Do let me give you some more chocolate, Mrs Quentin. There's still some in the pot. No? Then you have it, Kit. I'm full.'

Kit accepted and spooned the last of the cream onto it. Jill, in a momentary silence, thought how much the girls had left unsaid, in spite of their frankness. She had only a very hazy picture of their lives and scarcely any picture at all of their father's. How does a man cope with a wife who drinks – and over such a long period of years? If it had begun when Kit was only two, and the wife had died only – was it eighteen months ago? Already, Jill found, various details of the story were eluding her. She would have liked to get them straight and also ask for more details but hardly felt she could, especially as the girls had now let the subject drop and were talking generally.

Fairly soon Robin said, 'I think perhaps we should go now. We have to help Father entertain some local bigwigs at lunch. Kit, you have a blob of cream on your nose.'

Back at the hotel, the girls went on duty with their

father, and Jill, having collected sandwiches, went on duty at the theatre.

She found Miles fairly pleased with the way the photo-call was going. But when, in the late afternoon, he got back from it he had changed his mind. He had just settled down to tell Jill all about this over tea when the three Thorntons, who were returning to London that evening, arrived to say goodbye. Miles at once switched off annoyance with the photo-call and asked them to come round and see him after the London first night.

'In your dressing room? Oh, marvellous,' said Kit. 'You *are* kind.'

He talked with the utmost patience until Geoffrey Thornton finally shepherded his daughters off – and then reverted to the photo-call while they were walking away.

Peter, it seemed, had treated young Cyril shabbily. 'Again and again he was in a bad position. Peter insisted on shots that favoured me. It's not fair, when the boy's made such a success.'

'Do be reasonable, Miles. It's photographs of you that'll draw people into the theatre, not photographs of Cyril.'

'Still . . . Anyway, I insisted on a couple of big heads of Cyril – and he's been photographed with his own fair hair, which means he'll be allowed to keep it for London.'

'Hardly his own, is it? What about that black line at the roots you told me about?'

'Oh, well . . . Why shouldn't the poor kid be fair if he wants to?'

'Have your tea, darling.' She had thought of telling him

of her outing with the Thornton girls but this was certainly not the moment for it.

The theatre was so fully booked that night that Miles had been unable to buy a box for her and she again stood at the back of the dress circle with Peter Hesper. For the first time, she was faintly dubious about the audience's reaction. There was some restlessness in the cheaper parts of the house and occasional giggles in the wrong places.

'New Town people, I gather,' said Peter. 'They get their pay packets on Fridays. I'm told tomorrow night will be worse. Apparently Spa Town people shun entertainments on Saturday nights.'

'Well, one must never be influenced by Saturday night reactions in the provinces,' said Jill. 'And the Spa Town reaction's a much better indication of how London will react.'

'In these days? I'm not so sure.'

It was the first time, since the triumphant Monday opening, that she had seen him look gloomy.

But at least the Saturday matinee went well. Jill got a seat in the stalls and listened to Spa Town old ladies praising Miles and Cyril across precariously held tea trays. She then went back to the hotel to pack, having made sure that a good dinner would be sent into the theatre for Miles to eat between the shows, and did not return to the theatre until the middle of the evening.

She had arranged to meet Peter Hesper at the back of the dress circle and had some difficulty in locating him as there was a double row of standees. He slipped his arm through hers and whispered, 'Agony, dear. Sheer agony.'

All over the house people were coughing, fidgeting, giggling. They weren't, she thought, inimical; sometimes they shushed each other. But they simply were not held. Towards the end of the second act, matters improved; Miles was playing superbly. Then came the dramatic climax. Young Cyril delivered his denunciatory speech at the top of his lungs. It was greeted by a huge roar of laughter.

'And, my God, who could blame them?' said Peter. 'Come on, let's get out.'

They eeled their way through the crowd on the stairs (the only remark Jill overheard was, 'Still, you must admit Miles Quentin takes his part well.') and out into Spa Street. The air was sultry. She said, 'Going to be a storm.'

'There is, and all,' said Peter. 'And you, my love, must now stick to the bargain you made with me on Sunday night.'

'What bargain? Peter! You can't mean you're going to re-direct, *now*?'

'Of course I must. Oh, I don't say London audiences will be as oafish as this one is, but they will be realistic and so, believe me, will the critics. We've just let ourselves be lulled by a lot of drooling old ladies. Let's go round and see how Miles feels.'

'You lay off Miles until the show's over – and if you've any sense you'll lay off him until tomorrow. We can talk on the train. *Could* you make the changes in time?'

'Of course. It's largely a matter of different positions and different lighting, plus a general toning down of that ghastly boy. Why the hell didn't we listen to Tom Albion?'

It began to rain, hard. They went back into the theatre and steeled themselves for the last act – which held rather better than they had expected. – 'And you know why?' said Peter. 'It's because it's almost entirely focussed on Miles. And that's how the whole play has to be.'

There was a fair amount of applause at the end but no real enthusiasm. Jill heard one illuminating remark. 'Old-fashioned, wasn't it? Funny, it didn't seem like that on television.' So much for Peter's ultra-modern direction, with its non-realistic sets and lighting. Perhaps they had showed up the play's old bones, like teenage clothes on an elderly woman.

Peter said, 'If you don't want me to start work on Miles tonight I'd better not see him at all. Anyway, I want to take a look at the script and have everything at my finger tips tomorrow. So I'll just have a word with the stage management and then clear off.'

It was still raining heavily so they went back-stage through the pass door; it was opened in response to Peter's thumping. Jill, glancing at the staff dismantling the set as she crossed the stage, thought of the many Saturday nights when she had been up till the small hours seeing the load out of provincial theatres. Thankfulness that those days were in the past made her less depressed about the present – for depressed she was: Miles was going to be worried about this last-minute contretemps.

But apparently he hadn't yet started to worry. He looked up from taking his make-up off and said cheerfully, 'Swine, weren't they? But it doesn't mean a thing.'

87

'*Of course* it doesn't,' she agreed, fervently. 'There's a cloud-burst outside. I'd better get the stage-door keeper to ring up for a taxi.'

'And say a soothing word to our leading lady, next door, will you? She says the audience hit her full in the solar plexus. Young Cyril took it like a trooper and an American trooper, at that. He said, "Just hicks, aren't they, Mr Quentin?"'

By the time Jill got back from ordering the taxi and soothing the leading lady's solar plexus Miles was almost ready to leave. He asked her to see if Cyril and his understudy would like to be driven home. 'They're on the next floor, Room 7.'

The door of Room 7 was open. She saw that the boys had gone. Sticking out of a wastepaper basket was the chocolate box with Spa Street on its lid – young Cyril obviously hadn't cherished it as a souvenir. She went closer and looked down on it, already feeling a whiff of nostalgia for the sunny Saturday afternoon just a week ago. She had thought, then, that the painting on the lid was better than most chocolate box art. Seen under the dressing room's glaring lights it was woolly and conventional. Perhaps her mood had supplied the touch of impressionistic atmosphere. Curious, that in her mind's eye, she could still see the picture as she remembered it.

Also in the wastepaper basket was a paper bag containing a few congealed acid drops. She particularly disliked the smell of acid drops and the very sight of them was enough to evoke it for her. They seemed, somehow, highly suitable for Cyril. For the first time, she admitted to herself that she, like Peter, found the boy repulsive. Well, all the more honour to Miles, for being so kind to him. She went down to the waiting taxi.

Spa Street now looked more like a river than a road. She hoped the shaving-brush chestnuts were enjoying their drench. Back at the hotel the golden lion shone wetly.

She remembered it, shining and streaming, just before she fell asleep.

⇤ 6 ⇥

Birth of a Teeterer

Jill unlocked the door of the flat and strode briskly through the hall, saying brightly, 'Nice to be back, isn't it?'

'Yes, indeed,' said Miles heartily.

She was pretty sure he disliked the flat as much as she did but neither of them had, as yet, admitted their dislike aloud.

The sitting room, in the early evening light, looked even more cheerless than usual as there were no flowers; and though the large windows gave an impression of airiness it felt airless. She flung the windows open onto the balcony but was not tempted to step out. After two months she still experienced vertigo when on the balcony; and Miles had recently confessed that he did too. It seemed a pity they hadn't pooled their vertigo before taking a tenth-floor flat.

She hoped that Miles was not, as she was, remembering many home-comings to their old Islington house where

Mrs Topham would have been on hand to welcome them – beloved Mrs Topham, none too clean but a glorious cook, who had been Miles's housekeeper long before he married. Alas, their leases on home and help had run out at the same time; the house was now demolished and Mrs Topham had retired on what she called 'me bits of pensions' – to which now was added one from Miles. Even the friendly old Islington furniture had gone into retirement, as this ultra-modern West End flat had seemed to call for ultra-modern furniture. They had chosen first-rate pieces; anyway, Miles believed them to be first-rate and she, most implicitly, believed in his good taste. She had felt sure she would get to like them but, instead, had come to hate their guts, and doubted if they had any.

'I ought to have asked Miss Linton to buy us some flowers,' she said, looking round the spacious, austere room. ('So wonderful to get such a large room in a flat,' kind friends said.)

'They would have withered at her touch,' said Miles, 'unless made of tin.'

Miss Linton spent two hours on three days a week keeping the flat scrupulously clean while remaining scrupulously clean herself in spite of the fact that she never donned an overall. She wore neat dark clothes, appeared to be middle-aged, and spoke only when spoken to. Jill had elicited from her that she lived with her mother 'very quietly,' but Miles insisted that she was really a robot who returned to a factory every night for servicing.

'Well, at least she's never obtrusive,' said Jill. Mrs

Topham had been very obtrusive, but the obtrusiveness had ranked as friendliness.

'What are you going to do about food? Why don't you change your mind and come with me to Peter's?'

She had refused Peter's invitation partly because she wanted to unpack and do various odd jobs but also because she thought Miles should go on his own. When he was with some of his oldest and best friends she had an idea that he and they occasionally found her presence inhibiting. Also she wanted Miles and Peter to consolidate the beautiful state of agreement they had now reached. During the discussion on the train Miles had surprisingly put up no fight whatever. He pointed out that he had always been willing to accept changes in the direction, once young Cyril had found his feet. And it now seemed that he had been more impressed by Tom Albion's criticisms than he had admitted, and less impressed by the Spa Town's approval than Peter had been. He was also, Jill guessed, feeling guilty towards Peter. 'I muddled you, Peter,' he said apologetically. 'If you'd had your way we'd probably have pleased the Spa Town fogies *and* the Saturday night toughs. It was just that I didn't want to hurt the boy.'

'Well, I'll handle him with kid gloves,' Peter had said, beaming with relief at having won Miles over. Jill was overjoyed at the sweetness and light in which he and Miles were now basking and they were welcome to an evening of it; also to an evening with Peter's manservant-friend, Gaston, whom she found trying. She assured Miles that she didn't fancy going out to supper. 'I'll just get myself something here.'

'There won't *be* anything here.'

'Yes, there will. I asked Miss Linton to get in some staples. And there's plenty of tinned stuff.'

'Why not ring down for a decent meal?'

She considered the restaurant on the ground floor charged impressive prices for unimpressive food. 'Well, I'll see.'

After he had gone she unpacked, got herself a drink, and then went into the small, gleaming kitchen. During a girlhood spent in bed-sitting rooms and boarding houses she'd had few chances to cook, and scarcely more during Mrs Topham's benevolent dictatorship. She had planned to cook at the flat but Miles preferred to go out for most meals. 'Anyway, you couldn't really cook in that kitchen,' he told her. 'It looks outraged if so much as an egg-boiler's out of its place.' Not that they had an egg-boiler.

She now wondered if she would attempt something dashing, then decided that toast and Gentleman's Relish would do very well – and coffee. The sitting room, when she carried her tray in, was now rather too airy. Before closing the glass doors she stood for a moment admiring the view, that view which had played a major part in attracting them to the flat (and if they had to leave their beloved old house, surely something quite new and stimulating was a good idea?). She could see the Houses of Parliament. Did the Thorntons live in Westminster? Yes, she remembered Geoffrey Thornton saying so, during

93

supper at the Civic Reception. Pleasant people. . . . Really, it was absurd: even to *think* about the drop below the balcony made the backs of her knees feel peculiar. She closed the doors and retreated to a nice, safe armchair.

Later, she wondered if there would be any interesting music on the radio, something like the Schubert Octet – how extraordinarily happy she had felt while listening to it. But though she twiddled with a will, even trying foreign stations, she could get nothing that pleased her. She settled for television. Miles, returning, found her fast asleep in front of it.

'You didn't have a proper meal,' he said, looking at her tray. 'I shall make you some bread-and-milk. I'll have some, too.'

She smiled. 'I wonder if we're really as fond of bread-and-milk as we think we are – or is it sheer association with that first time you made it for me? Anyway, it would be nice.'

The next morning, when they were discussing where they should meet for lunch, Miles asked if she could manage to give a party after the first night of the play.

She looked at him in astonishment. 'But you loathe even going to first-night parties, let alone giving them.'

'I know. They're ghastly if a play's gone badly – and even if it's gone well, one's never sure. But it's Frank Ashton's first production and a young author's first play. And I'd like to do a little something for the company. Everyone was a bit shattered on Saturday night.'

'You mean you want to ask the whole company?'

'Well, not unless you think you can manage.'

'Oh, I'll manage all right,' said Jill. 'But it won't be like one of our Mrs Topham parties.'

Mrs Topham could always be counted on for hot suppers served in enormous earthenware dishes, the contents of which combined tastiness with mystery. Guests had been known to penetrate her kitchen to ask for recipes, only to be fobbed off with, 'Oh, this and that, madam, depending on what I had by me.' There was, indeed, some truth in this. Mrs T. was as improvisatory as a Jazz player.

'How about getting in a firm of caterers'?' said Miles.

'I might. But their food's so conventional. Don't worry, I'll cope. Let's add up how many. Lucky the company's small.'

Still, with the understudies, the stage management, Frank Ashton, the author, Peter, the Albions . . . they were soon up to twenty.

'And how about the Thorntons?' said Miles. 'Those girls would love it.'

'They would indeed. Well, it'll be a squash but we ought to be able to manage with a room this size.'

'And if it's fine we can use the balcony – that is, people who aren't us can. I must go now. I said I'd meet Peter at the theatre. Let me know if there's anything I can do.'

'You can order a great deal of champagne,' said Jill.

'Right. I'll do that on my way.'

After he had gone she found the Thorntons' number in the telephone directory and rang it. Kit answered and accepted the invitation to the party ecstatically. 'Oh, roll on, Thursday. We're all gasping to see you again, Mrs Quentin.'

Jill found herself feeling cheerful. Somehow she would manage to make it a good party, not a formal, catered affair. The restaurant below should be bullied into sending up some really interesting hot food. And she would shop for exciting cold additions. She began to feel hungry – absurd, at ten in the morning.

Miss Linton arrived and, though unable to lend a hand at the party as her mother could not be left in the evening, showed willingness to wash all the glasses in readiness. Less robotish than usual, she remarked, 'This flat *needs* a party.'

'Of course!' Silly not to have realized that before. Miles would like the flat much better after a party, and so would she . . . perhaps. But she was in for a wild rush between now and Thursday night, what with the food and the flowers, getting her hair done and having a last fitting for her dress, buying presents for the whole company, meeting Miles for most meals, and spending much of Wednesday at the dress rehearsal.

The day sped by with far less accomplished than she had counted on. But she made better headway on Tuesday as she was off duty for lunch – Miles said he was going to take Cyril out for it, 'In case he's been upset by the morning rehearsal.' When she got back to the flat, after a satisfactory afternoon of present-buying, she found the boy in the sitting room with Miles. Cyril was looking distressed, she even thought he had been crying; (*impossible* to believe he was eighteen). Miles, with a slightly histrionic breeziness, said,

96

'We've been having a little private rehearsal. Cyril found things a bit difficult this morning.'

'Last-minute changes are always worrying,' said Jill sympathetically. 'But we all want to do what's best for the play, don't we, Cyril?'

Cyril merely nodded and gulped. Yes, he had been crying. She was wondering if she should offer him tea – or a drink, perhaps? – when Miles said, 'Now off you go, young Cyril. We'll have another run-through at the theatre in the morning, and you'll be as right as rain by the dress rehearsal.' He put his arm round the boy and steered him into the hall. Cyril barely managed a dejected 'Goodbye, Mrs Quentin.' Just before the front door closed she heard a short, low-toned conversation, out of which all that came to her clearly was 'I swear it, Mr Quentin. I won't let you down.'

'I take it things are difficult,' she said, as Miles returned.

'Well, those kid gloves of Peter's had holes large enough to let his claws through. Not that I altogether blamed him. The boy's just a drooling mass of self-pity.'

It was so unlike Miles to speak so harshly that she guessed he must be worried. 'Well, you've done all you can,' she told him. 'Just try to get your mind off his troubles.'

'That's easier said than done. You don't know the half of them.'

'And I don't think I want to,' said Jill firmly. 'Oh, I'm not unsympathetic but you really must relax. Now let's have a drink and then go out to an early dinner.'

She was thankful that he did not mention Cyril again all evening. And even more thankful that, as almost always, he slept well.

Next day the dress rehearsal, due to start at six-thirty, started only ten minutes late, but from then on it became a classic example of the bad dress rehearsal; indeed, there was a time when Jill thought it was going to prove a record-breaker for productions in which Miles had played. Scenery fell down, all the new lighting cues went wrong. No one, not even Miles, remembered the subtler points of Peter's re-direction, and Cyril reverted to the shouting performance he had given all the previous week; the end of Act II had to be done six times. Three people, including Cyril, wept. (Peter said, 'It's like hysteria going through dog kennels.') Miles and Peter had a shouting match across the (non-existent) footlights. Around one A.M. Frank Ashton, feeling he ought to make a noise like a management, came to Peter and said, 'Running a bit late, aren't we?' Peter, white with temper, said, 'Go away.' Frank Ashton, wisely, went. The author said miserably to Jill, 'I suppose this means we can't open?' She soothed him, handing out all the dope about bad dress rehearsals being lucky. And in the end the record remained unbroken as they finished at three A.M. She could remember a dress rehearsal that had lasted until five, and then the last act had been held over.

As she took Miles home she decided they lived in a lunatic world. None of this should happen – but again and again it did. And if the play succeeded one forgot about the nightmare, much as women were said to forget the agonies of childbirth.

But could this play succeed?

Some sixteen hours later, after working so late on last-minute preparations for the party that she barely had time to change into her new evening dress, she was almost past caring. She just longed to get through the first night and the party, and go to sleep. She gave a loving look at her bed, and then mentally shook herself. At least she didn't have to act, as Miles and the company did. And the stage management would be the tiredest of all.

She had invited Tom Albion and his elderly, still-handsome wife to share her box. She liked a box for London first nights, so that she could watch the audience and also avoid mingling with it, except for people who knew her well enough to come up to the box in the intervals.

'Well, here we go again,' said Tom, as the house lights dimmed before the rise of the curtain. 'Peter tells me I shall see quite a different play.'

'You'll be lucky if you see any play, judging by last night. I'm glad you weren't able to be there.'

But within ten minutes she had realized that, as so often, the first-night miracle had happened: chaos had been replaced by smoothness. But she did not think anyone was very good; even Miles seemed to her rather quiet. She turned her attention to the audience and decided there was nowhere near the enthusiasm of the previous week's first night. But she could not detect signs of actual boredom, let alone hostility. And the applause at the end of the act was good.

'Much, much better,' Tom pronounced.

'It didn't strike you as a bit tame?'

'Dear heart, it *needed* taming. I shouldn't wonder, now, if the damn thing didn't succeed.'

She looked him in the eye. 'You don't mean that, Tom.'

'I don't quite *not* mean it. I just don't know – yet. Come and have a drink.'

But she stayed where she was and chatted to friends who came up. They were all enthusiastic but she never believed a word anyone said on a first night.

The second act was even more tamed than the first. The less spectacular lighting made a surprising difference and there was a general toning down of melodramatic effects. Cyril (now 'Doug' on the programmes) remembered his new cuts and not to shout at the end of the act (no spotlight on him now, poor Cyril). Indeed, he mumbled; but Jill had recently decided that audiences no longer expected to hear fully; conditioned by ultra-natural television acting they took it for granted that they just had to guess. Anyway, Miles was superb and the end of the act now belonged to him. The applause, as assessed by Jill, was generous verging on handsome.

In the second interval, having located the Thorntons in the stalls, she beckoned them up to the box. She had arranged to meet them at the stage door and take them to see Miles. Now she had to tell them she wouldn't be able to. The play was running later than she had expected and she would need to dash off the minute the curtain fell – 'Otherwise I shan't be back to take in the hot food. And I've quite a lot to do before the party starts.'

'May Kit and I come and help?' said Robin.

'No, really. It's sweet of you but you want to go back-stage. Miles is expecting you.'

'We can visit him some other time,' said Kit. '*Of course* we shall come with you. Have you a taxi ordered?'

'I don't think you can order taxis to wait outside theatres. I was trusting to luck.'

'Oh, the commissionaire can manage something. We'll talk to him now, before the interval ends. Come on, Robin.'

Robin started off, then called back, 'What time's the curtain likely to be down?'

Jill made the best guess she could, then looked rather dazedly at Geoffrey Thornton.

He smiled. 'I know. They can be a bit over-powering. But you really will find they're a help. I'll let your husband know what's happened to them.'

'And to me, please. He'll be expecting me.'

During the last act she was more anxious about getting home than about the play, which continued to proceed smoothly. She was out of the box as the curtain fell and had the pleasure of hearing solid applause as she sped from the theatre.

The taxi was there all right, with the two girls standing by its open door. Jill, helped inside so firmly that she nearly fell on her face, had the sensation of being kidnapped.

They reached the flat in time to receive the hot food – or rather, the girls received it, decided it wasn't hot enough, and put it in the oven. They then got cold food from the refrigerator. Robin, dismissing Jill – 'Perhaps you'll want to do a little something to your lovely hair,' added, 'Don't worry about us. We really are terrifically domesticated. We have to be, to run our house with only a little help from a poor dear who used to look after Mother, and now needs looking after, herself. Oh, will Mr Quentin open the champagne? If not, we do know how, even though we don't drink it.'

Jill said Miles would cope, and then went obediently to tidy herself. 'And the odd thing is,' she thought, 'that I don't feel irritated by them. I just feel grateful.'

She was even more grateful a couple of hours later, for she realized that, without the sisters, the party would have been a dead failure. There was nothing wrong with the food or the drink, nothing she could blame herself for. The fault lay with the guests, who were quiet to the verge of gloominess and who resolutely refused to circulate. The senior members of the company clung together, preferably around Miles. The stage management remained with the small parts and understudies. Frank Ashton and the author sat together looking both shy and worried. Peter Hesper huddled with the Tom Albions, discussing a prospective job. And Cyril, his understudy and his understudy's Mum sat together but barely talked to each other, let alone to anyone else – until they were joined by Geoffrey Thornton who, presumably, thought this was the best way he could pull his weight. Jill went from group to group but did not feel she was proving stimulating. Only Robin and Kit – Robin in her gleaming satin sheath and Kit now in scarlet chiffon – infused some little gaiety. They offered food, replenished glasses, paid compliments and cracked jokes, somehow giving the impression the party was 'going'. Jill, in the kitchen making coffee, was asked by Robin, 'Truly, are we over-doing it?'

'Truly, you're not,' said Jill fervently.

'Then back to the good work. Perhaps coffee will wake them up a bit. Shout when it's ready.'

'Most of them are dead tired, poor loves. I hope they don't stay on and on just out of courtesy.'

It was the understudy's Mum who made the first move. On being conventionally begged not to break the party up she became – at last – voluble about the complications of her journey home. A few other guests drifted away at the same time. Jill, returning from seeing them off, noticed that Cyril was collecting empty plates and no-longer-needed glasses. Instructed by the Thornton sisters? She went into the kitchen and found they were already washing up.

'No, no,' she protested. 'There'll be someone to do that in the morning.'

'But not before breakfast, surely,' said Robin. 'And you couldn't face getting up, with all this about. Thank you, Cyril, but be careful not to sneak glasses from people who are still here. We'll do all the glasses afterwards, Kit, with fresh water. You can wash, then, because I polish glasses better than you do.'

Jill murmured 'Angels' and went back to the party, where she talked to Geoffrey Thornton until the next batch of guests had to be seen off. Cyril pounced on their glasses the instant they moved towards the door.

By two A.M. there was no one left but Peter Hesper, the Albions, the Thorntons – the girls still busy washing glasses – and Cyril, whom the Thorntons had undertaken to drive home. Miles said to Tom Albion, 'Come on, now. What's your verdict on the play's chances?'

Tom Albion looked round the room. 'Author gone, management gone, cast gone? Where's that boy?'

'In the kitchen, out of earshot,' said Jill. 'Come on, Tom.'

'Well, if you ask me, the damn thing's going to be my absolute *bête noire* of plays, a teeterer.'

No one looked puzzled but Geoffrey Thornton, who said blankly, 'A what?'

'A play that teeters between success and failure,' said Peter Hesper. 'Frank Ashton will probably feel he has to tide it over and wait for it to build.'

'And he's liable to lose a lot of money,' said Tom Albion. 'And I'm liable to lose a first-rate film contract for Miles. Yet I couldn't, with my hand on my heart, advise Ashton to cut his losses now. There's a *chance* of success.'

'Of course there is,' said Mrs Albion. 'You wait till you see the notices. Shall we go out and get the early editions?'

'Not for me,' said Miles. 'I don't want to sit up all night discussing them. The morning will be time enough.'

'Anyway, the notices will teeter, too,' said Tom. 'And I

doubt if Frank Ashton is over-burdened with courage.' He turned to Jill. 'On the whole, I still say what I said originally: three weeks.'

'Pay no heed to him,' said Mrs Albion, rising to go.

Peter went with the Albions. The girls stayed until the last ashtray was washed, and then Kit announced that she was going to do what she had longed to, all evening – 'go out on the balcony and look at the view.'

She took Cyril with her. Even Jill could not feel nervous for them, as the parapet, in their case, came chest high.

'Marvellous,' said Kit. 'I should like to sleep out here. Well, there's Big Ben calling us home.'

'And quite time, for shrimps like you,' said Robin. 'You'd better go to bed at seven tomorrow and try to grow.'

Between Today and Tomorrow

The notices in the morning papers undoubtedly teetered; none were really bad, none fully complimentary – except to Miles and even his were not the kind of 'raves' that can sometimes enable an actor to carry a play to success single-handed.

'But at least no one's feelings are going to be lacerated,' he said with relief. 'The author can cherish "promising", "an ear for dialogue" and "a sense of situation"; and Cyril can chalk up "Doug Digby is a likeable youngster", "sincere if inaudible" and less painful than the average boy actor.'

'And the Sunday papers and the weeklies may help,' said Jill. 'And of course the word of mouth.'

'From my own point of view I hope the thing doesn't run. Oh, I'm not ill-wishing it but that's how I really feel.'

'Because you want to do the film?'

'You know I loathe filming. But somehow the play seems to have gone sour on me. Well, I must churn up some enthusiasm.'

They had arranged to lunch with Peter Hesper. After commenting on the notices he talked mainly about the next job Tom Albion had lined up for him. Jill had often thought that, for directors, a play in rehearsal could occupy every waking hour, and then be shovelled out of mind immediately after the London production. Not that Peter was uninterested in the play's fortunes, as he was paid a royalty on the box-office takings; but he was no longer creatively concerned. He would have disliked holding another rehearsal.

She put in an afternoon and evening on typing thank-you letters for Miles's first-night telegrams, then called for him at the theatre. He reported that business and booking were, 'Just what one would expect with a teeterer. Anyway, optimism is the order of the day.' They then went out to supper. The normal, pleasant pattern of their life was taking over . . . except that it did not seem quite as pleasant as was normal.

She only fully realized this on the Sunday morning. The notices, again, were neither good nor bad, though bad in as much as they were brief and would do little to advertise the play. She had discussed them, read anything else in the papers that interested her, and then started to weed out the flowers which had died since the night of the party. Becoming conscious that Miles had stopped reading and was following her about with his eyes, she looked at him questioningly.

He said, 'Let's face it. Neither of us is happy in this flat.'

No doubt it *was* best to face it. She nodded acceptance. 'What shall we do, then? Get rid of the flat and find a house?'

'Running a house would be hell for you, without Mrs Topham. The flat's easier and I'll even admit this room has a certain beauty. But I don't feel I'm living in a home, just a *pied-à-terre*. Suppose we kept it as that, and got ourselves some little place in the country? I've been reading property advertisements. One or two cottages sound attractive. I mean for weekends and when I'm between jobs.'

'You're never between jobs for long. As for weekends . . . I doubt if there'd be late enough trains on Saturday nights.'

'Suppose we got a car and I took up driving again?'

'Oh, Miles, would you? Could you?'

It was some seconds before he answered. 'I think so. It wasn't a question of losing my nerve.'

'I've always thought it was more that you were punishing yourself – for something that wasn't your fault.'

'No use thinking about that now. What matters is that I'm willing to drive again. And I daresay you'd like to learn.'

'I'd have suggested that long ago if you hadn't said you didn't even want to have a car.'

'I know. You may be right about my punishing myself. I was extremely fond of cars and of driving. Well, then, how do we start?'

'I suppose we consider cars and enquire about cottages.'

'Just one thing. Will this be of real interest to you? You won't be doing it simply to please me?'

He was looking at her searchingly. And there was something about his expression that reminded her of that moonlight night a couple of weeks past when he had needed reassurance. Now, as then, she gave it.

'I shall love it, Miles.' But she felt vaguely uneasy. He seemed to have something on his mind. And was he perhaps thinking more of her than himself, in planning car and cottage? She had no desire for either. If he really wanted them of course he must have them, but she would take no steps towards them until he raised the matter again.

The next morning she received a letter from Robin Thornton who had already sent a punctilious letter of thanks for the party. The second letter read:

Dear Mrs Quentin,

I am writing this invitation, instead of just ringing you up, so that it will be easier for you and Mr Quentin to refuse if you want to. This is how it is. Our brother Julian is back from Scotland and mad with jealousy because we've met you and Mr Quentin and he hasn't. You see, he wants to go on the stage – oh, not yet, he'll be up at Oxford for a couple more years, so there's no chance of his asking for help in getting a job. But he would terribly like just to meet Mr Quentin and sort of ask his advice generally. So we're wondering if you could both bear to come to supper after the theatre on Friday – just us, no need to dress. And perhaps you would come a bit early so that Kit and I can have you to ourselves for a while.

We hope Mr Quentin will count it in our favour that we haven't sprung a stage-struck brother on him without warning. Still, we shall quite understand if we get a refusal.

Yours, with love
ROBIN

There was a postscript from Kit saying: 'Robin seems almost resigned to getting a refusal but I'm hopeful because Mr Quentin is so very kind. And we absolutely promise that Julian won't recite.' This was signed with a clever little drawing of Kit looking like a cat or a cat looking like Kit; Jill couldn't decide which.

Miles, after reading the letter, said, 'Of course we must go – if only to repay the girls for the way they worked at our party. And it'll be interesting to see the brother. I don't mind stage-struck youths.'

'Then I'll ring up and accept.'

After doing so, while her ears still buzzed with Kit's excited thanks, she remembered that she had never told Miles about the late Mrs Thornton's dipsomania. He'd better know now as they were getting on such friendly terms with the Thorntons. He listened with interest, then asked if she thought the girls could have been exaggerating.

She said, 'Somehow I'm sure they weren't. And they were perfectly cheerful, kept stressing that it was over for them, and for their father, too. They said he'd started a new life.'

'My God, he'd need to. I wonder why they upped and told you? Anyway, do anything you can for them – you'll have more chance than I shall. Though I could ask them to tea at the theatre and let them explore the stage. That usually interests the young.'

Getting into a taxi on Friday night (she had promised Kit, on the telephone, to arrive an hour before Miles did), she felt inexplicably excited, though a hint of an explanation came to her as the taxi drove past the Houses of Parliament – 'It's just that one's entering a new world' – she and Miles had no friends unconnected with the theatre. She wondered if Geoffrey Thornton would be inside the House of Commons. No, not in August, surely – though she was as vague about this as about everything else connected with politics.

The taxi was now driving through small, quiet streets of old houses. She felt a pang of loss for the Islington house – these houses were a little like it; but they were smaller, and even older, she thought, and most beautifully taken care of. Impossible to imagine a peeling front door or a broken window here, or any of the encroaching decay amidst which she and Miles had lived for the last years of his lease.

After she had paid the taxi off, she stood outside the Thorntons' house for a moment before ringing the bell, taking in the quiet street. At one end of it was a blitzed church, looking all the more romantic, against the still faintly luminous sky, by contrast with its well-kept surroundings. She now found that she was nervous, as well as excited. How absurd! She rang the bell firmly – and it was answered so quickly by both Robin and Kit that it seemed likely they had been at hand waiting for her.

'Darling Mrs Quentin,' said Kit, embracing her.

'You should never kiss grown-ups until they show that they want you to,' said Robin. 'Mrs Quentin may not like kissing.'

Jill said that in the theatrical profession most people kissed most people – 'And I'll admit that I don't always care for it. But I'm happy to kiss you two.' She now kissed Robin and then added, 'And I'd like it if you'd start calling me Jill.'

Kit said triumphantly, 'I told you, Robin. She really meant it when she said she'd be our friend.'

Robin said, 'We want you to come up to our room, if you don't mind a lot of stairs. This house is so small that we have to make do with the attics. Not that we mind.'

'No, indeed. We adore the attics.'

They proceeded upwards, not without difficulty as Kit kept her arm through Jill's and the staircase was barely wide enough for two to walk abreast. On the first floor a door stood open onto a doll's size drawing room. 'And that's Father's room at the back,' Kit explained, 'and up above there's our spare room and Mary Simmonds's room – I suppose you *could* call her our help – and then we're at the top. Do you need a rest'? No? Then on we go. We share a bedroom so that we can have the front attic as a sitting room. It's really nicer in the winter when

112

we can have a fire. Of course we carry the coals up ourselves.'

'It's nice enough now,' said Jill, looking round. 'What a lot of books.'

'They're mostly Kit's,' said Robin. 'Not that I don't like reading some authors, such as Jane Austen, Charlotte Bronte and Dickens. But most of Kit's modern authors are too much for me.'

'That's odd, really, seeing that in some ways you're so much more modern than I am. That's Robin's special wall.'

Over the fireplace was a large, canvas-covered board to which were drawing-pinned cuttings from magazines – reproductions of abstract painting, pop art, op art, recipes, extreme fashions in clothes and hair styles.

'I change the collection every month,' said Robin. 'Oh, could you bear to tell me frankly if this dress is too awful? I'm not sure me and me dressmaker didn't get carried away.'

It was a very short shift of felt, divided into quarters of black, white, grey and blue. Jill could, with sincerity, admire it.

'I tell her it looks like the flag of some new country,' said Kit.

'Father thinks it looks more like linoleum – but then linoleum quite often looks like Mondrian, so it was a sort of compliment.' She sighed. 'Of course what it really needs is the *authority* of a great couturier. But me and me dressmaker do our best. What do you think of Kit's dress?

113

It isn't usual for girls of fifteen to wear black but then she's not a usual girl of fifteen.'

The dress was long-fleeced black wool, trimmed with narrow strips of black rabbit. Jill said, 'If there was a black cat here I wouldn't know you from it, Kit.'

'Oh, lovely! I did want to have a little fur tail.'

'Me and me dressmaker thought that would be sheer whimsy,' said Robin, then suddenly swept her long, fair hair up onto the top of her head. 'I'm considering getting rid of my blinkers.'

'Do persuade her to, Jill, before she gets run over.'

Jill, realizing for the first time the beautiful breadth of Robin's brow and her admirable jawline, said enthusiastically, 'Oh, I like it up.'

'But I feel so much more frail and mysterious, just peeping out,' said Robin, dropping her veils of hair. 'And I can always watch the traffic lights. Now I'm talking too much about myself. Do tell us how the play's doing.'

Jill responded perfunctorily that the business was 'building', and proceeded to look round the room. 'You've got so many interesting things.'

'This is a kaleidoscope,' said Robin, offering it. 'You hold it up to the light and you can see fascinating patterns, a bit like kinetic art. It was our great-grandmother's when she was a child. So was the musical box. Shall I play it?'

'No, Robin,' said Kit. 'It's nice but it kills conversation.'

Jill was looking through the kaleidoscope, turning it to vary the patterns made by the tiny, brilliant pieces of glass.

Kit said, 'When I was young it used to sadden me that

114

patterns went for ever each time you changed them. It seemed like painting a picture and then destroying it. But in a way that's the beauty of it.'

'Like the way fashions change and never *quite* come back,' said Robin. 'Oh, I do love clothes. I think I have almost a religious feeling about them.'

Kit was now offering a glass paper-weight for inspection. 'Look, it's got an old print of Queen's Crescent on it. *That* was our great-grandmother's house. We loved it – but I think we love this one more, because it's so much older. But perhaps you don't like old houses.'

'We admired your beautiful modern flat,' said Robin politely.

'I can't say Miles and I do,' said Jill. 'We'd much prefer to live in an old house.'

'We *are* glad,' said Kit earnestly. 'Oh, not that you don't like your flat but that you do like old houses. We were so afraid you might not like this one.'

Surely her opinion could not be of such importance to them? She still found it puzzling, this liking the sisters had taken to her, still could not quite accept it at its face value. But she more and more found it pleasant. They continued to show her their possessions. They asked her opinion on clothes, life and literature. She did fairly well on clothes and life but was out of her depth as regards literature – though she was thankful to be able to say that she had read one book by Kit's favourite modern novelist, Ivy Compton-Burnett.

'If you only read *one*, you couldn't have liked her,' said Kit. 'People who do, read them all – and again and again.'

'I *almost* like her because she writes about families,' said Robin. 'But she doesn't tell one enough about their backgrounds, what the houses are like, what the women wear. And though everyone's always eating, we're never allowed to know what they eat.'

'Well, who wants to know what anyone eats?' said Kit impatiently. 'And she does say quite a bit about backgrounds. Sometimes there are cracks in a wall, or an overgrown creeper, or the rich people have cushions. One can do the rest from imagination. And the strange thing is that whenever I re-read one of the books I get a different mental picture of the house in it – and I can remember all the different mental pictures. Very peculiar, that. And the dialogue's so marvellous, somehow it's what the characters are thinking as well as what they're saying, so it ends by being what they *are*. People say the servants don't talk like servants and the children don't talk like children, but the servants just *are* our great-grandmother's chauffeur and lady's maid, and the children are *me*, almost before I could talk. And the plots are lovely, all the families have terrific secrets and scandals, just like our family – though Miss Compton-Burnett hasn't done a dipsomaniac nymphomaniac, which seems a pity. She usually deals with quite ordinary adultery, though sometimes it's murder or bigamy or incest, but the incest seldom comes to anything. I must say she's fussy about incest. After all, it's been highly thought of at many periods of the world's history, and it appears to work well in the animal kingdom.'

'Kit, dear,' said Robin, getting a word in at last. 'Jill isn't interested in Ivy Compton-Burnett.'

'I am, now,' said Jill. 'I'll try her again.'

'Try *A Family and a Fortune*,' said Kit. 'That's my absolute favourite. Though *More Women than Men* is rather a love. There's a most charming homosexual in it, the nicest character in the book. He marries eventually.'

'That's enough, Kit,' said Robin sharply. 'And now I think we should go down to Father. He nobly said we could have you to ourselves for a while but we mustn't go on hogging you. And Julian should be back soon. He went to one of the arty films he favours.'

'We like some arty films,' said Kit. 'Even some of the slow ones and some of the horrible ones. But we're not enthusiastic when slowness and horror are combined.'

'Julian thinks those are the best of all.'

They went down to the little panelled drawing room. Jill, greeting Geoffrey Thornton, thought how right the room was for him; it, too, had a small-boned elegance, though he was, as a man, considerably larger than the room was as a room.

'I've quite fallen in love with your house,' she told him.

He said he was wonderfully lucky to have a Westminster house just when he needed it. 'I bought the lease – or rather, my grandmother bought it for me – a good many years ago, when my political aspirations were relegated to the dim future. One reason I stood for Parliament was so as not to waste the right house,'

Big Ben – as if on cue, Jill thought – began to strike eleven. She said she was ashamed to say she'd never been in the Houses of Parliament.

117

'I'll arrange for you to come to a debate, if you'd like to. I'll guarantee not to be speaking.'

'But I'd rather come when you were,' she said.

'Then you'll have to wait quite a while. I've barely recovered from making my maiden speech.'

Robin had slipped out of the room. Kit, about to follow, turned to say, 'Please excuse us now, Jill. We want to see that all's well with supper.'

Thornton, looking after his daughter, said, 'Is it all right for her to call you Jill?'

'I asked them both to.' She was about to add that she hoped he would, too, but hesitated; there was always a hint of formality combined with his pleasant ease of manner. Still, it seemed stuffily unfriendly not to. But during her fraction of hesitation, voices were heard below and Thornton said, 'Ah, this will be Julian.'

The young man who entered was almost breath-takingly handsome – though 'beautiful' seemed to Jill a more appropriate word. He was as fair as Robin, and like her in other ways. Jill, remembering the girl with her hair swept up, realized that brother and sister shared a similar breadth of brow and clean-cut jawline. But Julian's eyes were a more spectacular blue; indeed, his whole appearance struck Jill as spectacular – hardly a word applicable to Robin, hiding behind her veils of hair. He seemed an unlikely son for Geoffrey Thornton, yet there was a definite resemblance: the jawline derived from Thornton and both father and son had particularly well-shaped, mobile mouths.

Having introduced Julian, Thornton occupied himself

with pouring out drinks, leaving Jill to talk to his son. She found him unforthcoming, almost enough so to seem discourteous. She wondered if he was shy, but there was nothing shy about the carriage of his head or the way he spoke when he did speak. It simply appeared that he expected her to make all the running. She asked him about the film he had been to, and received the kind of answer – brief, definite – which meant she had to think of another question. She asked if he enjoyed life at Oxford, to which he replied, 'Sometimes.' Even when she said, 'I understand you're planning to go on the stage,' he merely said, 'One has thought of it.' She was wondering if she would have to talk about the weather, when Geoffrey Thornton re-entered the conversation. Julian Thornton then retired from it, but she was aware that he was both listening to her and looking at her – so noticeably that it made her feel self-conscious. She was relieved when she heard the doorbell and guessed that Miles had arrived.

The girls came upstairs with him and, from then on, conversation was general and easy, though Julian still said remarkably little. She saw that he was now watching Miles, rather than herself. It was interesting to compare their good looks. Both were fair, both classically handsome. The great difference between them – apart from over twenty years in age – was that Miles's face was so alive, so expressive, whereas Julian's was as still as a face in a photograph.

A bell tinkled. Robin said, 'That means that supper's ready.'

The dining room, below, was as small as the drawing room.

'I don't know what we'll do when Father wants to give large, important political dinners,' said Kit.

'We'll cross that unlikely bridge when we come to it,' said her father. 'I'm more attracted by the idea of secret conferences at midnight, after the Prime Minister's said, "Don't come to me, I'll come to you."'

The first course, cold soup, was already in position. After that, hot food came up on a dumb waiter. Jill noted with what quiet efficiency the girls coped with serving the meal, which was very good and slightly mysterious; she could always identify what she was eating but the flavouring was both delicate and elusive. This supper was as good as Mrs Topham's Islington suppers, but in a very different way: lighter, less rich. Jill remembered the recipes pinned to the notice board upstairs; no doubt there were fashions in food, as in clothes.

Conversation came up against a brick wall early in the meal when Miles said to Julian, 'I hear you're interested in a stage career,' and Julian responded, 'I'd find it difficult to discuss that in the bosom of my family. Might I crave a few minutes alone with you, later on?' Jill thought the suggestion sensible but Julian's tone of voice and phrasing were extremely aloof. And though Miles said, 'Yes, of course,' he looked both surprised and rebuffed – but only for an instant. He then began a bantering conversation with the girls. And Julian – she was between him and his father – began to talk to her, rather more easily than in the drawing room; probably he *was* shy, and the shyness was beginning to wear off. Geoffrey Thornton said remarkably

120

little. As the table was round, the conversation could remain fairly general and she got the impression that he was deliberately not taking a lead in it. When he did speak, it was mainly to Miles and with particular courtesy.

As supper ended Jill happened to remark how little she knew Westminster – 'I'd no idea there were streets of old houses like this.' Kit instantly said to her father, 'Why don't we take her for a little walk, while Mr Quentin talks to Julian? That is, if you'd like it, Jill.' She barely waited for Jill's assent before continuing, 'I'll get your stole, to save you going upstairs.'

'And get my white boots,' said Robin. 'I can't walk in these heels.'

'Of course you can. It's just that you hanker for your boots. I think you're becoming a fetishist.'

As she left the dining room Jill managed to exchange a glance with Miles. Hers was intended to indicate a rueful sympathy. She interpreted his smile, accompanied by a barely perceptible wink, to be an assurance that he felt equal to the situation. Well, if anyone could set the boy at his ease, it would be Miles.

Thornton said, 'Are you sure you fancy this walk? There's no need for us to clear out – Julian can perfectly well get his aspirations off his chest in my study.'

But she said she would enjoy a stroll. 'It's such a beautiful night. And I could see so little of the neighbourhood, coming here by taxi.'

Kit returned with the stole and Robin's white boots. Miles and Julian went up to the drawing room. Jill and

Thornton went out into the quiet street. The two girls followed and walked a few paces behind. After a couple of minutes, Big Ben began to strike midnight.

Kit said, 'When I was a child I read in a story by Algernon Blackwood that, between the sixth and seventh strokes of midnight, there's a crack between today and tomorrow. And if you can think yourself through it, you can be outside time and space and be blissfully happy.'

'For ever – or just until the seventh stroke strikes'?' Thornton enquired.

'Well, they can be the same thing. Anyway, the sixth stroke's coming. So silence, please, while I try.'

The sixth stroke struck and then the seventh.

'Any luck?' said Thornton. 'You appear to be still in the flesh.'

'Well, I might be, to you – but not to myself. However, I didn't get through the crack that time.'

'Have you ever?' asked Jill.

'Frankly, no. But I go on hoping.'

'I doubt if you'll ever make it,' said Thornton. 'It would surprise me if, among your many talents, there's one for mysticism.'

'Oh, goodness, is that what it needs? Yes, of course it is. Then I shall never get through the crack – I'm terribly mundane. Ah, me! Well, there's the end of one of childhood's fancies.'

Big Ben was now silent and the night seemed more silent than before it had begun to strike. There was no traffic in the small, quiet streets they were walking through and no sounds issued from the houses, even when there were lights behind the drawn curtains. Robin suddenly giggled and said she had a wild desire to bang every knocker. 'Just imagine all the doors being opened by startled people.'

'Quite a number of whom would be my fellow Members of Parliament,' said Thornton. 'You'd get me drummed out.'

'It's the kind of thought that *would* come to a girl wearing white boots,' said Kit. 'And just when I was trying to think myself back three hundred years, to when these houses were built.'

'Perhaps not quite so long ago,' said her father. 'But some of these streets were certainly here by the end of the seventeenth century.'

After that, no one spoke for a while and the only sounds were their own footsteps and the dulled whirr of distant traffic. Jill became aware that there were no footsteps behind her. She looked back, then said, 'We've lost the girls.'

'I suspect their consciences smote them about not helping our very inadequate help. She's not strong in body or mind, partly as a result of her devoted service to us – or rather, to my late wife. I believe the girls did give you some idea of their poor mother's history?'

'I hope you didn't mind their telling me,' said Jill.

'Only because I feared it might have embarrassed you. Apart from that, I was glad for you to know. Incidentally, the girls weren't angling for sympathy or trying to make themselves important.'

123

'I didn't for an instant feel that.' All the same, she had never fully understood why they had told her. The reasons they gave hadn't seemed fully adequate. But she was not going to delve into that now. Instead, she went on in a lighter tone, 'They really are a remarkable couple. Surely it's not usual for such young girls to be such admirable hostesses?'

'Well, they work hard at it,' said Thornton, 'as they do at running the house, which sometimes makes me feel guilty. Not so much about Kit; she'll continue her education in the way that seems best to her and it will, almost certainly, *be* the way that's best for her. But Robin was still enjoying school last year, when she insisted on leaving. And she now secretly hankers to design clothes professionally.'

'Can't she design them as well as run the house?'

'It isn't just the designing. She really wants to be in business. You'll be hearing about a curious composite being, known as "me and me dressmaker". Oh, I hope to work things out for her eventually. At present I'm too unsteady on my newly found feet to resist my daughters' determination to let their lives revolve round me.'

They had come out onto the Embankment, close to the Houses of Parliament. Jill, looking towards them, said, 'Well, you have an important job to do.'

'I'm only a modest back-bencher; still, I've made a fairly good start. And, with the perversity of these things, I'm now being offered more briefs than I've time to handle – not that I'm complaining about that.'

124

'Which interests you most, politics or the law?'

'Politics will, if I can make real headway. But they're pretty precarious. I must hang on to my legal work for a long time yet. I ought probably to take silk reasonably soon – which means becoming a Queen's Counsel, if you didn't happen to know.'

She laughed. 'I did – just. But it's about all I do know about the law. I suppose it would add to your prestige.'

'It might also detract from my income. One can do better as a successful Junior than as a Q.C. who doesn't quite make the grade. You *see* –' He pulled himself up. 'I'm talking too much about myself. Forgive me.'

'But I'm interested. Please go on.'

He gave her a quick, eager look; then shook his head. 'I mustn't, now. We've left your poor husband stranded with my stage-struck son. I think we'd better go back.'

She accepted his complete change of tone and subject, and said, 'Oh, Miles won't mind. Are you happy about Julian's wish to go on the stage?'

'I shall be happy for Julian to do anything in the world he really wants to,' said Thornton. 'But I can't, as yet, take his stage aspirations very seriously. He's never so much as mentioned them until this last week.'

She got the impression that Geoffrey Thornton was less satisfied with his son than with his daughters.

They had taken a roundabout route to reach the Embankment. Going back took only a few minutes, during which neither of them spoke. Jill was glad to be in the quiet, old streets again. The Embankment, with its lights

125

and shining river, had been beautiful too, but more conventionally so. And the little streets had a reassuring intimacy. She was sorry that, so soon, Thornton was unlocking his front door.

The girls came hurrying up from the basement.

'Do forgive us,' said Robin. 'We suddenly remembered poor Mary would be trying to do everything on her own. We do have a dishwasher, but even so, after a party . . .'

Kit said, 'But all's well now, so please do stay a long, long time. So far, Mr Quentin hasn't shouted for help.'

Miles must have come near to doing so, Jill thought on entering the drawing room. He was sitting listening to Julian reading from a volume of Shakespeare.

'Julian!' cried Robin, in an outraged tone. 'We promised you wouldn't do anything like that.'

'Oh, I asked him to,' said Miles. 'Thank you, Julian; you read well. We must meet again later, when you're ready to make a start. And now, I'm afraid we ought to be going.'

The girls protested but Miles was firm. 'It's Saturday tomorrow and I never care to be up too late the night before I have to give two performances.'

This was news to Jill but she took the hint and backed his decision to leave, and a taxi was telephoned for. While waiting for it Miles arranged for the girls to have tea with him at the theatre the following week, and was his usual pleasant self. But she felt sure that Julian must have, in some way, discomforted him or he would not have been so determined to go. However, his manner, when he said goodbye, was as charming to Julian as to everyone else.

Julian, when he said goodbye to Jill, gave her a look so direct that it amounted to a stare, and then smiled very sweetly, as if with genuine liking.

In the taxi, Jill said, 'My poor Miles, did you have a difficult half-hour with that young man?'

Miles made sure that the division between them and the driver was closed, then said, 'I did indeed. Dear God, I've never in my life been more embarrassed.'

'Do you mean he has no talent at all?'

'For acting? I don't believe he wants to act. Oh, he says he does but he was most unconvincing. I got the impression he'd cooked the whole idea up simply to get a chance to meet me. I don't think I've ever been at the receiving end of such glowing admiration.'

'Glowing? To me, he seemed extremely cold.'

'And well he might, if my suspicions about him are correct. In fact, they're more than suspicions.'

'Miles! Oh, good heavens! Did he *say* anything?'

'That isn't strictly necessary, you know. If you mean, did he come right out into the open, then, no, thank God. But I was none too sure he wasn't going to. That's why I asked him to read aloud – *not* a torment I usually subject myself to. As it happens, he reads rather well and has an excellent voice. He might make an actor. But that wasn't his ambition this evening. Anyway, not in the normal meaning of the phrase.'

'One gathers he was out of luck, poor Julian. Did you let him see you disliked him?'

'I doubt if I'm capable of really disliking such a beautiful young creature,' said Miles. 'And I'm as vain as the next man – he said one or two things about my acting which were extremely perceptive. But in the circumstances, I don't want to see any more than I can help of Master Julian. I wonder if Thornton knows about him.'

She, too, wondered, remembering Thornton's lack of enthusiasm about his son. But she only said, 'We shall be free of the boy for a while, anyway. He told me that he's just about to go abroad. Well, apart from Julian, it was quite a pleasant party, wasn't it?'

'I didn't find Julian all that unpleasant,' said Miles.

❧ 8 ❧

A House Stained by Sunset

Miles gave the girls tea at the theatre after the next Wednesday matinee. At supper he reported to Jill – who always left him to be sole host at his occasional dressing-room tea parties – that they had appeared to enjoy themselves, especially when exploring the stage. Cyril had been included in the party; (though he was now Doug Digby on the programmes, everyone still called him Cyril).

'Kit made him play a dramatic scene with her,' said Miles. 'You'd be surprised how well he invented lines to fit.'

'Is his performance any better? You haven't said anything about him lately.'

'There hasn't been anything to say. No, I can't say he's improved much but he gets by. Poor lad, it'll be a catastrophe for him if the play doesn't run, and I'm more and more doubtful if it will. I *must* remember to talk to Tom Albion about him.'

The next morning, when Jill came back to the flat after doing some shopping, Miles informed her that Geoffrey Thornton had just rung up to offer them the loan of a country house.

She stared blankly. 'But how did he know we're interested in a country house? If we still are.'

'I happened to speak of it to the girls yesterday – oh, very casually, but I still like the idea. Have you gone off it?'

'Not exactly. But you didn't mention it again. And we could so easily make another mistake.'

'That's why I was attracted by Thornton's suggestion. He says we could try the place for, say, a couple of months and then, if we wished, rent it either furnished or unfurnished. It's in secluded country but only thirty miles from London. Somewhere in the Rodings, wherever they are – Essex, actually.'

'But we haven't bought a car and I haven't learned to drive. And your driving will be a bit rusty, won't it?'

'We could be driven down in a hired car or just go by train. What I have in mind is that if the play fails – and I should know pretty soon – we could dig ourselves in there for a while. The film Tom's still hanging on to for me won't start for at least a couple of months. I've worked up a picture of us spending a golden autumn in the country. Anyway, I could hardly refuse even to look at the place.'

'Yes, I see that.' It was foolish to be so against the idea just because she disliked the thought of living in the house where the late Mrs Thornton had staged her dipsomania – for that, presumably, must be the house in question. She tried to recall what the girls had said about it that morning in the Spa Street café, but found she merely retained a vague impression that it was old. Well, she and Miles liked old houses. 'All right, When do we inspect it?'

'*You* do. Thornton has to go down on Saturday afternoon and can drive you. I couldn't get back in time for our first show. If you think the house will do, I'll come and see it next week.'

'Did you tell him I'd go?'

'Unless you rang up to the contrary. He's calling for you at two-thirty. I thought you'd enjoy it. He said the girls would pack a picnic tea.'

'And I'll take some contribution.' She suddenly felt cheerful. It would be an outing such as they had all taken in the old Rolls.

But when, on Saturday, she went out to the waiting car – which couldn't have been less like the stately Rolls – only Thornton was in it.

'Where are the girls?' she asked, as the hall porter closed the car door on her.

'At home, entertaining friends,' said Thornton. 'Did you think they were coming?'

'Well, Miles said something about a picnic tea –'

'Oh, they've sent that, with their love.' About to drive off, Thornton hesitated. 'Does it matter? Were you counting on them?'

'No, no,' she said hurriedly. 'Of course it doesn't matter in the least.'

'Good. To be honest, I'm quite glad to have you to

131

myself; they do tend to monopolize you.' For a moment, he concentrated on getting out into the main stream of traffic, then added, 'But you may find me a poor substitute for them. I'm not good at talking when I'm driving in traffic.'

'I won't speak a word unless I'm spoken to.'

He laughed. 'Oh, it's not as bad as that. But if I don't answer, it's liable to mean that I didn't take in what you said.'

'The traffic really is awful.' She found that she noticed it far more than she did in taxis.

'It'll be bad until we're right out of London. The great thing is never to get annoyed with it.'

Watching him drive, she found it hard to believe that she could ever learn. But she must certainly try, if Miles wanted her to. Did he really intend to drive again himself? And how keen was he on 'golden autumn in the country'? She had an uneasy feeling that she had not, recently, understood him as well as she prided herself on doing but she could think of no reason for this.

Thornton was now talking casually – and, in spite of what he had said, it seemed to her that he could with the greatest ease talk while driving. She found herself watching his hands with interest; she had never particularly noticed them before. They were well-shaped, and though small – anyway, by comparison with Miles's hands – they gave the impression of being strong and highly efficient, very much the right hands for a man with his small-boned, resolute face. Turning to him, while they waited at traffic lights, at the same moment that he turned fully to her, she noticed how alert his eyes were; indeed, his whole expression was livelier than she had previously seen it. She recalled that on the first meeting, in the Spa Street café, she had thought his personality somehow veiled, muted, and she had gone on thinking it so. Now she no longer did. Barely had she formulated this thought when he said, 'Do you know it's just four weeks since we met at that chocolate counter?'

She opened her mouth to say, 'Talk about telepathy' but changed her mind. Instead, she said smilingly, 'And already you're offering to lend us a house. Surely we must insist on paying some rent?'

'Not until you've tried living there – if you're willing to try. I shall be only too happy to have you as caretakers. Old houses need living in.'

'You don't want to use the house yourself?'

'I can't afford to run two houses. The sensible thing would be to sell the place, but Julian thinks he might like to live there some day. Do you know this way out of London?'

'I don't know any way out of London, as we've never had a car. What masses and masses of suburbs there are.

'All pretty hideous, I'm afraid, though some of them are beginning to acquire a hint of period charm. The Saturday afternoon traffic's even worse than I'd remembered but it's pleasant seeing so many people starting out for holidays – all the little family cars packed with children and dogs. You can usually tell the holiday-starters by an exposed box of Kleenex.'

'I hadn't been noticing.' She noticed now. 'Oh, look, is

133

that an attractive golden dog – or a repulsive head of dyed hair?'

'It's a woman, I think – probably a mum-in-law. No! It's flapping its ears.'

'Well, I hope they all have *lovely* holidays.' She was at ease, enjoying herself.

Gradually, the suburbs were changing in character, beginning to have something about them suggestive of country towns. Fine old houses still survived, even if come down in the world; and to Jill, Epping Forest seemed like deepest country.

'It's wonderful how it manages to remain a real forest,' said Thornton, 'in spite of all the hikers and picnics. But it survives through careful preservation. We're still quite a way from real country – though now I come to think of it, you may find it tame, compared with the Forest. Agricultural land is seldom romantic, not in these days.'

After Ongar, they lost the holiday traffic; indeed, there was little traffic of any description. And soon they were in what, she guessed, he considered real country. It certainly wasn't spectacular.

She said, 'What's happened to all the hedges?'

'Cut down, burned down, torn up – as the farmer's fancy takes him. I'm against it, and not merely because it ruins the beauty of the countryside. It's also hell for the birds and means that no saplings are preserved to grow into trees. Of course there are two sides to the question, but taking an overall, long-term view –' He pulled himself up. 'But I think we'll drop that subject and we won't even begin to discuss the horrors of chemical sprays and factory farming. I'm afraid the general behaviour of farmers is something I'm apt to lose my temper about.'

'Somehow I can't imagine your losing it.'

'Oh, I do – but in a nasty, tight-lipped way, much worse than just letting fly.'

'In fact, you never lose it at all.'

'How well you already know me. But there's nothing commendable about it, I'm just thoroughly repressed. I take it you don't admire this type of country?'

'Well, it's beginning to grow on me. It's so nice and empty. And I like it because it isn't beauty-spotty.'

'Some of the villages are pretty enough for that.'

He slowed down so that she could admire one. She noticed that some of the plastered, gabled houses had been carefully restored and, obviously, were no longer inhabited by villagers. Thornton said he found some of the restorations a trifle self-conscious – 'But one's thankful to see the old houses preserved so lovingly. So many of them fall into disrepair and are condemned and demolished.'

She said, 'Miles would love this village.'

'In that case he may not like Hallows. It isn't spick and span like this well-kept little street.'

'Oh, he won't mind that. You should have seen our Islington slum. But I think he may hanker for more trees.' It might be difficult to stage a golden autumn in this shorn landscape – unless the gold of the stubble fields would be enough.

'Well, there are plenty of trees around Hallows and the

135

height of the hedges is a scandal – even to a man who, like myself, loves hedges. My wife refused to let them even be trimmed, and I've still done nothing about them.'

How long ago had his wife died? Had the girls said eighteen months? Yes, surely; anyway, Jill wasn't going to ask him. She found herself disinclined to talk about his wife. Instead, she asked what the name Hallows derived from.

He said he'd been unable to find out. 'It's hard to trace the history of old houses unless they have some claim to fame, and Hallows is only a farmhouse; though there's a bit that's said to have been part of a priory – the name might derive from that. But it's more likely to be the name, or the corruption of the name, of people who once lived there. The title deeds give no information about it. My wife's family bought the property about a hundred years ago. It then included five hundred acres but most of them were sold, by degrees. My wife only inherited eighty, which are let off to a farmer. Are you noticing the place names? Any novelist who invented them would be accused of whimsy.'

She began reading aloud the names on signposts and he added to the collection from memory. Good Easter, High Easter, Abbess Roding, White Roding and masses of other Rodings; Margaretting, Shellow Bowells, Pharisee Green – sometimes she accused him of making them up, and then saw an even more fantastic name. Somehow the names increased the charm of the countryside, and charm it certainly had. She no longer missed the hedges, and there were still a few fine old trees; and so many unspoilt inns, farms and cottages.

He stopped the car on the top of an incline scarcely high enough to be called a hill and invited her to get out. 'From here you can see where Hallows is, and that it's fairly close to two villages, and there are other houses quite near. It's not as isolated as you might feel it is, once you're there.' He then directed her attention to a wood surrounded by stubble fields.

She said, 'There are certainly plenty of trees. But where's the house?'

'In the middle of them. We're not quite high enough for you to see the chimneys.'

'Don't the trees make the house dark?'

'Well, there's a fair-sized garden between them and it – though there's not much in it but grass, now. I suppose you may find the house a little gloomy; so many of the windows are small. A pity the sun's gone in – though perhaps it's best that you should see the place at its worst.'

Hardly that, she thought. It would be worse in a downpour. And this open country might be grim in winter. But she liked it now – and more and more, out here in the air. One never quite got the feel of anywhere from inside a car.

It would have been easy to miss the narrow, over-grown lane that led across the fields. 'The surface gets bad in winter,' said Thornton. 'And it's my responsibility. I suppose I ought really to sell the property.'

'Or let it advantageously, to someone who would live

137

here all the year round and keep it up – as we couldn't.' It seemed wise to get this said. Even if Miles fancied a golden autumn here she doubted if he would want to take a long lease.

So high were the hedges that they did not see the house until they drove through its open gate. Then it was so suddenly visible that the effect was startling. About a third of it was of crumbling rose-red brick. The remainder was plastered and painted a pink almost as dark as the brick. The plastered part had two wide gables and a smaller one between them. No two windows seemed alike; some had diamond panes, some were Georgian sashed windows, some looked Victorian. A few in the brick portion of the house were filled in and only traceable by their stone mullions.

'What a beautiful old house,' said Jill. Well, it *was* beautiful, but she could no more imagine living in it than in the Tower of London.

'It ought to be repainted,' said Thornton, 'but it's hard to get the colour that pink has weathered to. This grass needs cutting.'

'Must be quite a job.' The house was surrounded by a large expanse of grass, broken only by the gravel drive. She could see no flowers at all. Beyond the grass rose the surrounding hedge – she guessed it to be well over twelve feet high – and beyond the hedge was the surrounding wood.

'My wife had an almost pathological dislike of flowers – well, quite pathological, really. She said they made claims on her, always wanting to be watered, or pruned, or arranged or something. So after she decided to live here she had all the flower beds turfed. Not that she was any too keen on grass. She once said concrete would have been less trouble.'

He got out of the car and helped Jill out, then unlocked the door of the house.

The wide hall smelt damp. She avoided commenting on this by so much as a sniff but Thornton himself drew her attention to it, adding, 'You can get rid of that by having the central heating on for a couple of days. It's very efficient. We usually kept some of it on right through the summer.'

'Miles would love this old furniture,' said Jill. But would he? It might be valuable but it was extremely heavy; Jacobean, she thought. And there was a great leather-bound chest which somehow suggested to her that it was housing a corpse.

Thornton opened a door: more heavy furniture, a refectory table, leather-backed chairs, a large oak dresser. 'We seldom had meals in here. There's a pleasant little breakfast room which I used when I could get down for weekends. The nicest room's at the back, used to be the drawing room. Sylvia turned it into a bed-sitting room.' He showed Jill in.

It had possibly been a pleasant, if conventional, drawing room; the flowered carpet, gilt-framed water colours and satin-wood furniture had a touch of Edwardian charm. But as a bed-sitting room it was dreadful. The late Mrs Thornton

139

had merely plonked a four-poster bed and a huge Victorian wardrobe into it.

'Those ought to have been moved,' said Thornton.

'It's a very fine bed,' said Jill, looking at it in horror.

'By the way, my wife didn't die here. She needed day and night nurses and someone to wait on the nurses, and it couldn't be managed here. And in the end, I doubt if she minded where she was.'

He opened the French window, outside which was only grass, bordered by the towering hedge which gave no access to the wood – or the world – beyond. Jill pictured his wife taking exercise here as if in a prison yard. 'Poor woman,' she murmured; it was a comment both on his speech and her own thoughts. She then felt impelled to say cheerfully, 'Well, I'm sure this could be a delightful room.'

He smiled and said, 'It must be embarrassing to be shown over a house by its owner. I assure you there's no need to be polite but you'll probably go on feeling you ought to be. So how would it be if I left you on your own? I have to see the woman who's supposed to keep an eye on the place and I'd like to get it over. Then we can have tea. I shan't be gone more than twenty minutes. All right?'

She agreed thankfully, adding, 'One can take in a house's possibilities better when one's on one's own.'

'And its impossibilities. Don't worry, my dear. Just pretend you're going round the Chamber of Horrors.'

'No, really –'

He cut her short. 'We'll talk when I get back. Don't *worry*.'

He gave her a parting smile of such intimacy that she felt

140

he must know all that was going on in her mind. She stood in the hall until she heard the car being driven away, then mentally shook herself. It was absurd to feel . . . whatever she did feel . . . excitement, apprehension, almost panic – what utter nonsense! He did *not* know what was going on in her mind, not even the portion of the turmoil which was connected with the house. Oh, he might suspect she didn't like it but what did that matter? She only had to say it was too big, a little lonely; there was no need to go on being insincerely polite, and perhaps she could find things she could praise with sincerity. Anyway, she must explore. And there was no point in harrowing herself by thinking about his wife's miseries. But what about *his* miseries? Well, he'd survived. Concentrate on that.

She found a room which was a cross between a study and an office, a well-equipped kitchen, reasonably cheerful, and leading off it, the little breakfast room. At the end of a passage a door opened into the older part of the house, which appeared to be used only for storage purposes. It had a dungeon-like atmosphere. She came back hastily to the lived-in rooms – an absurd description for them now. Then she went upstairs and into five bedrooms, one of them minus its fourposter and wardrobe. In all of them the old furniture was good, but most later additions and all decorations – which looked as if they belonged to the days of his wife's parents – were in bad, charmless taste. How could the man who now lived in the admirably furnished Westminster house have stood this place even for weekends? Well, compared with the horror

141

of spending weekends with a dipsomaniac wife, surroundings could hardly have been important.

There was an attic storey reached by a narrow staircase, at the top of which she stood and took in that one long, raftered room ran the full length of the house. She saw some broken furniture, a few pieces of old luggage, and a pile of photographs, their silver frames now black, She examined some of the photographs and came across a wedding group in which Thornton was the bridegroom. As a young man, and obviously a very young man, he had been debonair, conventionally good-looking, and slightly reminiscent of a *jeune premier* about to break into a song and dance. His bride looked innocuous, just a slim, fair girl, resembling Robin but less pretty and with a weak chin. There was a striking old woman in a particularly graceful hat – Thornton's grandmother, Jill felt sure, recognizing a masterpiece from the Spa Street milliner. The only other person whose identity seemed guessable was an elderly man who suggested an actor playing a tipsy part in an old film: the bride's father, perhaps, as the girls had said her alcoholism was inherited. Poor girls, terrified of what might be their own inheritance.

Well, she'd done her duty by the house. She gave a last look at the boyish face in the photograph, then went downstairs and out into the front garden. She would, on his return, again praise the beauty of the facade. There was nothing else she could, with even a show of sincerity, praise.

The sky was now heavily overcast yet, looking back from the gate, she saw the rose-painted house as if in the light of a lurid sunset. The illusion lasted for only an instant – the sun would not set for hours. The house was lit by its own perpetual sunset. She imagined describing this to Miles. Then she heard Thornton's car returning and found herself revisited by panic.

It must have shown in her face; for Thornton on getting out of the car at once said, 'What is it? What's the matter?'

She said faintly, 'Nothing. Nothing whatever.'

'But there is. You're trembling.' He put his hand on her arm to steady her. 'Is it the house? Were you frightened to be alone there?'

The house had depressed her but not frightened her. Indeed, concentrating on it had driven off the panic now returned. But she said at once, 'Yes, it was the house,' and went on trembling.

'I was a fool to leave you there. You'd better sit down – in the car, if you're frightened of the house.'

'No, I shan't mind it now.' She detached herself from his grip and walked towards the house.

'What you need's a drink – and there's no drink here these days unless it exudes from the walls.'

'Tea will be better.' She sat down in the hall.

'I'm afraid the tea's chocolate. The girls said you liked it. And they don't think tea's good out of a thermos.'

'Chocolate will be wonderful – really. I'm all right now.' It was true; anyway, she had stopped shaking. And it was certainly better to have found out what was the matter with her; she had done so when he gripped her arm. Now she could concentrate on not letting *him* find out.

143

'I'll get the picnic case. Will you mind being alone here for a couple of minutes?'

'Not in the least. I brought some marrons glacés. They're in the glove compartment.'

She watched him as he hurried out to the car. Of course, it was all very dreadful but no one but herself was going to know about it – and if one felt marvelous, well, one did, and that was that. One felt all the more marvellous because one had forgotten how marvellous feeling marvellous was. She wanted to laugh aloud but that would hardly be suitable for a woman supposed to have been terrified by a haunted house. She composed her features as Thornton came back with the picnic case.

He said, 'Where shall we have it? The little breakfast room, I think.'

'Why not the kitchen?' It had seemed to her the one cheerful room.

'All right. But we can't boil a kettle or anything. We always cooked by the Aga stove.'

'We don't want to boil a kettle or anything. Come on. I liked the kitchen.'

'It's the one room that had to be done up regularly. Otherwise we couldn't have kept any help. Sylvia never went near it. She liked rooms to remain unchanged; it became a sort of mania with her. Any sort of change frightened her. Did you really feel that she haunts this house?'

'Sort of,' she said, untruthfully.

'She'd be a most unwilling ghost. And I'm afraid the

poor dear will be furious if she finds she has an immortal soul. She once said she'd like to rub herself out, not only from existing but also from having existed. She had the most absolute will to oblivion.'

'Was she quite sane?'

'Probably not, towards the end. But she was always too sane for any escape into insanity, and too sane for one to feel one could justifiably force anything on her, such as so-called cures or psychiatric treatment. But we won't go on talking about her. I'll take your sympathy for granted, if I may – both for her and myself.' He was unpacking the picnic case. 'I think those dear girls have over-estimated our appetites.'

'Oh, I can eat quite a lot,' said Jill cheerfully.

'You're really feeling better? It never occurred to me that the house could have any effect on you, beyond boredom. I'd have said it was too utterly dreary to awake your imagination.'

She'd better get this said: 'Did you really think Miles and I would want to stay here?'

'Not for a moment.' He had spread out the tea, opened a thermos, and was now pouring out chocolate.

'Then why did you bring me here?'

'I fancy you know the answer to that one. But you're entitled to get it in plain English. I wanted a few hours alone with you.'

'But you invited Miles too.'

'Having chosen an afternoon when I knew he couldn't come. Anyway, I had an idea that Miles, out of the

145

kindness of his heart, would let you come alone. Jill, I know about Miles.'

She considered looking blank and saying, 'Know what?' but decided it would be futile, the kind of dialogue that always put Miles off a play. She substituted, 'I suppose quite a lot of people do.'

'In theatrical circles, perhaps, but it's not at all obvious. I was astonished when the girls told me.'

'*The girls?*'

'Kit, actually. She's known about homosexuality since she was ten years old when she asked what crime Oscar Wilde committed. My grandmother, who had met and liked Wilde, obliged with a straightforward answer couched in such a way that Kit accepted homosexuality as being neither right nor wrong, despicable nor pitiable, but simply existent. She wasn't particularly interested; unlike many children, she's never had much sexual curiosity. But a couple of years ago, when Julian was involved in a school scandal, she said to me, "I feel guilty at being so ignorant," and promptly read the subject up. She now knows more about it than I do. Here, do eat something.'

She found herself quite willing to. But before embarking on a sandwich she said, 'Are you telling me she actually spotted Miles?'

'Far from it. She thought him – to use her own words – "tremendously male". But she happened to write a postcard to Julian telling him she'd met you both and she got back a letter saying "Don't get too worked up about your gorgeous Miles Quentin because my information is

146

that he's a homosexual." I'm taking it you'd like the plain truth about this, Jill.'

'Of course.' It now seemed perfectly natural to be sitting here eating cucumber sandwiches (so suitable, in view of the mention of Wilde) in this matter-of-fact way. 'Julian's one, too, is he?' Her tone would have been much the same if she'd been enquiring if he was a Boy Scout.

'Now there you have me,' said Thornton. 'He was acquitted at school – in my opinion, unjustifiably, but I don't think he's actually opted yet. Still, my general impression is that he will be.'

'Don't you mind?'

'Well, naturally I'd prefer him to be normal but one can't coerce normality. And I'd rather he was a happy homosexual than an unhappy heterosexual. Anyway, I shan't have any say in the matter. At the moment, I'm furious with him. We had one hell of a row before he blithely skipped off abroad. He treated Miles disgracefully. Did Miles tell you?'

'He said Julian – well, made overtures. I can assure you they were discouraged.'

'My dear son didn't report that – he's probably too conceited to have noticed it. I ought, in justice, to say that he was well-intentioned as well as curious. He said he wanted – well, to investigate the whole situation, before backing up his sisters. I'm afraid it's been quite a conspiracy. Are you angry? Have some more chocolate.'

'Yes,' she said. 'I mean, yes, more chocolate. I don't seem to be angry – except a bit with Julian on Miles's account. But I don't understand, really I don't, Geoffrey. Is that what you're called? Not Geoff, or anything?'

'Geoffrey is fine.' He handed the chocolate. 'Let me tell you what my daughters did towards the end of our week at the hotel. They came to me together and, with intense gravity, Kit informed me that they were quite sure you and I *liked* each other – she used the word my grandmother would have used even to describe what Tristram and Iseult felt for each other – and they had, that morning, had the information about Miles, so I could with a clear conscience take you away from him.'

She said dazedly, 'But I thought they liked Miles.'

'They do. They admire him as an actor and as a man. I tell you, they don't *disapprove* of homosexuality. But they don't feel a homosexual should have first claim on a woman they want their father to have. I know it's preposterous, ludicrous, even. But it's also good sense.'

'But how could they know that you felt anything at all about me – let alone what I felt about you?'

'They're very deeply attached to me, and they became attached to you with astonishing swiftness. And I suspect that, to the eyes of love, love shows. I knew about you, as well as about myself, almost from the beginning.'

She was becoming more and more dazed. 'But you couldn't have known about me, any more than they could. I didn't know about myself – not until today, when I was alone here. Those children made the whole thing up and put the idea into your head.'

'It was in my head from the first day I met you. Oh, I

148

don't say I fell in love at sight but I did feel very much attracted. And if you'll look back honestly you'll find that you . . . well, at least felt *something*. I've a great many faults but I'm not particularly conceited and I tell you I knew. There was . . . something in your eyes.'

Already a retrospective self-knowledge was rushing at her. 'Oh, my God, was there something Miles could have seen? Was that why you thought he'd let me come alone today?'

'I don't know that he saw a thing, as regards you. But my own feelings were so strong that I should have thought anyone could see them. And I can't imagine Miles behaving like a dog in a manger. Does he usually?'

'There's been no question of it. I've never –' She broke off, shaking her head hopelessly. 'Oh, you've got it all wrong.'

'Are you telling me you've never had any lovers?'

'Not since I married. There were some before.'

'Then is Miles bi-sexual?'

'No. He's completely homosexual. Though he would, if I'd wished it . . .' She shook her head. 'That doesn't mean that I don't love him. It's just that it's not that kind of love.'

'Then all these years there's been *no one*?'

She smiled. 'Perhaps I'm what Kit says she is, frigid. Though I wasn't in my unregenerate youth.'

He, too, smiled. 'That's surely a matter that's easily decided.'

He came round the table, pulled her to her feet and took

her in his arms. Her response to his kiss was so over-whelming that she had to cling to him for support.

'Oh, dear,' she said weakly. 'I do apologize.'

He laughed. 'Apologies were never less called for. All the same, as we've rather a lot to discuss, we'd better leave it at that for the moment. Well, almost at that.' He kissed her again, less lingeringly, then settled her back in her chair. 'Drink some chocolate. Have a piece of cake.'

'Let them eat cake,' she said balefully. 'Oh, Geoffrey, need we talk – now?'

He placed the cake knife on the kitchen table. 'Look, there's the drawn sword between us. Obviously one needs protection from frigid women. My dear love, of course we must talk. When will you tell Miles? Or rather, when will you have it out with him? I'm sure he knows already.'

She said thoughtfully, 'I think you're wrong about that. Even if he knows about you, he couldn't know about me – when I didn't know myself.'

'All right. Let's say it was all wishful thinking on the part of me and my children. It doesn't matter now.'

'But of course it does. If Miles doesn't know yet, why should he ever, if we're discreet? I can't bear the thought of his knowing.'

'My dear Jill, one can't divorce a man without his knowing.'

She sprang up so suddenly that her chair overturned. 'You must be mad. I couldn't conceivably divorce him.'

'Then let him divorce you. Though I should have thought, when it's not a real marriage –'

'Marriage isn't only sleeping together. I've had years and years of loving kindness from Miles.'

'And God bless him for that. But surely –' He came round to pick up her chair. 'Well, don't back away from me. I'm not going to rape you.'

'I don't mind your raping me. I'm all for it, in fact. But I'm not leaving Miles. I *couldn't*, Geoffrey. Oh, dear, I quite see that you want a wife –'

'I don't want *a* wife, I want you. Did you really think I'd settle for an affair? Remember, my children are in on this.'

She was shaken by sudden fury. 'Blast your children. The nerve of it – you and them. The great Thornton take-over bid! Well, it isn't going to work. Oh, God!'

He had taken her in his arms again.

'It's not fair,' she said at last. 'You know I'm in love with you and you're just taking advantage of me.'

'Oh, no, I'm not. Now or ever.'

'You mean you're going to hold out for marriage? How bloody priggish. Darling, please, even apart from Miles, I'm not suitable for you. I don't belong to your world. And I wouldn't begin to know how to be a politician's wife. I haven't even any political opinions.'

'Then you can try mine on for size. Jill, none of that matters.'

She said earnestly, 'But you know it does, when it comes to marriage. Why can't we just be lovers? The children needn't know. And probably Miles needn't, though if he did there'd be no trouble. I even think he'd be glad for me.'

'I daresay. But I'm not sleeping with you by courtesy of a queer.'

'There we have it,' she said with bitterness. 'That's how you really feel about him. Oh, you pretend to be tolerant and enlightened but it *is* pretence. You really despise him.'

'I don't, and I'm deeply sorry I said that, though it's not really a derogatory term. I've heard many homosexuals use it about themselves.'

'It's all right for queers to call each other queer, just as it's all right for Negroes to call each other niggers. Anyhow, the *way* you said it was insulting.'

'Was it? Yes, it probably was. Listen, we'd better get this clear. I like and admire Miles. And my tolerance – even the word's an impertinence; let's say my enlightenment – anyway, it *is* genuine. But I can't quite control my resentment that a completely homosexual man should have married a normal and obviously highly-sexed woman. No doubt it's a convenience to have a wife –'

She interrupted him. 'It's got nothing to do with that. He married me for *my* sake, not for his. You don't understand all he's done for me, all we've meant to each other all these years. You don't understand anything.'

'Then make me,' said Thornton.

❧ 9 ❧

Snow on a Warm August Afternoon

But could she? Could she even bring herself to try?

He said persuasively, 'Come on, now. And remember I want to know all about you, as well as about your relationship with Miles. It's an extraordinary feeling to be so much in love with a woman I know so little about. I'm like those people who say they know nothing about painting but know what they like – only I want to find out *why* I like.'

'Perhaps you'll just find out that you like me less,' – and remembering her past self she thought this very possible. Well, that might be no bad thing; not that she wanted him to stop being attracted by her, merely to stop wanting to marry her. Anyway, she'd try to be completely honest. 'I'd better begin with my despised girlhood,' – despised, certainly, by her and if anyone had *not* despised it, that fact hadn't come to her notice.

'Go back further. What were you like as a child?'

'Horrible, I should think, and generally miserable. Oh, perhaps not really miserable, just deadly bored and uncomfortable and so often cold. My father was a stage manager, usually on tour; in those days – I mean when I was really small – there were still a good many touring companies. My mother and I trailed round with him. I've heard old pros describe theatrical lodgings as cosy but they never struck me that way. And there were the dreary Sunday train calls.'

What she called her camp-following days had ended when she had to go to school – 'You can't think how nasty cheap boarding schools can be.' And even the cheapest cost more than her parents could well afford so that twice, when her father had stage-managed West End shows, she'd been brought home (always theatrical digs) and sent to the nearest day school – 'Then off they'd go on tour again, and once to Australia, and I'd go back to boarding school – a different one, the one I'd left not being keen on such an impermanent boarder. I doubt if I'm much better educated than gipsy children.'

She had left school for good at sixteen, to work as her father's assistant and also keep house for him, as her mother had died. 'I probably didn't miss her as much as I thought I did. Perhaps I just thought I was entitled to feel forlorn and motherless. And from seeing too little of my father, I then saw too much. He was quite a kind man but short-tempered, also he was an old-fashioned stage manager and thought it necessary to bully people and use foul language. The comic thing was that he could switch the foul language off whenever he was with my mother and me. But once I was in the theatre, working for him, he didn't think it necessary to. I found it humiliating when he swore at stage hands in front of me – and sometimes at me in front of them. I suppose it made me feel a bit extra inferior. Silly, really, as when my father swore it meant no more than when a dog barks. And he trained me well; by the time I was eighteen I was a good A.S.M. in spite of loathing the job. Oh, God, do you really want to hear all this stuff?'

'Every word. Go on and don't skip anything.'

She spoke of various jobs, with and without her father. When she was twenty he had gone to Australia again. He could have taken her as his assistant but she'd just landed a fairly good job and preferred to stick to it. 'I never saw him again. He stayed out there, married a woman who owned a small hotel, and died four years later.' She paused, conscious of a disinclination to talk about her life after her father left England. But she must, of course, because it was the mess she had made of things then that had led up to her marriage, or more specifically, to her gratitude for it, and it was the gratitude she had to make clear.

'What happened after you were left on your own?' Thornton gently prodded.

'Nothing pleasant, and no wonder. You can't imagine how ghastly I was at twenty: gawky, badly dressed, with the most awful hair. Either it was lanky and greasy, or frizzed up by a cheap permanent wave. I'm not at all sure I was even clean – no, really; I always seemed to be in the kind of rooms where you felt dirtier after getting out of the bath than before you got into it. Oh, no doubt I managed badly about my looks and clothes, but an A.S.M. gets no time for private life, especially on tour. By then there weren't so many regular tours, but I had a genius for getting into pre-London try-outs that went on for weeks and then didn't get to London. But my real trouble –'

She broke off, unwilling to describe that real trouble to a man to whom she wanted to remain attractive. But this was all part of the credit Miles deserved and she was going to do the job thoroughly. 'Let's face it,' she said at last. 'I was sex-mad and sex-starved. It's a repulsive combination – and anyway, my whole life was in the theatre where there are always plenty of attractive girls around. I was twenty-two before anyone obliged by seducing me. He was fifty and the occasion couldn't have been less glamorous. Can I skip it?'

'No,' said Thornton. 'Back in the witness box, my love.'

'I'd almost forgotten you're a barrister as well as an M.P. – doubly out of my world. Well, onward with True Confession. . . .'

She had taken a job with a repertory company which, at Christmas, had put on *The Importance of Being Earnest* – 'Funny I was thinking of it just a little while back, when I was eating all your cucumber sandwiches. Well, they'd engaged a West End actor to play John Worthing. He was much too old, of course, but he wore his clothes well and still looked handsome in his make-up. We were staying at the same horrid little hotel, so we got together a bit – anyway, we did on Christmas Day when we were at a loose

156

end because there was no performance, I mean in the theatre.' She broke off to laugh. 'Oh, dear, no girl could have had a more putting-off introduction to sex. He hadn't known I was a virgin and he *hated* it, both morally and physically one might say. I'm not sure I wasn't still a virgin when it was all over. For the rest of the Christmas season we barely spoke, and then when he left the company he tried to be gallant and said, "Thank you, dear girl, for a memory I shall treasure." And believe it or not, that was quite a comfort to me. I pretended to myself that I'd been in love with him and he with me and it was simply his conscience that had come between us. Perhaps I've always been able to let one half of my mind fool the other half. But in the end, I see what I've been up to.'

She had looked away while describing what she had come to think of as a ludicrous episode. Now she offered a rueful grin, and was worried by the gravity of his expression. She instantly wondered if he had found the story in bad taste – as she now instantly did. Even while telling it – and before – she had disliked the tone of her voice and the words she was choosing. It was as if the girl she had been was taking over from her present self. But perhaps her present self was only a veneer; if so, he'd better know it. She looked away again, quickly, and pressed on.

'Well, after that, I was out of work for some time, and then in some plays that never came to London. There was no one I could even pretend to be in love with and life was just a monotony of hard work and discomfort. I remember sitting in that Spa Street café where we first met thinking that if I could be peacefully dead by just wishing it, I probably *would* wish it – well, it was raining and I was extra full of self-pity because I'd been hankering for clothes in the Spa Street shops. And there was worse ahead of me because I was then with yet another play that folded on tour, after which I was out of work for months. But eventually I landed another job – and in London; the best job I ever had, as a matter of fact, only – I'd better warn you that what's coming isn't pretty, but it's important if you want to know why I married Miles.'

She had fallen in love with the stage manager she worked with and she still considered him worth falling in love with. 'He was superb at his job – great authority and without shouting and swearing. And he was as good with the company as he was with his staff. Some stage managers bully the staff and toady to the company – that is, the important members of it. But he was just universally both kind and firm. He was the first man – the only man – to teach me that our job was to keep the company happy. And we were always *partners* in the job, not just the boss and his run-about. Naturally, I adored him, and I'm sure he was fond of me, perhaps even a little in love, though I always knew he really loved his wife. Anyway, we had an affair, a real affair, it lasted a whole year.'

She broke off, and sat staring at the stopped kitchen clock, wondering how best to convey what that year had meant to her, which was all the more difficult because it now meant so little; indeed, she couldn't remember when last she had thought about it. And yet . . . Perhaps talking about the past stirred a flicker in the embers. After a moment, Thornton said, 'Does the memory still distress you? Have a rest. There's another thermos of chocolate. And how about some more cake?'

'I've already had two pieces. Still . . . it's such very good cake. You'll be thinking I'm a compulsive eater.'

'You well might be. Women who sublimate their sexual life to the extent you must have been doing are liable to compensate with food.'

'Oh, God, are they? I don't *think* I do, though there *was* a time when – I don't *need* this cake.'

He looked at her amusedly. 'It wouldn't worry me even if you were a glutton – which you couldn't be, with your figure. Eat your cake. And then tell me about your nice stage manager. Were you happy at last?'

Had she been, even for so much as a day out of the whole of that year? 'Well, I was happier – or rather, I was fully alive at last; sometimes I was more acutely unhappy than I'd ever been, because I knew he didn't love me. And he was apt to make that painfully clear. It's surprising how unkind fundamentally kind men can be when they feel guilty – as he did, towards his wife. And then it was all so *difficult.* He had to be at home every night and on Sundays. Of course we had the theatre to make love in but what with eight performances a week and understudy rehearsals we didn't have too much time. And cleaners are always liable to barge into dressing rooms – which, anyway, aren't the cosiest of love nests. Once or twice we went wandering round the dust-sheeted theatre, looking for somewhere

private. There was a top box . . . Oh, dear!' She broke off
and took a drink of chocolate.

'Sounds an exciting setting,' said Thornton, encour-
agingly.

'It didn't excite me, just terrified me. But I was almost
always terrified – of being discovered, of his getting tired of
me, of not giving satisfaction.'

'Hardly conducive to fun.'

'Fun? That's something I quite gave up hoping for. I
didn't mind too much. I concentrated on love. And it was
love all right, on my side. Well, eventually his wife came to
the theatre one afternoon unexpectedly, got as far as his
office door and heard enough. She didn't come in – at least
I was spared that. She just went home, and had it out with
him that night. I guessed he was quite glad to be forced to
give me up, and the play was due to come off so it was all
very convenient. He got work with a company that was
going to Australia – I think my telling him about my father
put that idea into his head. And off he went with his
forgiving wife.'

'Leaving you flat.'

'Not as flat as you make it sound. He fixed a job for me,
in a play that was going on tour for a month with a London
theatre already booked. Miles was the leading man. He'd
just blossomed into being a star, not as big a one as he is
now but, in a way, more exciting because he was a newer
one. And, goodness me, was he handsome! And not just
boringly handsome; he's never been that. There's always
been something off-beat about his good looks which saves

them from being conventional. Lovelorn though I was, I was sure that, well, if I hadn't been lovelorn I should have fallen for him. I felt distinctly swindled when I learned that he was a homosexual.'

'You knew that from the outset?'

'Yes, indeed. Jack – my stage manager – told me. He'd stage-managed a show Miles was in and liked him very much. Jack also told me that Miles lived with a boy – well, a man; he was thirty, only a couple of years younger than Miles and they were completely devoted to each other. They'd been together nearly ten years. Alan – Miles's love – was a small-part actor, not very good and he didn't get a lot of work, but he was a dear. He came to several rehearsals. Miles introduced him to me and he was particularly pleasant to me, as Miles always was – though Miles was more than pleasant, he went out of his way to be kind to me, as he always does if he sees anyone is unhappy. And in my case it didn't take much seeing. Night after night, as soon as I got into bed, I'd start thinking of the past year and then I'd put in a couple of hours crying. Naturally I looked like hell in the morning – no one ever looked more hideous than I do after crying. Really, I wonder that I held that job down; but my work was all right. Don't look so worried. None of this harrows me now.'

'It does me,' said Thornton. 'Have some more chocolate.'

She laughed. 'No, thanks. *You* should, as you're the harrowed one. Well, the show opened – in Brighton and it was a great success. Our next date was Manchester. Most of the company travelled by train on Sunday, but Miles went back to London on the Saturday night because he wanted to collect Alan, who was in a play that finished its run that night. They'd planned to drive to Manchester. Managements don't much like members of a company to travel by car but Miles was allowed to. It was foggy on the Sunday and Alan, who had a horror of driving or being driven in fog, suggested they should go by train. But Miles wanted to have the car with him for the rest of the tour and the fog wasn't at all bad and he thought it would probably lift. So off they went and took their time. But in the late afternoon, just as it was getting dusk, the fog got much worse and they ran into a car that had got onto the wrong side of the road. It wasn't a bad crash as both cars were crawling – no one in the other car was hurt and Miles was only bruised, even the cars weren't badly damaged – but Alan had been leaning out of his window, trying to see the kerb, and when his door shot open he went out head first into a stone wall. He was killed outright – suddenly gone for ever. And he hadn't wanted to come in the fog. Well, you can imagine the horror of it all, and Miles had to play in Manchester the next night. You'd never have known anything was wrong with him. Oh, that's not so remarkable, really; just the old tradition of "the show must go on", lots of actors could have done it. What *was* remarkable was the way he behaved off-stage. He sent a message to the company asking that no one should mention the accident to him, and he somehow carried his stage performance – he was playing a very debonair part – right out into the wings. He actually joked with people, and the company played up like mad and joked back. It was so extraordinary that I wondered if he did, really, mind very much about Alan's death, and then I happened to catch sight of him in the wings when there was no one with him and his face was like a mask of tragedy. That same night I was asked to run after him with some message and I didn't catch up with him until he was going into the Midland Hotel, where he was staying. He simply switched on cheerfulness and insisted on my having supper with him.'

'Perhaps he was glad to have someone he had to act to.'

'Probably. But I think it was kindness, too. By then I must have been looking more woebegone than ever as I'd realized that I was pregnant. Such a charming situation. Jack was in Australia and I'd promised not to write to him –'

'But surely in the circumstances –'

'No. Because the circumstances were my fault. I'd hung round his neck for "one last time", when he wasn't expecting it. By now my father was dead, and I hadn't even a woman friend I could consult. In the theatre you make friends in dressing rooms, and I was seldom in dressing rooms. There seemed no one I could turn to. I remember thinking how extraordinary it was, me with my miseries and Miles with his, just eating supper and chatting about the show. After supper he saw me back to my digs and before I went in he put his arm round me and kissed me on the side of the head and said "Bear up" and I said "You, too" – and just those two words of sympathy were more than he could stand. He simply dashed away into the darkness.'

She paused, collecting her thoughts. Every word she said was convincing her more and more that she could never leave Miles, and she must now convince Thornton too. Surely she could? Surely what she was going to tell him now would make him *see?* She hurried on to the last week of the tour.

She'd found herself staying in the same digs as Miles. Usually he stayed at hotels but these were good, old-fashioned rooms where he'd once stayed with Alan. He'd booked a bedroom and sitting room before the tour began and let the booking stand. She'd had a little combined room. Miles had asked her to have her meals with him, so they'd seen a good deal of each other, and half way through the week, when they'd finished supper after the show, he'd let his facade of cheerfulness break up and talked to her about Alan and the accident. From then on they'd been much more at ease with each other. On the Friday night it had been bitterly cold and the landlady had made up a specially good fire, given them a supper of bacon and eggs, and brought in a second pot of tea before she went off to bed.

'You'd think we'd have turned to something stronger than tea for comfort but, with Miles, excessive alcohol acts as a depressant, and I'd never drunk much – couldn't afford to. Anyway, we just went on coaxing cups of tea out of the teapot, while we sat up over the fire. He'd told me several days before that he'd guessed I was unhappy and I'd admitted I'd had an unhappy love affair but given him no details. Well, that night he asked me point-blank if I

164

was going to have a child. There was nothing anyone could see yet, so I suppose it was just intuition; Miles is like that. Anyway, I didn't deny it and he asked me what I was going to do. I said I was still hoping things would come all right, especially if I could find something to take. He said that was a crazy idea, probably wouldn't work, might make me ill, and even affect the child. If I was determined to get rid of it I'd better have a proper operation and he'd pay for it, but he was dead against it. So was I. Somehow "taking something" hadn't seemed to me like abortion. Then he asked me if I was quite sure I didn't *want* the baby – and God knows I was; I just wanted it to go away. I hadn't really thought about it as a baby, only as a terrifying thing that had happened to me. But the way he talked about it made it real. He said he'd help me until it was born and then I could get it adopted – or why shouldn't I keep it? I could always get jobs – his agent would help over that. And his housekeeper might know of someone who would look after it well; it was the kind of thing she always seemed to know. And anyway, I was to stop worrying. Whatever I decided, I could count on him to help.'

She found herself momentarily recapturing the enormous relief she'd felt that night. And at breakfast next morning he'd again told her not to worry. But she hadn't felt any too well and Saturday was the worst day of her week – 'Two shows and then I had to see the load – the scenery and everything – onto the train, and then walk back from the station. It was colder than ever, snowing a little. By the time I got in – it was long after midnight – I was frozen, especially my hands. Miles had waited up for me. He said the landlady had left me some cold supper but he thought I ought to have something hot so he'd explored the kitchen and organized some bread-and-milk, he could do with some too, as he'd finished supper two hours ago. So he got it while I took off my coat and got into some bedroom slippers; I'd been on my feet, almost solidly, for over twelve hours. And even when I'd settled down by the fire I could hardly hold the spoon for my bread-and-milk because my hands were still numb. He warmed them between his and said my job was too hard for me, anyway it would be soon. Then, still holding my hands, he said, "Now don't die of shock but I've been thinking, sitting here waiting for you, why don't we get married? I like children and I shall never have any of my own" – during that week we'd talked quite a bit about his homosexuality – "and I could make everything easy for you. And you needn't feel tied –"' She broke off, wishing she hadn't spoken the last words.

'Did he say you could always have a divorce if you wanted one?'

'Well, yes, but the situation's different now. Neither of us could guess how we should come to feel about each other.' She slid back into the past. 'It shames me to remember that, in spite of feeling grateful to him, I was – well, almost horrified. Oh, even then I was perfectly tolerant about homosexuals but somehow the idea of marrying one did stagger me. But I don't think I let him see I felt anything like that. I said surely he'd want to set up

166

house again with someone like Alan, and he said never. What he'd felt for Alan was the love of a lifetime and both he and Alan had felt it would last a lifetime. For the moment he couldn't imagine ever being even attracted by anyone else. Presumably he would be some day but if so it would only lead to . . . I think he said there might be "interludes", though he hated to think there would be. Anyway, they surely wouldn't affect me, and he would sincerely *like* to marry me; being able to help me would somehow help him as well. Then he told me to eat my bread-and-milk before it got cold. He ate his too, sitting on the other side of the fire, and talked about his house in Islington and how he was dreading the thought of going back there without Alan. I knew he was trying to make me feel I'd be doing him a favour – and I believe he truly did want me to say yes on his account as well as my own; already there was something real between us. I never did actually say it, but I got as far as "Well, if you're absolutely sure . . ." and then he plunged into making plans. Funny the things one's memory hangs on to. Just beyond his head was a huge framed photograph of the landlady's dead husband, enlarged from a snapshot and all blurred, like a spirit photograph. I'd have said I remembered everything about that room but I find I can only see the firelight and that man's face; he had a waxed moustache. And Miles, of course, though in a way I see him as he is now. I wonder how much all this is conveying to you.'

'At least it's conveying that Miles didn't exactly victimize you,' said Thornton soberly.

'Oh, *good*. One thing more, something I specially like remembering. It was nearly three when we decided to go to bed – by then there was no more coal. Miles parted the curtains to see what the weather was like; I'd told him it had been snowing and we had an early train call. Then he said, "Put the lights out and come here." It must have gone on snowing – the whole street was white, under a bright moon. Normally it was a hideous street of drab, uniform houses with horrid bay windows, but it looked quite beautiful. I remember saying, "Transformation scene!" and Miles put his arm round me and said, "It'll be all right, you know. We shall get through." And we did.'

'When were you married?'

'Soon after the play opened in London. Miles got some kind of a special licence. And he tried to avoid publicity, but what a hope! Really, those weeks were fantastic. Miles was in love with a dead man and I with a man who was dead to me, and yet there was . . . well, a sort of spurious happiness, excitement, congratulations, and me making what seemed a marvellous match. Not very many people knew about Miles's homosexuality, and some of those who did know thought they'd made a mistake, or that he'd reformed or something. Even now it's far less known about him than about most stage homosexuals. Oh, God, when I look back! Do you know, I hadn't taken in that he intended to treat me like a wife in every way but sleeping with me – I mean technically; we've always shared a bedroom, always wanted to. He showered presents on me. When we went shopping, if I said I liked something and then wasn't sure, he'd say, "Buy it and find out." Can you imagine what that was like to a girl who'd had as little as I'd had? Even the food . . . I told you there was a time when I compensated with it.'

Thornton smiled. 'Pregnant women are entitled to considerable gluttony, and God bless Miles for feeding you well. What happened to the baby?'

She said, trying to sound merely matter-of-fact, 'Oh, I had a miscarriage three months after we married. Miles had got me released from the show ages before that and I'd been taking every care. But it happened.' From now on there was much she didn't want to tell; indeed, couldn't have told coherently, so long was it since she had let herself think about it. Perhaps she needed to now – or rather, when she had time to think. For the moment she finished up, 'We were both of us desperately sorry and I was very ill. Miles was wonderful to me. And I'm sure you've now had more than enough of my sob story.'

'That's a superficial remark that's unworthy of you,' said Thornton. 'And there's still a lot more I want to know. But I'll admit I'm beginning to find this kitchen chair a bit hard.' He got up and began re-packing the picnic case. 'What's your deadline for getting back? Make it as late as possible.'

'I needn't call for Miles until half-past ten.'

'Then there's plenty of time for what I have in mind. But I'd like to get you out of this house now. It's even more melancholy by twilight – and the glare of electricity makes it still worse. If you're interested in what my daughters call "the girls" there's one off the hall.'

'Thoughtful,' said Jill.

'One learns to be, with daughters.'

Studying her face in the looking glass of the little lavatory she experienced a fractional shock. She had been so immersed in the past that, for a split second, she expected to *see* herself in the past, with lank hair, drooping features. She was thankful to be herself as she was now, even with a smear of chocolate on one side of her mouth. Also – let's face it, she thought, and faced it with the utmost eagerness – she now felt pleasurably excited, as excited as when alone in the house but without any trace of panic. In fact, the excitement was now exhilaration.

When she came out into the hall Thornton was returning from carrying the picnic case to the car. He said, 'Out with us, quick, and no backward glances. And if I've left a cigarette burning, the house has my delighted permission to go up in flames.'

'Wouldn't you mind, really?'

'Only because I feel old houses should be preserved. Apart from that, a fire would be a splendid solution. Don't worry, anyway. I never do leave cigarettes burning.'

As they walked towards the car she said, 'Wait a minute. I want just one backward glance.'

Beyond the woods at the back of the house the sky was now flushed a deep rose, by contrast with which the house no longer glowed with its own fictitious sunset. It merely looked dark and unutterably sad. She felt pity for it.

'How much of it did you explore?' asked Thornton.

'Most of it – I even went up to the attic. Did you know all those photographs were there?'

'Oh, yes. Sylvia turfed them out, said they reminded her of people.'

'There was a wedding group. You looked so young. How old were you?'

'Twenty-two. So was she. We met when I was stationed at an airfield near here. Of course I'd no idea then – But I'm not going to tell you the story of my life; anyway, not now. Probably not till we're safely married.'

'Geoffrey, for pity's sake! You're not still counting on that, not after all I've told you about Miles?'

He said calmly, 'My dear love, you've told me many things about yourself that I didn't know, all of them valuable to me. But, as regards Miles, I'd already guessed he was a nice man, a good man, and nothing you've said has convinced me that you ought to stay married to him. Now stop worrying and let things sort themselves out. Either you'll give in and marry me, or I shall give in and have an affair with you – but I'm ninety-nine percent certain I shan't do the giving in.'

'And if I won't either? Do we just say goodbye for ever?'

'It's conceivable, I suppose. No, I refuse to consider it. Anyway, whatever the future brings, let's just be happy for the rest of our evening. Please! Will you try?'

She said, 'Try? God help me, I'm practically delirious already.'

⇥ 10 ⇤

A Teddy Bear and the Kama Sutra

When they were on their way he said, 'You'd probably like us to stop somewhere for a drink, wouldn't you?'

Something in his tone made her say, 'Not unless you particularly want to.'

'Me? I loathe drinking in pubs, even in so-called cosy village inns. As a matter of fact, I seldom drink anywhere unless it seems to me a social necessity.'

'You gave us a very good hock, that night we had supper with you.'

'Which my daughters eyed as if it were prussic acid. They have a real horror of alcohol. I'm not as bad as that so do say if you'd like us to call in somewhere.'

She said she was none too fond of pubs herself. 'I suppose they're most people's idea of heaven, judging by the dozens of pub scenes in television plays. But they're apt to make me feel gloomy, on or off the screen.

Anyway, I'm at present doing very nicely on auto-intoxication.'

He laughed. 'So am I. And I'd hate to associate this evening with that faintly sour smell so many pubs have. But I'll feed you on the way home, in a place I associate with happiness.'

'Heavens, I don't think I can eat after all that tea.'

'Well, we'll see.'

The sun was almost down now and a large, pale moon was rising. It gave her pleasure to see sun and moon together. But everything she now saw gave her pleasure. Every village they drove through looked enchanting – she refrained from mentioning that the lit-up bars of inns now struck her as fetching. The hedgeless fields had become delightful. The vast, cloudless sky shared by sun and moon seemed to her so beautiful that she longed to look up at it unobstructed by the car roof. At last she said, 'Oh, please stop a minute. Let me out so that I can get the *feel* of everything.'

He drew up, helped her from the car and across a ditch into a stubble field. There was no cottage in sight and, even in the distance, only a square church tower indicated a village. She said, 'You wouldn't believe how seldom I get into the country. Comes of having no car. Well, Miles thinks he'll drive again.'

'Good for Miles. But it's no concern of yours – sorry I said that; we're not going to argue this evening.'

She said earnestly, 'But, Geoffrey, there are some things I must get into your head – now, before we go any further.

Surely everything I've told you today must have made you see I'm unsuitable to be your wife?'

'Don't repeat yourself. You've already mentioned that you've no politics.'

'There's more to it than that. My upbringing, lack of education –'

'Don't be snobbish.'

'Me, snobbish? I'm being the reverse.'

'You're being snobbish towards yourself, which is one of the worst forms of snobbishness. *And* you're trying to make a snob of me. I shall be extremely proud of you as a wife. And if it's any comfort to your snobbish soul you speak far better English than my children and I do. You don't – to use Robin's phrase for it – "mince deplorably".'

'That comes of living with Miles. I've always imagined it was because of Miles your children made friends with me.'

'Well, you're a half-wit if you still think that. The girls adore you. Even Julian fell for you – though he did have an idea, before he met you, that you might be what he calls a "cover woman".'

'Blast Julian!' Then she added soberly, 'But it's true in a way. I've always done everything I can to safeguard Miles's reputation. That's one reason why I've avoided making real women friends; one gossips to women friends. And it's an extra reason why I'll never divorce him.'

'Is there anything I can do to stop you arguing?'

She looked around. 'Not here. There isn't any cover. Not so much as a haystack.'

'Well, I don't know what your plans for the far side of a haystack were but at least, in a good cause, I'll risk a kiss.' After a moment, he added, 'And my God, kissing you *is* a risk. I'm thankful there isn't a haystack.'

She said weakly, 'I've never felt like this before. It's frightening.'

'It certainly frightens me, in view of my honourable intentions. We're going back to the car, my girl.'

They drove on through the gathering dusk. At last Thornton said, 'This is where we leave the real country. From now on I shall be chaperoned by civilization.'

'Did you say something about eating? Not that I'm ravenous but I daresay I could manage something. And it ought to be fairly soon if I'm to work up another appetite for supper with Miles.'

'Why not tell him you've had supper with me?'

'I'm not going to let him know I've been out with you for so long. You're supposed to be a casual acquaintance – well, almost – and I shall have been with you' – she counted up – 'it'll probably be eight hours. That might make him suspicious. Oh, not resentfully suspicious. But I don't want him to be any kind of suspicious.'

'I do – though I really want him to be certain. Anyway, the place I'm taking you isn't far off. You may hate it. Perhaps I only like it because I went there with the girls, the last time they came to Hallows with me. They hated coming but there were things we had to decide about the house; it was a few weeks after their mother died. We were absolutely flattened by memories, regret, pity – though Kit says she can't feel pity for her mother; I think she would if she'd seen her during her last illness. When we were on our way back to London she said, "Well, now it's ended. And we're all going to admit that we're relieved. In spite of everything, you've managed to give us a pretty happy childhood but we couldn't be really happy when we knew all the horror you had to cope with. From now on we're all going to be *madly* happy. And I should like *my* equivalent of getting dead drunk. Let's go to an Espresso." And we went.'

'And that's where you're taking me now?'

'If you're willing. I suppose it's sentimental of me but somehow the girls are so much involved with what you and I feel for each other. Aren't you conscious of that yourself?'

She nodded and said – but this time without rancour – 'The great Thornton take-over bid. If only you'd chosen someone who was free.'

'I'm afraid the thought of rescuing you added to our zest. And it's no use saving you're not in need of rescue. Any right-minded person –'

'Don't talk to me of right-minded persons. Masses of them would like to jail Miles for life.'

'Surely not nowadays?'

'Yes, indeed. I've heard them on television, *screaming* with indignation.'

The café, which they shortly reached, was in a small town which resembled an overgrown village and still belonged more to the country than to London, though the wide High Street was garishly lit. The café, by contrast, was a dim, smoky cave. There was barely enough light to reveal the tropical decorations on the walls, which contrasted oddly with the pink and white striped awning over the counter. Except behind the counter Jill could see only young people, all of them talking with surprising quietness, or not talking at all. The only raucous sound came from the juke box, which was blaring out a rhythm rather than a tune.

'I'm afraid it's rather full,' said Thornton. 'Of course, it's Saturday night. If you'd rather not –'

'Looks gorgeous to me,' said Jill, though it was the clientele rather than the café that she liked. The boys and girls in their very 'with-it' clothes looked untidy and none too clean and yet somehow attractive. And each group seemed to her perfectly composed. 'See, there's a free table.'

They managed to slide into it. The clientele took not the slightest notice of them but a woman from behind the counter came to get their order.

'The girls and I had some good toasted sandwiches,' Thornton told Jill. 'There were cheese, and bacon and tomato.'

'Sounds wonderful.'

He ordered – 'And coffee now, and more when the sandwiches are ready. Shall I come over for the coffee?'

The woman smiled (sweetly, Jill thought). 'Well, it'd be a help. We're busy tonight.'

Left momentarily to herself she gazed around. Every face she studied struck her as beautiful. She did not usually admire long-haired young men but she thought those she now saw resembled Renaissance Italians painted by Old Masters. As for the girls, most of them were pale and even sickly-looking yet even so had a wan beauty. She wondered about them. The eyes peering from beneath long fringes were waif-like, vulnerable, and not at all innocent. One girl was cuddling a snow-white teddy bear; another was flicking over the pages of the *Kama Sutra*. Well, she hoped they were all happier than she had been at their ages but doubted if they were as happy as she was now . . . just for tonight, anyway.

Thornton returned with the coffee. She said, 'I love this place.'

'I don't suppose you often go to Espressos now. And they'd hardly be in when you were young.'

She stared at him with mock-indignation. 'They certainly were. I once worked in one, between stage jobs. Anyone would think I was Methuselah.'

He laughed and apologized. Then, after stirring his coffee, remarked, 'While we're on the subject of age, do you mind clearing something up for me? Kit told me Miles married ten years ago – she looked it up in some reference book – but from various things you said today it seemed you were only in your middle twenties when you married.'

'That's right. I was twenty-five.'

'Then you are now thirty-five?'

'I shall be, soon. What's so funny?'

He had started to laugh. 'Oh, my God!' He passed his hand across his brow, still laughing. 'I thought you were much older. I thought you might even be older than I am. I'm forty-two.'

'*Geoffrey!*' She gasped, between laughter and outrage. 'Surely I don't look – I suppose it's my grey hair.'

'Your hair's lovely and so are you. It's simply . . . I must explain this carefully, it's important.'

'I'll say it is,' she said ruefully.

'It has nothing to do with your looks. It's more . . . I will *not* use that awful word "poise". The nearest I can get to what I felt is that you have too much dignity for a woman of the age you really are. And the day we first met you spoke of yourself as having been plain as a girl in a tone which implied that your youth was long ago. Even the way you dress . . . Do you always wear shades of grey?'

'I suppose I do now, unless I wear black.' She looked at her summer suit. 'But this is quite a *light* grey.'

'It's charming – all your clothes are beautifully chosen. But I'd like to see you in flaming scarlet – or better still, chalk-white; a long Grecian evening dress. I'd love that.'

'So would I, now you mention it. I wonder why I've bowed out of, well, noticeable clothes. Perhaps it's because of my height.'

'Your height's a great asset. The real reason is . . . Do you remember when we looked at that hat together? You said something about women who were old enough not to compete. Well, you unconsciously joined them. You stopped competing.'

If that was true – and she instantly felt it was – why and

179

when had she stopped? She said slowly, 'That needs thinking about.'

'And give some thought to the fact that your life with Miles is plunging you into middle age years and years too early.'

'What a ghastly thing to say to a woman! You'll have me taking to thigh-high skirts.'

'All you need is to take to me. Oh, my dear, if you knew what joy it is to know that you're still so young. And of course, it makes me all the more determined to have my way.'

'But it's my way too, if only you wouldn't insist on marriage. *Why* can't we . . .' She lowered her voice and the juke box chose that moment to erupt into a record of unbelievable stridency. Thornton, leaning closer, said, 'I didn't quite catch . . .' Jill, feeling that even a shout would be inaudible at the next table, said loudly into his ear, '*Why* can't we just be lovers?' – and looked up to find that the woman from behind the counter had brought their toasted sandwiches and more coffee.

'Do you think she heard?' said Jill, when the woman had gone.

'Of course,' said Thornton cheerfully. 'But never mind, this isn't my constituency. Though perhaps she'll now take up her ballpoint and write to the National Press.'

'Oh, God, do you really think she recognized you?'

'It seems a bit much to expect of her, as I only appeared once on television and it's months ago. But seriously, my dear girl, and you are only a girl, at thirty-four, I'm not going to be your lover. Neither my constituents nor my daughters would like it.'

'Need any of them find out?'

'My daughters find out everything. They didn't at all like it the last time I had a mistress. Kit said they understood and even wished me joy but she thought it a very un-family thing. I found that distinctly off-putting. Now eat your sandwiches and give the juke box best for a while.'

She did as he told her, until the juke box, having achieved an ear-splitting volume of sound, stopped playing altogether.

'Odd, one quite misses it,' said Jill. 'Can these sandwiches really be as good as they seem to me?'

'Have another.'

'No, really. But I'd like some more coffee. Heavens, that'll be my third cup.'

'Kit had five, on what she called our day of liberation.' He signalled with his glass coffee cup to the woman behind the counter and held up two fingers. Someone fed the juke box, which responded with a gentle crooning – a very mawkish melody, Jill felt sure, but she basked in it. Thornton went for the coffee. She observed the clientele with envy; most of it was by now indulging in unabashed affection. Thornton, returning with the coffee, said, 'As we don't want to be conspicuous, we'd better at least hold hands.' They held hands in silence until she forced herself to say, 'We really ought to go. I'd like a little while at the flat before I call for Miles, just to get back to normal.'

'You mean to abnormal, surely? That very peculiar life in which you are Mrs Miles Quentin, aged say forty-five.'

'Geoffrey, you didn't really think I was as old as that?'

He grinned. 'Well, I was sure you were under fifty.'

He had already paid. Jill, at the door, looked back. The clientele no more noticed them go than it had noticed them arrive. On the way to the car she said, 'How beautiful they were!'

'What, the sandwiches?'

'Oh, they were, too. But I meant the boys and girls.'

'I can't say I was concentrating on them. Sorry the juke box was such hell.'

'I even liked that,' said Jill.

While they were waiting at traffic lights on the outskirts of London, he said, 'When do we meet again, and where?'

She told him he could come to the flat any evening but Sunday – 'Or on Wednesday afternoon, when Miles has a matinee. And on Saturdays he plays two shows so you could come any time after four-thirty.'

'I'll come on Saturday at five. That'll give you a week to think about things.'

'And you do some thinking too. Please, Geoffrey –' The lights changed and he concentrated on driving. After a few minutes she said, 'Could we park somewhere, just for a few minutes? There's something I want to say and I need every bit of your attention.'

He turned into a street of drab little houses, drew up, and stopped the engine. She said, 'Will you let me put a few ideas into your head – for you to think about before we meet again? Will you listen, and not shut me up?'

He smiled and took her hand. 'All right. State your case.'

'Geoffrey, it isn't only that I don't want to hurt Miles, or that I know I'm not a suitable wife for you. It's me. I'd feel lost in your world. Surely the *sensible* thing to do is to have an affair? And if the girls *have* to know, I think I could make them see my point of view. I'm in love with you and God knows I haven't tried to hide it. But I love Miles too, in a different way. Please don't try to break up my whole life. I'd have thought you'd feel it was unscrupulous to be so determined to take another man's wife. Oh, yes, I know the answer to that one. I suppose you wouldn't have tried if I'd been married to a normal man.'

He said calmly, 'That's an interesting point. Faced with a normal marriage I might have had more scruples. But, on second thoughts, no – not once I saw that, as Kit put it, you liked me.'

'Anyone would think I was sending up signals calling for rescue. I wasn't. I didn't know anything about it.'

'I doubt if you've been very honest with yourself for a good many years, Jill. You said this afternoon that you've always been able to let one half of your mind fool the other half.'

'I also said that, in the end, I see what I've been up to.'

'Well, I hope you see it now, about your life with Miles. Anyway, give it some thought during our week's amnesty. And don't forget all those years I added to your age. My dearest Jill, it's utterly wrong that you should be tied to a homosexual.'

183

She was staring through the windscreen at the drab little street where they had parked. The vista of uniform bay windows reminded her of the street where she and Miles had been staying when they decided to marry. The memory, combined with the tone in which Thornton spoke the word 'homosexual,' caused her to turn on him. 'God blast you,' she said angrily, 'don't be so bloody smug. And you're hard, Geoffrey – sometimes your face looks as if it's carved out of granite. And what right have you to be so damned sure of yourself? How do you know you could make me happy? Oh, God, I didn't mean to say all that. And I'm mad about your face really.'

He had looked both startled and stricken but her last words made him laugh. 'It's no use cursing me if you finish up that way. Please don't think me smug. And I didn't know I was hard.'

'You're not, really. No one could see you with your daughters and think you hard. But you're being hard with me. And don't say it's for my good.'

'You know it is. As to whether I can give you a happy marriage, I can only say – well, what Miles used to, when you went shopping and weren't sure if you liked something, "Buy it and find out." Which reminds me, did you ever buy that hat I showed you in Spa Street?'

'I'm afraid not. Miles didn't approve of it.'

'What cheek! You wait till you're married to me. I'll show him how you ought to be dressed. And now, alas, I should hand you back to him, if only for a week.'

'Geoffrey, I'm *not going to leave him.*'

184

'Ssh. The argument's over.' He re-started the engine.

They spoke little for the rest of the journey. He would not let her re-open the argument and she felt incapable of small talk. But when he drew up outside her block of flats and she saw the porter coming towards the car, a host of things she wanted to say sprang into her mind. She asked hurriedly, 'What will you tell the girls?'

'The truth, in a very short version. And I promise they won't molest you. See you this day next week at five.

'It's a long time off. I'll be alone every evening, if you should want to come – or perhaps to ring up.'

He shook his head. 'I'm going to leave you on your own, to think. And I'll think, too. I promise.'

The porter opened the car door. Suddenly self-conscious, she got out instantly, and then felt agonized because she had not said goodbye. She looked back from the entrance to the flats and for a moment they smiled at each other. Then she went through the door the porter held open for her.

Up in the flat she got herself a drink, which reminded her that even her very mild consumption of alcohol might shock the Thornton family. But she must not let herself think about anything now except presenting a normal appearance at the theatre. She carried the drink to her dressing-table and looked at herself. She had more colour than usual but powder took care of that. Far more noticeable was the brightness of her eyes. She tried to look lack-lustre and achieved a hang-dog expression that made her laugh. Perhaps a black dress would have a toning down

185

effect. She hastily changed into one and, while doing so, visualized herself in a chalk-white evening dress and wondered if she could really wear scarlet. As a girl, she had loved bright colours but looked ghastly in them – but she had looked ghastly in everything. Perhaps now . . . She pulled her thoughts up. There was something she had to decide before meeting Miles: what was she going to say about the Thornton house? There seemed no reason why she shouldn't describe it truthfully – and thank goodness, it would be easy to talk about.

It took the porter some little while to get her a taxi and when she reached the theatre the house was coming out. It seemed to have been quite a good one, but a show had to be doing atrocious business not to achieve a fair house on Saturday night, so she was barely surprised when the stage door keeper greeted her ruefully.

'Sad news of the play tonight, madam. And I did think we'd got a success this time.'

'Oh, dear – is the notice up?'

'Went up this afternoon. And yet they all tell me that Mr Quentin's wonderful.'

Passing through the swing doors she reflected that, as far as she knew, no stage door keeper ever saw a play.

She paused at the notice board. A week's notice was being given. The run would then have lasted three weeks and three days. She remembered Tom Albion's prognostication at the Spa Street theatre. He had been rather less right when he described the play as a teeterer. A real teeterer would have teetered longer.

The girl A.S.M. greeted her in passing, adding, 'Isn't it bad luck?' Particularly for the stage management, thought Jill; all the hard work of rehearsals plus the provincial and London openings, and no chance to dig themselves into a run. And then there was the poor young author and – oh, dear! Cyril-Doug Digby came down the stairs, much of his make-up still on. He paused on seeing Jill at the notice board. 'I can't understand it, Mrs Quentin. We had a smashing house tonight. And audiences *like* us. I've had letters asking for my autograph. Why don't they advertise on the telly? That'd bring people in.'

She explained about the enormous cost of television advertising but saw she was making little impression. So she just said she hoped he would soon get another job.

'Oh, I'll be all right,' he said, cockily. 'Mr Quentin's sending me to his agent. He'll get me on TV again. Bye-bye for now, Mrs Quentin. My brother's waiting for me.'

She glanced after him as he opened the swing doors and saw a tall youth mainly dressed in black leather. Well, it was kind of him to call for his kid brother – not that Cyril really was a kid; she always found it hard to remember that.

Miles, when she reached his dressing room, was commiserating with his leading lady. Jill continued the commiseration, while he finished removing his make-up. She waited until the leading lady had gone before saying, 'I'm so very sorry, darling. How much do you mind?'

'For myself, not at all. It means I can do the film. But I'm sorry for everyone else. Well, tell me about the

Thornton house. Is it a possibility? I rang Tom after the matinee and he says I can have at least six weeks before the film starts.'

'The house is utterly out of the question. I'll tell you at supper.'

Miles's dresser returned – Jill guessed he had tactfully made himself scarce on the leading lady's tearful invasion. He was Miles's favourite dresser; someone else who would be affected by the play's closure. It was at that moment that she first asked herself how the closure would affect *her*. If Miles wanted her to take a holiday with him . . . He interrupted her thoughts by saying, 'Darling, don't look so worried.' She must control her expression – which would necessitate controlling her thoughts.

They went to a Soho restaurant for supper, rather than to one of their usual haunts where friends were likely to enquire about the play. Miles said, 'When a show's coming off one should appear both decently sad and commendably brave. And as I'm not sad, and have no need for bravery, I'm liable to sound callous. I believe the food's good here – not that I'm particularly hungry.'

'Nor I,' said Jill, wondering how she was to eat anything at all; those toasted sandwiches had been extremely filling.

'What time did you get back? I telephoned just before we rang up on the second house, but could get no reply.'

'I must have come in soon after.'

The waiter hovered. They ordered. Then Miles asked what was wrong with the Thornton house. She described it at length, stressing its lonely surroundings, its strange

188

pink colour, its over-grown hedges and general air of decay.

'Sounds attractive to me,' said Miles. 'Unspoilt.'

'But the inside, Miles –' She talked about it until the waiter had served their meal when she concluded, 'Anyway, apart from being depressing, it'd be an impossible house for us to run.'

'Did you bow out of it, then? I hope you were tactful. It was so very generous of him to offer to lend it.'

'I think I managed all right. I stressed that it was too big for us and too isolated. He quite understood.'

'Well, we'd better entertain him and the girls as soon as I'm free. Were they there today?'

'No, to my surprise.' She was thankful to have got that said. 'I somehow gathered from your telephone talk to Thornton that they were going to be.'

'Isn't it time we started calling him Geoffrey? I suppose the gesture should come from me as I'm probably older than he is.'

'The same age – he happened to mention that he's forty-two. I did call him Geoffrey today, because he called me Jill. But somehow I shall go on thinking of him as Thornton; it suits him better.'

'Why?'

'It's a harder name.' She realized that she had a desire to talk about Thornton and must pull up – though it scarcely mattered, as she had said something faintly derogatory.

'Do you mean he's hard in looks or in character?'

'Looks; I don't know enough about his character. Oh, it was just an idea.'

'Still, I know what you mean,' said Miles. 'There's a touch of rigidity about his whole personality.'

She was instantly defensive. 'Perhaps it's just that he belongs to a different world from ours – less emotional.'

'Could be that. Anyway, I find him likeable, not to mention good-looking.'

That gave her great pleasure but she managed to sound dubious. 'Is he good-looking?'

'Oh, surely. They're a good-looking family. Any news of the ravishing Julian?'

'Only that he's gone abroad.'

'Ah, yes.' Miles concentrated momentarily on his supper.

Had she managed well, sounded natural, casual? She thought so. Relieved, she almost shovelled in her Sole Véronique, barely conscious that she was eating, let alone what she was eating.

'You're liking that better than I am,' said Miles. 'But I'm just not hungry.'

She switched to talking about the play's failure and worked hard at it – for whenever the conversation flagged she began to think. And she wasn't going to allow herself the luxury of thought until she was in bed and Miles was safely asleep.

Only then did she relax and let herself re-live her day; the drive amidst the holiday traffic, the first glimpse of the melancholy house, herself alone in it, Thornton's young face in the photograph, his face as it was now, the moment when he had first kissed her – at the memory of which she experienced a vertigo not unlike what she felt on the flat's balcony, except that this present vertigo was wholly pleasurable; all the same it was alarming because she had never experienced anything like it before. Even for Jack, in those days she had so vividly remembered this afternoon, her desire had been more emotional than physical. Well, ten years of repression accounted for much, and she must beware of being fooled by her body, particularly as its sensations had never come up to her expectations in those days of love making in dressing rooms and on the hard floor of that blasted box. I am *not*, she told herself, a really physical woman . . . and then blissfully sank into sleep.

≈ 11 ≈

An Unidentified Flower

She awoke to find it was ten o'clock and Miles was already up. She could not recall having outslept him since the earliest days of their marriage, when it had been a toss-up which of them slept worst, woke earliest. She was further reminded of those days when he arrived with a breakfast tray, saying, 'It's a long time since I had the chance to do this for you.'

She said she couldn't think why she'd slept so late.

'Perhaps it was the country air you breathed in yesterday.'

'Precious little of it. I was mainly in the car or in the house.' To have agreed that the air might have affected her would have been a bit ridiculous. 'Just a minute, darling, while I freshen up.'

When she came back from the bathroom he had brought his own breakfast tray and settled back in bed, having supplied them both with Sunday papers. This was the way their Sundays usually began except that, normally, she was the one to bring the trays and papers.

She drank her coffee and gazed unseeingly at a front page; little short of a declaration of World War Three would have rivetted her attention. Anyway, one could not cope with a grapefruit and read. She put the paper down.

But one could cope with a grapefruit and think and her thoughts were not welcome – though no doubt they ought to be, as part of the stock-taking she must do during her week of armistice. Miles's arrival with the tray had so vividly brought back the time when they had first come to count on each other's kindness. Those interminable nights . . . they had tried various sleeping pills but none of them had proved too satisfactory and, anyway, Miles had a horror of becoming dependent on them. So they had chucked the lot away. *Her* worst times had been when they put the light out and she remained utterly wakeful. He would then recite to her, in a veiled, monotonous voice which always ended by soothing her to sleep. (He once said, 'I shall never dare to play Shakespeare again after using him as a soporific') *His* worst times had been just after dawn when he would wake with a devastating realization that Alan was gone for ever. He would try not to disturb her but it seemed that just his need of her woke her. They would then talk and she found that her best way of distracting him was to get him interested in doing things for her, taking her somewhere, buying her something. (She once said, 'Getting your mind off your troubles always ends by being so expensive for you.') He would fall asleep again eventually but, one way and another, they hardly had good nights. Yet in retrospect those nights had charm for her, a heart-breaking charm.

Well, so had the days, with Miles always behaving as if she was the one woman in the world for him (which, in a sense, she was). All their sight-seeing and shopping, she remembered buying her first fur coat –

Miles, looking up from his paper, said, 'Will you need a new fur coat this year?'

Extremely startled, she gasped, 'Goodness, no. I had one last year. Whatever made you ask?'

'I've no idea.' He glanced back at his paper. 'Yes, I have. There's a picture of a girl in a fur coat. I suppose I noticed it unconsciously.'

Well, maybe. But they so often experienced flashes of telepathy, and at present she wanted no leakages from her mind to his. She must lay off private thinking when he was at hand. She finished her breakfast hurriedly, trying to concentrate all her thoughts on it . . . grapefruit, scoop it, eat it; coffee, pour it, drink it. (And why, in the midst of this, did she suddenly think of the Taj Mahal?) She took a final gulp of coffee and said, 'All right if I have the first bath?'

He said, 'Surely,' without looking up from his paper.

Relaxing in her bath she took up her thoughts where they had broken off. (Presumably a solid wall precluded telepathy.) But soon she reached the memory of her miscarriage and after that came the time she had boggled at thinking about when talking to Thornton, and she still boggled. That must wait until she was sure of being alone for a good long while, with the whole flat to herself. Good heavens, she couldn't turn off all secret thought for every minute she was with Miles. Perhaps it would be all right if she now definitely decided she wasn't going to leave him; that would somehow act as a safety device on her thoughts. Anyway, she would decide it for today. Unfortunately, this decision made her feel more in love than ever with Geoffrey. It was the first time she had thought of him as 'Geoffrey', not 'Thornton' – though one really thought of people as they existed, more than by name.

She got out of the bath, dressed, and busied herself with washing up and bed making. Miles, when he was dressed, went back to the papers.

On Sunday, they generally lunched at a hotel, their usual restaurants being closed or apt, somehow, to seem off-key. Today Miles chose the Ritz and, with slightly histrionic determination, treated the occasion as a celebration. When he ordered champagne she blankly said, 'But why?'

'Because we must think of ourselves as at the beginning of a holiday. Any ideas, now the Thornton house has fallen through? Would you like to go abroad?'

'Me?' She never went abroad with him nowadays. For years his (less and less frequent) 'I think I'll go abroad for a while' had meant just one thing. As far as she knew, all his affairs were now conducted on the Continent and she rarely knew with whom they were conducted. He had become more and more secretive about his sex life. And as, in the days when he had talked more freely, she had never shown the slightest disapproval, she could only take it that he had come to prefer secrecy. Now she hastily followed up her astonished 'Me?' with 'Yes, if you'd like us to.' It was the last thing she wanted – though perhaps she ought to welcome the delay.

He began to talk of various possibilities, almost as if trying to sell them to her. Then he said, 'Oh, well, let's just toy with the idea. Get some travel brochures if you like. But we'll only go if you really want to.' The last words were accompanied by a particularly kind, direct look. She feared she hadn't shown enough enthusiasm, and instantly said she would get the brochures.

Back in the flat after lunch they watched television. And in mid-afternoon Peter Hesper rang up and asked them to supper. Miles relayed the invitation.

Jill said, 'Not me, but you should. Do! I'll promise to order myself a good meal.' And she would tonight. Although not hungry now, she felt sure she would be if she could be left on her own.

'All right, then.' Miles accepted for himself, then hung up and said poor Peter was out of luck – 'That job he was expecting has fallen through and now Gaston's insisting on being taken on a Continental holiday which Peter says he can't afford.'

'I wouldn't break your heart. Peter makes plenty. I'll get tea. Would you like toast and jam?'

'I like the *sound* of toast and jam. It suggests a cosiness we

196

never achieve in this flat. But unfortunately I couldn't eat a bite.'

When she came back with the tea he was staring at the window. Rain was driving across the balcony. He said gloomily, 'I wonder what this room will be like in winter.'

'At least it'll be warm – plenty of central heating.' It flashed through her mind that she might not be there in the winter, but she reminded herself that her decision for the day was not to leave Miles.

Soon after six the rain stopped. He said he would start early and walk. 'I need exercise. Oh, I might be late getting back. Peter wanted me to go to some party with them.'

She said, 'Good idea. I won't wait up,' – and thought, after the door of the flat had closed behind him, that he could hardly have said anything more liable to liberate her – for the evening, anyway. She had a shrewd idea of what kind of party Peter would be taking him to. Was it only now that she felt a twinge of resentment or had she, in the past, fooled herself about not feeling it? Which brought her to something which had been trying to invade her thoughts all day. Could one really be dishonest with oneself? Had she, in fact, known all through that sunny week in the Spa Town that she was falling in love?

She had certainly been particularly happy and had sometimes come near to forgetting the very existence of the play Miles was acting in. She'd felt guilty about that afterwards, especially that morning when she'd looked through the telescope and seen Miles at the window of the Lion. And even before that there had been her experience when listening to the Schubert Octet. She had told the girls about her mental picture of a comic little town band, but not about what she had pictured during the last movement ... someone, some woman, escaping, running towards joy, under the blossoming chestnuts. But had she equated the woman as herself? And anyway one couldn't accept a childish bit of imagination as a proof one had fallen in love, and with a man she had only met a few times. Of course one could fall in love at sight but not without knowing, surely? She remembered her first meeting with Geoffrey, the walk to the hat shop, and the memory gave her such pleasure that she now felt she must have known even then.

Was one some kind of schizophrenic? Three weeks ago she had sat in this room while Miles, as now, had gone to Peter Hesper's, and she'd been utterly unaware of what it now seemed she must have been aware of. She couldn't have been sane. But she was sane enough now, and particularly clear-headed; also in very good spirits. And having spent the day on Miles's side, as it were, she was going to spend the evening on Geoffrey's.

She telephoned the restaurant below for a fillet steak, zabaglione, and a large pot of black coffee. Then she got herself a drink.

On Geoffrey's side now: surely being the wife of a Member of Parliament couldn't be so very difficult? She could learn to open bazaars and even do a bit of canvassing, especially if the girls came with her. She longed to see them again. Why did they like her? Even the lordly Julian wanted her in the family. It was the first time in her life that she had made a personal success – not that she'd really felt any lack of success since marrying Miles; his friends had accepted her and he had more and more made her feel her importance to him. And she had always enjoyed *his* success, been proud of it on her own account, as well as his, because she had continued to think of herself as a little (if lanky) nobody who had made a marvellous marriage (if with a catch in it). And now that same nobody had the chance of another marvellous marriage (which wouldn't, anyway, have the same catch in it). Very, very ego-inflating. She remembered once looking up the word *hubris* because it occurred in a part Miles was playing and neither of them knew what it meant: insolent pride or security. Oh, she must beware of *hubris*!

The doorbell rang. It would be the waiter with her meal. She went to let him in.

He proved to be a pleasant Austrian boy who had served food in the flat before but not for some time, nor had she lately seen him in the restaurant. She asked him, while he set the meal out, if he had been away. Yes, he had been home for a holiday. And home, it turned out, was in a valley near Innsbruck. She knew it, to his delight, and had lunched in the village he came from – 'But it was a long time ago, let's see . . . over nine years.' She couldn't remember the name of the inn, not even when he told her the name of all three inns.

But she could *see* the inn and, once the waiter had gone, she saw it too vividly for her liking. For the inn, its surroundings and, above all, a mountain meadow she and

Miles had walked up to after lunch, were all part of the memories she had up to now boggled at. They were definitely not on Geoffrey's side, nor did they promote enjoyment of her meal. She left much of it uneaten, then returned to her armchair, taking the coffee with her. Now memory must have its head.

She was back in that dazzlingly green meadow, marvelling at the contrast between the vastness of the mountains rising all around and the tiny, fairytale villages dotted along the valley below. Had it been May'? No, she'd had the miscarriage in May and been too ill to travel for several weeks. It must have been June – late June, because it had been the last day of their holiday. Miles had taken a couple of weeks off between the closing of one show and rehearsals for another.

She had been feeling wonderfully better, physically and mentally, at times almost happy and all the more so because she believed Miles was becoming less unhappy. Sitting in the meadow, they had talked with a gaiety which was not just the surface gaiety with which they encouraged each other but – in her case, anyway – a genuine light-heartedness which had something of the serenity of the mountains and the sky. She was therefore a little surprised when, after a few minutes of joint silence, he'd said, 'Are you still minding very much about losing the baby?'

She had answered, 'Oh, it's getting easier.'

'You're sure? Because if not . . . well, to the best of my belief I'm perfectly capable of fathering a child. And with you, I'd be willing.'

She had said instantly, 'But you don't *want* to, Miles.'

He hadn't contradicted this. Instead, he'd tried to make her understand his particular kind of abnormality. As far as she could make out, only for men could he feel a love which had for him, as well as physical satisfaction, beauty, charm, romance. For women – anyway, for her – he could feel the warmest friendship, tenderness, affection, indeed love, but it was a love which had nothing to do with being 'in love'.

How, then, she'd asked, could he bring himself to sleep with her? He'd pointed out that plenty of marriages, such as *mariages de convenance*, were consummated without anywhere near the affection they felt for each other. It would have been unthinkable for him while Alan was alive, but now . . . He had taken her hand and said – she could remember his exact words – 'You are the one person in the world I truly care for and, apart from any question of a child, if it would give you pleasure it would give me pleasure too.'

She'd said she would like to think it over, and he'd said of course. All through the conversation she had been staring at a flower he had picked and handed to her on their walk up to the meadow, a very strange flower with hairy petals, pink stained with green. She did not know its name and she had never thought about it since. But she could now see it with the utmost clarity and remember stroking its petals. And yet she could not remember how the conversation ended or what they had talked about, walking down to the village.

Had she then begun to realize what was happening to her? Certainly the full realization had come that evening, when they were back at Innsbruck, and in their historic old hotel bedroom, getting ready for dinner. He had asked if she was sorry their holiday was ending and she had said yes, in a way, but it would be fun to be home. And she had suddenly felt flooded by happiness and known that she was in love with him – and surely he would not offer to be a real husband if he was not more attracted by her than he was admitting to himself? Everything would come right. She would tell him now that she had made up her mind – no, she would wait until later tonight. This darkly romantic old room would make a good setting. It would be the perfect ending to their holiday.

They had dined in a cellar-like room, all antlers and beer mugs. At a near-by table had been a group of very young men, talking and laughing loudly. Miles had said, 'I fear we're in for a noisy meal.' The waiter had handed large, confusing menus. She had studied hers for a few moments and then looked up to ask Miles for advice. He was gazing, over his lowered menu, at the group of young men, and there was an expression in his eyes she had never seen before. Usually they were reflective, sometimes sad, always kind. Now they were brilliantly alive, his whole face was more alive than she had ever known it to be. Only a few seconds passed before he turned to her, smiling and helpful; but in those seconds she had realized that one – possibly all – of those casually-seen young men attracted him more than she ever would. It didn't change her feelings for him but it did stop her telling him about them. And that night, when they took a last stroll round the moonlit town, she said she thought their relationship had better remain as it was. She had been almost sure he was relieved, though he had finally said, 'Well, the offer remains open.'

A month later he'd had his first affair since Alan's death. He told her about it and she had found herself painfully jealous though she knew that, in the circumstances, she had no right to be. She had forced herself to be sympathetic and had most determinedly hidden the jealousy. But had she always hidden it? Perhaps by degrees he'd guessed and tried to spare her by becoming secretive about his affairs none of which had lasted long or affected their life together. She wished now that she could have let him know that she'd minded less and less, no doubt because – though she had come to admire him more and more and to grow even fonder of him – she had ceased to be in love. Except . . . sometimes when watching him act, when by imagination and skill he could represent a completely masculine man, she could again feel both emotionally and physically attracted, and these fleeting experiences had a value for her which lasted on into the long periods of unexciting affection. But they were as nothing compared with what she now felt for Geoffrey Thornton.

Well, where did all this get her? And why had it seemed a duty to remember that day in the mountains'? And why had she, before this, sheered off from remembering? That strange flower had today come back with the startling authenticity of a completely new-minted memory.

Did she feel guilty because she had turned from Miles's willingness to make their marriage a real marriage – or was it sheer regret she felt, had always felt, and had tried to shut her mind to? Anyway, she had now faced . . . whatever she had been averse to facing. And all she knew, sitting alone here in the long dusk, was what she had known before: she still deeply cared for Miles and was wildly attracted by Geoffrey.

She heard the front door open and close. It must be the waiter – though trays were not usually called for until the morning. And how had he acquired a key? She was just wondering this when Miles entered the room.

'What, no lights?'

'I was too lazy to put them on. Do, if you like.'

'The room looks better as it is. Twilight softens it.' He sat down without putting the lights on.

'Surely you're back very early?'

'Peter wanted to start for the party. It's some way off – in stockbroker Surrey.'

'Really? Sounds unlikely, somehow.'

He laughed. 'Oh, there are stockbrokers and stockbrokers.'

'You didn't fancy going? Will it be a gorgeous orgy?' The phrase was an old joke between them.

'I grow less and less interested in them. Even in my riotous youth I wasn't much of a one for gorgeous orgies. Alan rather liked them. They're a curious mixture of the lyrical and the ludicrous. Well, I hope you ordered yourself a decent meal.'

'More than I could eat. That nice Austrian waiter's back.'

'Oh, good. By the way, how would Austria be for our holiday? You liked it, didn't you? All those flowers – though there wouldn't be so many at this time of the year. Do you remember that mountain meadow near Innsbruck?'

She told herself it was perfectly natural he should speak of Austria, her mention of the waiter must have reminded him. And yet . . . but surely thoughts could not linger on in the air? 'Yes, I remember,' she said, with no comment in her tone.

'I've often wondered if we made the right decision.'

'About what?' She said it to give herself a moment for thought but found herself incapable of thought.

'If you don't remember, we probably did.'

There was enough light for her to see that he was smiling at her. She said, 'I do remember now, of course I do. And right or wrong, it was *my* decision, wasn't it? And I think it was for the best.'

'Very possibly. And anyway, you always knew it wasn't irrevocable.'

'I did indeed. Funny we should talk about it after all these years, just because I spoke of the Austrian waiter. Would you get me a drink, darling?'

He rose to get it while she carried her tray to the kitchen. When she returned he had put the lights on and picked up a paper. She did not now think that either the waiter or telepathy had led him to say what he had said, though her reference to the waiter had given him an excuse to say it. She thought he was, with extreme tact, offering himself as a substitute for Geoffrey Thornton. And it made her problem infinitely more difficult.

⇥ 12 ⇤

Three Children on a Doorstep

But by the next morning she had changed her mind; let herself off, as it were. She could not believe that Miles, if he did know about Geoffrey, would have played such a scene with her. Even in a play he would have thought it, well, stagey to put up such veiled competition. Indeed, she doubted if he would think it fair to put up any kind of competition. He would either have come out into the open and wished her luck, or ignored the whole situation – and in the latter case, he certainly wouldn't have mentioned the mountain meadow. So she could take it that he simply didn't suspect, and his mention of Austria had been *only* due to her mention of the waiter. Unless . . . she felt a faint undercurrent of anxiety in case his reminder of their long-ago conversation was symptomatic of some present need of his own, some dissatisfaction with life (it must, as far as she knew, be well over a year since he had been involved in any affair) but she tried to put this idea out of her head. And he seemed his normal self on Monday morning.

She had quite a lot to do. It would take the whole day to buy Miles's last-night presents for the company. He always gave last-night presents as well as first-night ones, and when she pointed out that this play's first night and last night came pretty close together he said that was all the more reason for the last-night presents and they had better be specially good ones. She took trouble over the job and was glad to be occupied by it. She was also glad that Miles had to be at a conference about his forthcoming film so she did not have to meet him for lunch. She spent the evening in the flat, mentally going over her Saturday outing with Geoffrey – until she firmly snapped out of this and set about seeming like her normal self when she met Miles for supper.

On Tuesday she came to the conclusion that no amount of thinking would change her basic point of view, which was that she wanted to have an affair with Geoffrey but go on living with Miles. It would be *sensible*, kind to Miles and, in the long run, kind to Geoffrey. She tried to rehearse ways of making Geoffrey see this but always ended up by just longing to be with him again. And she still had five days to wait – well, four and a half, counting Saturday as a half-day. She even counted up the hours.

She had a bad moment on Wednesday, suddenly remembering that she usually went to the last night of Miles's plays. Would she, then, have to cut Geoffrey's visit short? But mercifully there was to be, on Saturday night, a television play by a young author Miles was interested in and which he asked her to watch. She hoped Geoffrey would be willing to watch it too.

Thursday seemed interminable – but terminated. Friday was bearable – so close to Saturday. She went to the hairdresser, wished she had bought a new dress. And in the evening she paid her last visit to Miles's play. The house was barely half full. Miles was still admirable but the show, in general, had deteriorated. As for young Cyril, he had reverted to his out-of-town performance and was shouting his head off.

She commented on this to Miles at supper. 'How long's that been going on?'

'It's been creeping in for a week but it's never been as bad as tonight – he had some free seats for his little friends. Well, at least he woke the house up a bit.'

'You were good as ever, Miles.'

He looked pleased. 'Really? This last week I've relied more on technique than feeling, but having you in front helped.'

She felt a pang. Good though she had thought him, she had not once experienced even a hint of that attraction which his acting had so often awakened.

He asked if she had collected the travel brochures. For several days she had quite genuinely forgotten – and been reminded by him. Now she was able to say that she had the brochures, though she hadn't yet studied them.

He said they could do that together. 'Once the play's off, we can concentrate on them.'

On Saturday they had lunch at the flat (not, to her relief, served by the Austrian waiter) and Miles left for the theatre soon after four – grumbling, as he often did, at having to play two Saturday evening houses – 'I don't mind normal matinees, with a rest before the evening show, but I hate jamming two shows so close together. It means I give my worst performance of the week to the biggest house.'

'You don't give worst performances, Miles.'

'That's all you know. Anyway, I shall be glad when tonight's over. I've had to simulate so much gloom this week, in order to keep down with the company Joneses, that the gloom's becoming genuine. See you at supper.'

Now that she could expect Geoffrey in less than an hour, she found herself in a state of nervous joy that was positively dementing. And why, why hadn't she bought a new dress? Her wardrobe was packed with black dresses, gun-metal dresses, grey dresses – but nothing she could imagine pleasing him. Even a black and white striped silk dress Miles had thought too striking now seemed to her suitable for a dowager at a garden party. But in the end she put it on. Anyway, no dowager would have worn such a short skirt (and she hitched it up a bit, with its belt) or such very sheer stockings.

'And now, I suppose, he'll be late,' she thought, as Big Ben began to strike five.

On the third stroke, the doorbell rang. She hurled herself across the sitting room and the hall, and flung the door open. He stood there exactly as she had remembered him: cool, calm, collected, a barrister and a Member of

Parliament, a man belonging to an utterly different world from any she had ever known. 'Oh, come in, come in,' she gasped, and barely managed to get the door closed before she was in his arms. Later she hoped that, as regards this, he had taken the initiative, but gravely feared she hadn't given him time.

After a few minutes, during which they somehow managed to arrive in the sitting room, she said, 'Oh dear, you'll think I'm sex-starved or something.'

He laughed. 'Well, of course you're sex-starved. You have been for ten years – and even before that, I doubt if you ever had a good square meal. Oh, dear God, how relieved I am to find I like you as much as I thought I did.'

'Me, too.'

'That's a very lurid dress. But after seeing you in it I shall feel much fonder of zebra crossings.'

'Oh, Geoffrey –' They had sunk onto the sofa. She edged nearer.

'Just one minute,' he said firmly. 'I dropped a parcel in the hall.'

'You did? I never noticed. *Dropped* it?'

'Well, I put it down very hastily.'

He retrieved the parcel and sat beside her untying the string. 'A habit inculcated by my grandmother. This is from the girls. It had to be camouflaged in brown paper or it might have looked conspicuous.'

The parcel was about a foot square. When the brown paper came off she saw a very decorative box tied with silver ribbon. He undid the ribbon, saying, 'They found this vase in an antique shop and filled it with flowers. Robin does flowers rather well, with Kit standing by as a stem critic.'

Jill lifted out the vase. It was small and exquisite, a miniature urn delicately painted with flowers. And the real flowers, moss rosebuds, love-in-a-mist, and some tiny white stars, were little larger in scale. 'It's enchanting,' she said, suddenly near tears. 'Does it need water?'

'Not for the moment. They wrapped the stalks in wet moss.'

'The darling girls. Geoffrey, what did you tell them about me?'

'What I said I would: a shortened version of the truth.'

'Were they shocked?'

'Deeply – oh, not *at* you; for you. Robin wondered how we could ever make up for all you've been through. And Kit said, "It was sad for Mr Quentin, too, losing the baby, because I'm sure he'd have been a wonderful father." Then they jointly cooked up a scheme for Miles to remain a family friend. Kit said, "Perhaps we could always lay a cover for him at our table – like the Thrales did for Dr Johnson."'

Jill laughed weakly. 'He's not very good casting for Dr Johnson.'

'But seriously, we could remain friends with him. I'd be more than willing, if Miles would.'

For a moment she tried to visualize herself installed in the Westminster house with Miles trotting in and out almost like an extra member of the family. *Was* such a state of affairs conceivable? Well, not by her. She said, 'Geoffrey, have you given one moment's thought to letting things be as I want them'?'

He said he had indeed, and had discussed it with the girls. 'And Kit at once said, "But then we should never get her free. Besides, she wouldn't be *ours*." You see, my love, what you rightly called "the Thornton take-over bid" is a family affair, not just a bid from me.'

She felt a mixture of love and resentment towards the girls but love predominated, which was why she anxiously asked, 'Did you tell them I'm not really fifty'?'

'I never thought fifty or anywhere near it. Yes, I told them you're only thirty-four.'

'Were they surprised?'

'Frankly, yes. Also delighted. And Kit said she hoped you'd forgive them for treating you with too much respect.'

Jill, gazing lovingly at the vase of little flowers, said, 'You have powerful allies. Do they want to see me?'

'Of course. But they'll wait till you're willing. And in case you're anxious, I've muzzled them. Kit was all for rushing to Miles with the glad news. She said such a generous man would instantly let you go.'

'Well, so he would. Oh, dear, I hadn't thought of Kit lending a helping hand. You're sure she won't?'

'I am now. She at once saw *you* must make the decision. But has it occurred to you how horrified he'd be if he knew you were even considering remaining with him against your will?'

'But I still don't know what my will is. Geoffrey, could we stop talking for a little while?'

'Well, if it'll clarify matters for you,' said Geoffrey, almost resignedly.

After a fairly lengthy interlude he released her, saying, 'And now, as we're not going to bed – no, really, we're not – could you bear to behave like a grey-haired lady of fifty?'

'You underestimate ladies of fifty. Lots of them would have got you to bed long before this.'

'I assure you, no. I'm a man of iron resolve . . . I hope.'

They gazed at each other lovingly and blearily. Then she earnestly enquired if he would like some tea.

'No, nor a drink, nor a cigarette, nor any bloody thing but some solid sense from you. Now sit still and concentrate.'

'Well, for a little while.' She made a sudden dive and kissed him on the ear, then retired to the far end of the sofa.

'Why my ear, for God's sake?' he said, rubbing it.

'I sort of fancied it. Well, turn on the solid sense.'

'It's needed from you, not me. Now, will you tell Miles tonight?'

'No, Geoffrey. I can't face it yet.'

He said quickly, 'Does that mean you've made up your mind to, eventually?'

She hastily denied it – to herself as well as to him – adding, 'Have you the faintest idea what it would mean to him?'

'I'm not completely lacking in imagination. But you *can't*

214

go on with him, not if you're really in love with me. Perhaps you aren't.'

'Damn it, haven't I shown I am?'

'Oh, that might be sheer physical attraction, and partly due to the inhibited life you've been leading.'

She had thought that, herself, but wasn't pleased with him for mentioning it. 'Well, it feels more than that. But I do keep remembering that I was quite happy with Miles up to last Saturday.'

'Really happy?'

'All right, let's say contented. And that's a hell of a lot compared with the miseries of my youth. I couldn't face anything like that again.'

He was silent for a moment. Then he said, 'You probably wouldn't care to say this, so I'll say it for you. In your youth you were poor. I know your contentment has mainly been due to the affection you and Miles have for each other, but it's also been due to his money. Well, if you marry me I can ensure by a settlement that, even if the marriage fails, you'll be in out of the rain.'

She was glad she could say with truth that she hadn't thought of that side of things – 'Though I suppose I took it for granted you'd hardly chuck me out to starve. And I'll admit I wouldn't like to be poor again. But . . . no, nothing to do with that worries me.'

'Then is it only your dread of hurting Miles?'

'It's also dread of hurting myself – of losing Miles and then disappointing you. I think I'm a little frightened of you.'

215

'Because my face looks as if it's carved out of granite?'

'*Chiselled* out, very neatly. You have the nicest nose and chin. I bet you look gorgeous in your barrister's wig.'

'Superb. I only wish I'd brought it with me.' His smile faded. 'Seriously, Jill, why are you frightened of me? Perhaps you think I drove my wife to drink?'

She turned to him in horror. 'Geoffrey! You can't possibly believe I think that.'

'It would hardly be surprising, seeing that I sometimes think it myself. You'd better have an outline of the case.'

'But there's no need –'

'Yes, there is.' He was now speaking in a tone so unemotional that it was almost cold. 'The girls can't have given you the full facts because they don't know them. And I want you to have them. Much as I want you to marry me, I don't want to cheat you into it.'

'All right, then.'

She put out her hand as if to encourage him, but he ignored it, got up, and sat on the arm of a chair at some distance from her. He'd said she'd better have an outline of the case, and she guessed he was going to present that case as calmly as he would have presented a case in court. After a moment, he began.

'Well, I think I told you we married young. There was nothing to stop us; a fair amount of money on both sides, Sylvia's father – her mother was dead – was all for it, and my grandmother, the only relative I was closely in touch with, approved of early marriages. Incidentally, after meeting Sylvia and being charming to her, she left us alone

216

as she didn't believe any young married woman would want to see much of a grand-mother-in-law; I think she only came twice to our London flat – where we lived very comfortably, looked after by Mary Simmonds, the woman who's still with us. She'd been with Sylvia's family for years. As you know from that photograph at Hallows, Sylvia was very fragile-looking but she seemed perfectly healthy, and normal in every way. After a couple of months she began drinking perhaps a little more than I cared to see, but a few weeks later she became pregnant and went off drink altogether, so I never gave the matter another thought. Well, Julian was born and she was the most enchanting mother, nursing him herself and utterly absorbed in him – in fact, I was a bit out in the cold, but I didn't mind too much as I was working very hard. She was anxious to have another child soon, said she wanted a girl, and I'd nothing against it, so Robin was born before Julian was two. Again, Sylvia was a devoted mother; and poor Julian, like me, was out in the cold. But Mary Simmonds looked after him and I thought things would straighten themselves out once Robin grew beyond the baby stage. I also thought that two children would be enough – for the present, anyway – and Sylvia's doctor agreed with me. He said there was nothing really wrong with her, but she wasn't particularly strong. She didn't seem to hanker for more children but she did – rather vaguely – dislike the idea of any form of contraception. Eventually she asked me to leave it to her and not mention the matter again or she thought it would put her off making love. I did as she

217

asked and in no time at all she was pregnant again. I just accepted it but after Kit was born I took care of things – not that I'd much occasion to, as Sylvia was completely absorbed in Kit. Robin had now joined Julian and me in outer darkness. I put in all my spare time trying to console them.'

'Was she actually unkind to them?'

'She snapped at them, and sometimes doled out slaps. I remember my grandmother, on one of her rare visits, saying, "She's like a mother cat whose half-grown kittens hang around when she's got new ones," – but she said it quite affectionately. And she thought things might be better if we weren't so on top of each other, so she bought a long lease on the Westminster house, and found us an admirable Nanny, because Mary Simmonds couldn't possibly run the house, look after Julian and Robin, and wait hand and foot on Sylvia – who soon decided she loathed the house and that the Nanny was trying to take Kit from her. By then I'd realized I was married to a neurotic but there didn't seem anything I could do – her doctor said a psychiatrist would upset her and she just needed patience. And things weren't quite as bad as they may sound. Mary Simmonds looked after her and Kit, and the Nanny looked after the other two children.'

'And who looked after you?'

'Oh, Mary gave me breakfast and sometimes a meal at night. And I was tearingly busy. One just lived from day to day – until Kit stopped being a real baby. Then there was a wild flare-up. Sylvia said she couldn't stand the house or the Nanny a moment longer. She wanted to take the children and Mary, and spend the summer with her father at Hallows. Well, that seemed all right. I didn't know her father well but I quite liked him – I hadn't the faintest idea he drank – and there'd be some local help so Mary could concentrate on the children; and I'd come down every weekend. Actually, I only went one weekend. Sylvia put me off twice, made some quite convincing excuse about having decorators in the house and there being nowhere for me to sleep – she said she was sleeping with the children. Then I couldn't go one weekend – I was doing a rush job on my first really important case. So I hadn't seen them for nearly a month when I got a postcard, written in block capitals, from Julian, who'd been bright enough to send it to the hotel I'd moved to. All it said was: PLEASE COME QUICK. I got it in the middle of the week but, by the grace of God, didn't have to be in court that day, so I could drive straight down. I tried to telephone but was told the telephone was out of order.'

'Were you terribly worried?'

'Not too desperately. I'd telephoned at the weekend and been told by Mary that all was well except that Sylvia had a cold and didn't want to talk. I took it for granted that someone would ring me up if anything was seriously wrong and I imagined that Master Julian, who was then rising six, was bored. However, I got there as fast as I could. I found the three children sitting on the doorstep, simply waiting for me. They rushed at me and the girls burst into tears. Julian remained calm. He said – and even at six he could speak with hauteur – "It may interest you to know that our mother and our grandfather are drunk, and Mary is down in the village burying her father." He then pointed to a shocking bruise on his forehead and said, "So sorry to worry you but I feared one of us might get murdered." I believe those were his exact words.'

Jill, too, could believe it, and pictured Julian as an icy child of six. She said, 'Oh, God, how awful for you, Geoffrey.'

'At first I didn't realize *how* awful – oh, I knew something must be very wrong but I thought Julian must mean "ill", not "drunk"; I didn't think he knew what "drunk" meant. Anyway, I comforted the girls and then went into the house. Julian came with me; the girls hung back. I went first to the old man's study – he *was*, by the way, an old man; he'd been nearly fifty when Sylvia was born. I found him heavily asleep on a sofa and there was plenty of evidence that it was a drunken sleep all right. Then I went upstairs. Sylvia was in bed with her eyes closed, looking terribly frail. I felt sure hers really was a case of illness – until she opened her eyes and said thickly, "Well, fancy seeing you! Just go away and take the bloody children with you." And then she closed her eyes again. Even then I couldn't quite take it in that she was drunk. I asked her what was wrong and went on and on questioning her. She took no notice. Then Julian, with a sort of precocious showmanship, waved his hand towards some brandy bottles and said, "I *told* you."'

'And you'd never seen her drunk before?'

'Never. And except during the first few months of our marriage I'd hardly seen her drink anything alcoholic at all. I was so bewildered that I was barely capable of thought, but I knew I must get the children away. So I asked Julian if there was anyone who could pack some of their clothes. He said not until Mary came back but he and I could make a start and the girls could help – he thought they'd be willing to come upstairs if I'd see them safely past their mother's door. So we got them up. Even at four, Robin was clothes conscious and very sensible about what they'd need. I told them I hoped to take them to my grandmother but I'd have to ring up first and the telephone was out of order. Julian said, "It's just that Grandfather won't let it ring when he's like this. I'll show you." So we went down to the study and I found the old man had taken the receiver off. He never even stirred while I was telephoning though I had a bad line and had to shout. Mercifully, my grandmother said, "Stop trying to explain. You want me to take the children and I will – as soon as you can get them here. That's all we need to say now." Marvellous woman. Just as I came out of the study Mary Simmonds came bicycling back from her father's funeral.'

'She really had been to it?'

'Oh, lord, yes. And one way and another she was in a state bordering on collapse. But I did get some truth out of her. She said Sylvia had had drinking bouts even in her teens but there'd been none since her marriage, until she came down to her father. Even then, there'd been nothing serious to begin with. Sylvia had kept on pulling herself together. Mary swore only the last bout had been really bad. I asked why she hadn't let me know and she said Sylvia had forbidden it – and anyway, Mary had thought I'd be down the next weekend. And then her father had died suddenly. Of course she oughtn't to have left the children but it was no use reviling her; she was sick with guilt and misery – in fact, she rushed away to be physically sick. After that, she helped to finish the packing. I told her I'd get back as soon as I could, probably late that night, and then I drove the children off to my grandmother's. At least I knew Mary would look after Sylvia.'

He paused for a moment, and Jill visualized the arrival at one of the tall houses in Queen's Crescent. She said, 'It's a comfort to think of the children safely out of Hallows.'

'That most unhallowed house – though I feel more kindly towards it, now I can think of you there.'

They smiled at each other. Then, still unemotionally, he went on.

'Well, I didn't get back until nearly midnight. Poor Mary was waiting up for me. She said she'd got the old man to bed, and Sylvia was asleep, and I'd better sleep in a spare room and not talk to her until the morning. I tried to get some more facts but didn't have much luck. I can only remember Mary saying, "It's not her fault. She got it from her dad – it's in the blood. Everyone round here knows."'

'What did your wife say when you talked to her?'

'She insisted it was just a freak thing and wouldn't

happen again. But she wouldn't come back to London with me, said she must stay with her father as he was seriously ill. So he was; a month later he went into a nursing home where he died. She still wouldn't come back to London and when I went down for weekends she was antagonistic; said I got on her nerves. But there was nothing to indicate she was drinking. Then Mary rang up to say she was as bad as ever. And that's how it went on. She'd be all right for a while and then break out again; only the periods between the outbreaks got shorter. And she wouldn't cooperate, see doctors or psychiatrists. I tried taking them down as if they were ordinary guests, but she always found out and locked herself up.'

'Did you go on loving her?'

'I don't believe I felt any genuine love for her after that day I found the children huddled on the doorstep. But of course I felt completely responsible for her and there were times when I did greatly pity her. There was one particular occasion, when she'd been at Hallows about two years. She'd just recovered from one of her worst bouts and, for once, she'd been apologetic. After I was back in London I got a little scrawl from her saying, "Sorry, sorry, sorry. God, I wish I was dead." I felt I must make some new effort to cure her and I wondered if it would help if she had another child. You see, she'd never drunk while she was pregnant or feeding a baby. No one I'd consulted had been able to say if that was due to will power or just to revulsion from alcohol, and it was far from certain if it would work again. Also I was none too sure she was fit to have another

223

child; not to mention that she'd shown no willingness to sleep with me – but I thought that might be because she guessed I'd no desire for it. Anyway, I decided I'd at least discuss the idea with her while she was in her present mood and – well, try to be a bit lover-like, *ask* her for love. It wouldn't have been too hard, because I felt so much pity that it almost amounted to a return of love. Well, once I'd made up my mind I drove straight back to Hallows. Mary stopped me in the hall and said Sylvia was out walking, and why didn't I go to meet her? I was just about to when I heard Sylvia's voice upstairs and then I heard a man's voice. After that, I got the facts out of Mary. There'd been men for most of the time Sylvia had been at Hallows – even local tradesmen. By the way, the girls know nothing of this side of their mother's troubles.'

Jill nodded acceptance. There was no point in undeceiving him.

'I just drove back to London. And I never again considered sleeping with her. I didn't feel I could divorce her, and if she'd had a child I hope I'd have treated it as my own; but I wasn't going to risk not knowing if it was my child or some other man's. Mercifully, she never did have another child. Well, that's about all, really. I went on seeing her and even took the children. She wanted them sometimes but not for long; and their visits were apt to prove disastrous. Eventually, Kit refused to go near her. The outbreaks of drinking finally led to a long, fatal illness.'

'How many years did it all last?'

224

'From the day I found out to the day of her death it was eleven years. Her doctors – of course, long before the end I'd had to force doctors on her – couldn't understand how she could go on and on, especially as she showed no desire to live. Well, now you know – enough, anyway.'

She said briskly, 'I certainly know enough to be sure you weren't to blame. And I can't believe you think you were.'

He smiled. 'How I admire that brisk, matter-of-fact tone. I hadn't realized you and Kit had so much in common. Oh, I'll admit I behaved reasonably well during those ghastly years. My crime was in ever marrying Sylvia, in ever believing we could make each other happy. She was an incredibly *silly* girl – and I knew it and didn't think it mattered. My God, I must have been a patronizing young bastard. How bored she must have been, with me, my clever-clever legal friends, even with her own highly intelligent children. She wanted to escape from the lot of us. If I drove her to drink it was just by being myself. Perhaps you're right to be frightened of me.'

'But I'm not, any more . . . and I never was, really. I see now that I was only frightened *for* you – and I still am. Oh, Geoffrey – !' She broke off, suddenly knowing that she did not want to say what she ought to say, did not any longer want to put him off. Sometime during his unemotional narrative she had realized that he was quite as vulnerable as Miles, and it was as hard to think of denying him anything as it was hard to think of hurting Miles.

He came and sat beside her. 'Why are you frightened *for* me?'

'Because you're trying to make the same mistake again. Compared with you, I'm as silly as she was.'

'You're *not* silly.'

'Unsuitable, anyway. And so utterly limited in outlook. The theatre's such a self-absorbed world. But I've told you, I've told you from the beginning.'

'And I've told you it doesn't matter. Though if you do want to widen your interests my children are panting to help you. And now, please, could we just sit quietly, not talk, not make love, just *be* together?'

He put his arm round her and she leaned against his shoulder. And after a few minutes she gave a little sigh of absolutely peaceful pleasure.

⊰ 13 ⊱

Little Letter from Cyril

She had intended to tell Miles of Geoffrey's visit, very casually, during supper. But she found that Frank Ashton and the play's young author had been invited to join them, so the conversation was devoted to cheering playwright and impresario up. As Frank Ashton had plenty more money to lose and the author had already sold a new play for television, Jill did not feel too harrowed. But when it struck her that but for the recently dead play's production at the Spa Street theatre she would never have met Geoffrey, she felt a sudden fondness and regret for it, though this did not prevent her from being bored by the long suppertime postmortem.

In the taxi, on the way back to the flat, she mentally rehearsed various casual mentions of Geoffrey's visit but spoke none of them aloud. Only when she entered the sitting room and came face to face with the little urn of flowers did she manage to get out, 'Oh, look what the Thornton girls sent me. Geoffrey brought it round this afternoon.'

Miles, having said it was charming, appeared to be gazing at it with extreme concentration for so long that she feared he might be wondering why the girls couldn't have brought it themselves. Then he spoke, and she realized that his concentration had really been on the travel brochures, which were close to the flowers, for what he said was, 'Jill, would you very much mind if I went abroad on my own?'

Of all the unexpected miracles! It was hard to keep intense relief out of her tone, to sound merely kind and unresentful. 'Of course I wouldn't, darling. I think it's a very good idea – more of a change for you.'

But who was going to constitute the change? She had seen no indication that he was interested in any young man. But one had to face the fact that it could be just a chance acquaintance. Her job now was one she was accustomed to: she must show no curiosity and yet somehow demonstrate a warm friendliness which would encourage him to talk, if he wanted to. But he obviously didn't for he merely said, 'Bless you for being so understanding. Let's get to bed. I'm dog tired.'

She did not even ask when he would go, but a few moments later he said, 'I'll probably be off tomorrow.' She could hardly believe her luck – to be free to think her own thoughts, free to be with Geoffrey and the girls! And the fact that he was launching into an affair made her feel less guilty – though so great was her affection for him that she almost wanted to warn him, to cry out, 'Don't make it easier for me.'

While sitting with Geoffrey in the twilight she had remembered the television play she had undertaken to report on. (Miles seemed to have forgotten all about it.) Geoffrey had watched it with her and they had enjoyed it, though she guessed their enjoyment had been largely due to the shared occasion and the pleasure of exploring each other's opinions. It hadn't really been a good play and they had both of them disapproved of a noble and mawkish husband in a wheelchair. But she had provoked Geoffrey to delighted laughter by suddenly declaring, 'Though if *you* were paralyzed from the waist down, I'd still want to spend my life with you.' In view of which, he could not have been particularly worried that she still had not, in so many words, promised to marry him. But she had – more or less – undertaken to tell Miles, 'very soon, just give me a few days.' Ought she to tell him before he left for the Continent? No, she couldn't face it. And perhaps he might be at the beginning of some grand, consoling romance, so that it would be *easy* to tell him when he got back. But she knew only too well that he always returned from such trips more devoted to her, more dependent on her, than ever.

On Sunday morning he packed a single suitcase. Had they been going on tour she would have packed for him but many years ago he had made it clear that, on occasions such as the present one, he wanted no help. This was all part of the secret mood which took possession of him: if she helped she would have to be told what clothes to pack and that might have indicated where he was going, which she was never allowed to know. Nor was she told how long he would be away. And while away he would not write her so much as a postcard.

He excused himself from lunching with her, went out, and did not return until the late afternoon, when he did some last-minute packing. He then bade her a more affectionate farewell than she was expecting – often he merely smiled and said, 'See you soon.' This time he kissed her, asked if she was sure she would be all right, told her to take care of herself, and finally said, 'See something of the Thorntons, won't you? Why not give the girls some outings? They'll be company for you. And tell them how much I admired their flowers.' He then kissed her again and, with surprising swiftness for a heavy man burdened with a suitcase, whisked himself out of the flat.

She had never before seen him go without experiencing a mixture of regret and resentment, the resentment quickly censored and transmuted into a loving tolerance. Today, she was only conscious of relief.

About to telephone Geoffrey, she was smitten with nervousness in case Miles came back for something. So she waited an hour – and was then deflated to find that the whole Thornton family was out. (The wraith-like voice that told her so would be that of Mary Simmonds.) She left a message, but not until nearly midnight was she rung up, by both Robin and Kit, one of them on an extension line. On hearing that Miles had gone away they were ecstatically excited. Their father had driven to his constituency and would not be back until Tuesday evening. But would Jill come to them the first thing in the morning – or would she come now, and spend the night – or should they come and spend the night with her? Was she sure she wouldn't be lonely? Jill, who wanted a good night's sleep, was quite sure. But she would be with them by eleven in the morning. 'Such ages Father's been holding us at bay,' Kit complained. 'But it'll be all right now, won't it? And soon we'll have you for good.'

Jill protested that nothing was decided yet, but was so heavily over-borne by both girls that she hastily brought the conversation to an end and rang off. In the ensuing silence, she found that she *was* lonely. Oh, she wasn't missing Miles or even, at the moment, Geoffrey. She just felt regretfully cut off from the girls' happy voices.

When they opened the door to her next morning they were wearing tights and sweaters patterned with black and white lozenges. Tartan kilts, barely a foot long, were slung round their waists.

'You look like harlequins,' said Jill.

'All but the kilts. Robin calls them minus-skirts.'

'For once I'm trying to get ahead of fashion,' said Robin. 'Oh, darling Jill, how marvellous to see you.'

As on her previous visit, Jill found her progress upstairs painful. Kit edged her into the banisters. Robin bumped her from the rear. They were all three laughing in a way that unco-ordinated their movements.

'It seems like months since you were here,' said Robin.

'Actually, it's two weeks and three days,' said Kit.

To Jill, it felt like light-years.

This morning there was a fire in the attic sitting room.

'We thought it was just cold enough for one,' said Robin.

The little room, in morning sunlight, looked even more attractive than Jill's memories of it. Beyond the roof tops of the houses opposite, white clouds were scudding across patches of blue sky. A pigeon on the window sill had just discovered crumbs put out for it.

Jill, steered to an armchair, sat back and inspected the girls' outfits more fully.

'You should have one like them,' said Kit. 'And look like our sister.'

'Oh, do, Jill! We could get the tights and sweater in your size, and me and me dressmaker could fix you up with a minus-skirt.'

'Tights are so marvellously comfortable. And so decent when one feels the need to lie on one's back and wave one's legs in the air.' Kit, on the divan, performed some contortions which looked liable to break her neck.

'I'm much too old,' said Jill. 'Both for tights and waving my legs in the air.'

'What, at thirty-four? That's young enough for anything,' said Robin.

'Oh, how awful that we thought you were so much older! We can see you're not now. Perhaps you were thinking elderly thoughts, trying to reconcile yourself to being married to dear Mr Quentin.'

'But I didn't need to reconcile myself, Kit. I love him very much.'

'Of course. So do we. And I'd be honoured to marry

232

him myself in a year or two, if he'd have me. Really, it might be a good idea, seeing I'm more and more sure I'm going to be frigid. But not you, dear Jill. You're the last woman to be married to a homosexual.'

Jill said uncomfortably, 'I can't get used to your knowing about such things.'

Kit, bringing her feet down and sitting cross-legged, regarded Jill judicially. 'Will you kindly tell me why? Do you consider homosexuality an unmentionable crime?'

'Of course not, Kit, darling. But somehow . . .' She shook her head, at a loss for words.

'Just not a suitable subject for little girls,' said Kit, with a cat-like grin. 'And should they also be debarred from discussing colour-blindness, or left-handedness, or – for that matter – genius? Should nothing that isn't one hundred percent normal be mentioned by pure little lips?'

Robin said, 'It seems to me that homosexuality is neither a wrong thing nor a right thing. It's merely something that exists. Children should learn about it at the same time that they learn about normal sex – and they should learn about that jolly early. And they shouldn't be told that normality is necessarily right.'

'We're not convincing her, Robin. She still thinks homosexuality's *wrong*. You do, don't you, Jill? In spite of being married to such a very good and kind homosexual.'

She would have liked to say she didn't. But these children deserved complete sincerity. The best she could manage was, 'Not wrong, exactly. But I do think it's a pity. Surely you agree with me about that?'

'I don't,' said Kit. 'That is, not unless it's making people unhappy. Considered objectively, I think it ought to be encouraged. Everyone knows the world's population's exploding. There should be *dedicated* homosexuals, much honoured.' She flung herself backwards on the divan and executed a somersault.

Jill, laughing, knew that the girls had freed her of inhibitions far more than ten years of marriage to Miles had. But were things quite so simple? To the pure all things were pure . . . but only to the pure.

'How soon can you marry Father?' said Robin.

'Oh, Robin, darling –'

'Don't worry her, Robin. Father said we weren't to. We rang him up this morning, Jill, and he said we were just to give you a happy time. There's a thrilling exhibition at the Tate – we could go this afternoon – and a good concert tonight; you did enjoy that concert in the Pump Room.'

'And I thought we might take you to a dress show tomorrow. But of course you must say if any of our ideas bore you.'

'Nothing is going to bore me,' said Jill, with conviction.

Already the girls had new possessions to show her, new interests to discuss. Their energy, both mental and physical, was infectious and she was suddenly aware that she was feeling particularly *well*. Idly, she picked up the kaleidoscope which had delighted her on her first visit. But she put it down without looking through it, succumbing to the quick clutch of superstition. Soon after she had last looked, the pattern of her life had changed so drastically. She did not now want it to change again. Already happiness was hinting at its inbuilt snag: fear that it might not last.

When it was lunch-time Robin said, 'We hope you won't mind that we're having it in the basement breakfast room. We always do when we're on our own and Mary Simmonds has it with us. Father's told you about her, hasn't he? We'll all be very grateful if you can manage to like her.'

'Of course I shall,' said Jill, with histrionic heartiness. She found herself unwilling to meet Mary. It was as if the link with the late Mrs Thornton cast a shadow across the day's brightness. And the shadow intensified when, in the breakfast room – which opened on to the small back garden – she met the thin, pale woman who seemed incapable of taking part in the general conversation. Try as one could, Mary Simmonds again and again relapsed into silence. But it was not a gloomy or sulky silence. It suggested rather that she only wished to speak if others wished her to; there was nothing *she* wished to say. Only at the end of the meal, when she took scraps of food out to the birds, did she show signs of animation.

Robin, starting to clear the table while Mary was outside, said, 'She loves birds and flowers – she works quite hard in the garden. Do tell her she must have green fingers. It's a frightful cliché but she loves to be told it.'

Jill obliged, and talked about flowers and birds extensively. Mary seemed pleased but volunteered no information, merely answered questions. Jill eventually ran out of them, and then she and Mary went through into the kitchen where the girls, having stacked the dishwasher, were tidying everything up. They did not leave until Mary was settled in her armchair – Jill saw that the breakfast room was also Mary's sitting room. She had television, a radio and a stack of magazines. Robin, setting a tea tray beside her, said, 'Now you're not to do a stroke of work until six o'clock, and we'll be back in time to help dish up dinner.'

'They spoil me,' said Mary.

It was the first statement not elicited by a question Jill had heard her make.

When they had mounted the narrow stairs from the basement Robin said, 'Do you find her very depressing?'

'No,' said Jill, wondering why she didn't. 'Perhaps she's not definite enough to be depressing. She's like a whisper.'

'We think she's fairly happy,' said Kit. 'She enjoys quite a lot of things, particularly children's television. I used to feel I ought to watch it with her but we've discovered she likes to spend a lot of time alone. It's tricksy, making sure she isn't lonely and yet not making demands on her by being there.'

'And it's tricksy about work,' said Robin. 'One has to let her do enough to feel valuable but not enough to tire her. She'd be at it from morning till night if we didn't stop her. By the way, she's a very good cook, provided one writes everything down for her. Oh, there's a lot to be said for Mary.'

It dawned on Jill that Robin was trying to sell her Mary, was nervous for Mary's future. This brought home to her, as nothing else quite had, that she would eventually be living in this narrow, intimate old house. She said reassuringly, 'I can imagine getting very fond of her.'

'Oh, *can* you?' Robin positively sighed with relief. 'Kit and I have had to work hard at it, because we somehow linked her with Mother. But the poor dear had nothing to live for when Mother died, so we just had to have her here. At first we only pretended to like her, but now we really do.'

'And so shall I,' said Jill, knowing she meant it. There was so much love in her heart, for the girls as well as for their father, that there'd be some overflow for Mary.

She found the exhibition at the Tate Gallery immensely stimulating, partly because the girls were stimulating companions but also because she was in the mood to be stimulated. Indeed, her enjoyment was so intense that she became a little exhausted and the girls, instantly motherly, decided that a concert that evening might be too much for her. 'Father said we weren't to overdo it,' said Robin. 'Besides, there's so much to talk about.'

They had a good, rather feminine dinner, in the dining room, minus Mary. 'Mary,' Kit explained, 'does not dine. She sups, on a tray. Incidentally, she would be shocked at the idea of sitting down to a meal with Father. She accepts us – just – because she knew us as children; but she considers Father should be served, not hobnobbed with. She'll probably feel the same about you, once you're married to him. At present she thinks you're *our* friend.'

'The classless society will never get any kind of boost from Mary,' said Robin. 'And yet she's never obsequious. She has a sort of dignity which belongs to the country, not to towns.'

At ten o'clock Jill considered going home and found she disliked the idea. She had a mental picture of the flat waiting for her, empty, aloof, a home that had never been a home. And when she reached it – not much before midnight, as the girls' unwillingness to let her go equalled her dislike of going – it was even worse than she expected. All day she had kept thoughts of Miles at bay, but now they rushed at her. How was she going to tell him? Should she receive him back as if all was well and then, gradually . . . She imagined it as a scene in a play and thought, 'But it's unwriteable, unplayable.' Then she wrapped herself in the day's happiness and the prospect of the next day's. Whatever happened, she was going to enjoy her holiday – and, damn it, presumably Miles was enjoying his. For the first time, she encouraged a resentment she had never fully admitted to feeling.

She had invited Robin and Kit to lunch with her and suggested they might bring Mary but they assured her Mary would die with embarrassment if she had to lunch in a restaurant. The girls arrived at twelve o'clock and were greatly impressed by the flat in daylight.

'I suppose you'll go on living here,' said Kit, 'and Mr Quentin will go somewhere else. You can't stay here together or you'd never get a divorce.'

'It would be nice if you could move in with us,' said Robin, 'but I suppose you'll have to wait till the divorce goes through.'

This conversation raised problems which were even more to the forefront of Jill's mind during the dress show the girls took her to after lunch. She saw several dresses

238

she would have liked to buy – but what with? She and Miles had a joint bank account and, within reason, she bought anything she wanted. She could not go on using Miles's money but she had no access to Geoffrey's. Robin chose that moment to say, 'That dress would be splendid on you, Jill – just right for your trousseau.' Who was going to pay for that trousseau? It might be distinctly inconvenient to be between husbands. She was thankful that at least she had no shortage of ready money, having recently cashed quite a large cheque. Of course the money in her handbag was just as much Miles's as the money in the bank but it somehow helped that, when she cashed the cheque, she hadn't decided to leave him.

Geoffrey got home shortly before dinner, when she and the girls were together in the doll's size drawing room. He kissed her, but in much the same way that he kissed his daughters. And even when she was alone with him, after dinner, he did not so much as hold her hand. No doubt he was digging himself in for a long, respectable engagement. And sitting there in the little panelled room, occasionally hearing the girls' voices from below, she felt she could happily accept the respectability.

When he saw her home, he excused himself from coming up to the flat. She said, 'You'd be safe enough. I've given up hope of seducing you.'

He smiled and said, 'Thank God for that. If I gave in I still might not get you away from Miles.'

'Yes, you would. Truly. I'll promise you now, if you like.'

'I do indeed like. Still, I shan't feel quite safe until you've told him. Good night, my love.'

The next morning, she woke later than usual and found herself likely to be late for an early appointment at the hairdresser's. There were, she noted, a fairly large number of letters, all for Miles and most of them forwarded from the theatre. She glanced at the envelopes while she was hurriedly drinking some coffee. No handwriting was familiar. Probably they would all be fan letters. Anyway, they could wait until after lunch, when she would have time to cope with them. She was not due at the Westminster house until late afternoon as Geoffrey would be tied up till then and the girls, they had regretfully admitted, were booked to meet some ex-school friends.

She got back to the flat soon after three o'clock and settled down at her desk. Miles liked his fan mail to be answered without delay; and as she had no idea when he could deal with this batch it seemed best to send short notes saying he was on holiday.

She had finished the job and was about to put her typewriter away when she saw one last letter, which had fallen to the floor. It was addressed to the flat, not the theatre, but judging from the handwriting it, too, was from a fan and a very young one. And the writing was so illegible that she doubted if she could read it. She turned to the signature, which was 'Cyril'. Oh, dear! Well, she would just have to wrestle with the writing. What she eventually made out was:

Dear Mr Quentin,

I would not write this if I could help it, after you been so kind, though my brother says no credit to you, seeing' what you wanted. But I still think you were kind except that day at your flat – and my brother says what makes it worse is that I just told you how young I really was. You said not to tell what happened but my brother got it out of me when he saw how upset I was. And now I don't know what to do as Mr Albion says no work for me and my brother is out of a job. He says I should go to the police and you would have to pay me damages. But they might send you to prison and that would ruin you and you such a great actor. And if I could have a hundred pounds it would see us through for a long time. But not to send a check or write. Put the money in an envelope and bring it to that pub behind the theatre on Friday night at nine. And someone will be there, no one you know but he will know you. Then everything will be O.K. And I am truly sorry, Mr Quentin, but have no other course. But not to worry, I know you could not help it. I hope you are well.

Cyril

Even when she understood the sense of the letter, it took her a moment to realize its full meaning. Master Cyril-Doug Digby was implying that he had been assaulted, and he was attempting blackmail.

⚅ 14 ⚅

Tom Has Been There Before

Of course the letter was a vicious invention. Unless . . . she vividly remembered coming into the flat that afternoon when Miles had been rehearsing with Cyril. The boy had been in tears. Miles had put his arm round him to escort him to the hall. Could that – or some other gesture of comforting kindness, occurring before she came in – have been misconstrued, and its significance further exaggerated by the brother, that black streak she had seen at the stage door?

She read the letter again. It didn't read like an invention. Perhaps the little idiot *had* misunderstood, really felt justified . . . No. Nothing justified blackmail. And if the Digby brothers could blackmail, they could invent the reason.

What the hell was she to do? Ironically, had Cyril merely written a begging letter she would have sent him, well, say twenty pounds, knowing that Miles would wish her to. He rarely refused a loan (which almost always proved to be a gift) to a fellow professional; and he had, of course, shown Cyril special kindness. But she couldn't send money now. One couldn't be blackmailed. Perhaps she ought to go straight to the police. No, not while Miles was away – and she didn't even know in which country.

Could she get advice? Suppose she told Geoffrey? It would be a relief but somehow a betrayal of Miles – though would it, when Miles was utterly innocent? Perhaps she feared Geoffrey would not believe that.

Suppose she told no one – and did nothing? It was now Wednesday. Someone would go to the pub on Friday evening to meet Miles and Miles would not be there. But surely Cyril and his brother would not then rush to the police, thus losing their chance of ever getting any money? Unless – There was a sentence in the letter . . . she found it. 'And he thinks I should go to the police and you would have to pay me damages.' Nonsense, surely, but the Digby brothers might believe it. And if they did go to the police, if they accused Miles . . . Even if he cleared himself – and how *could* he clear himself? It would simply be his word against Cyril's.

Should she go to the pub herself and hope whoever came might know her by sight and make contact with her? She could explain that Miles was away, offer to tide Cyril over with a little money. No. It would be tantamount to admitting . . .

Get advice from someone she simply must. And it now

243

struck her that Tom Albion was the obvious person. As Miles's agent he would be vitally concerned in protecting Miles's reputation, and he was, too, their very good friend. Also it was just conceivable that Miles might have left, say, some poste restante address with him in case of some business emergency. Yes, of course she must talk to Tom – and please God he was in London.

She rang the agency and was put through to him. Cutting through his pleasant greeting she said she needed to see him urgently. 'Can I come at once?'

He said, 'Of course,' without an instant's hesitation. She was grateful for that.

In the taxi she had qualms. Ought she to show the letter even to Tom? Suppose he believed Cyril's accusation? But he wouldn't – no one who knew Miles would. He'd probably laugh at her fears, say the whole thing was impertinent bluff. She felt a warmth of reassurance even as she climbed the once beautiful old staircase that led to his ramshackle premises. He was always saying he must move out of Soho but she doubted if he ever would unless the house fell down on him – and it rather looked as if it might. Entering the agency she had affectionate memories of conferences punctuated by the entrances of secretaries bearing strong cups of tea, with slices of heavy fruit cake which acquired added heaviness from slopped saucers.

One such cup of tea, with its attendant cake, accompanied her into Tom's office today. Settling her into an armchair facing his desk, he asked if she'd rather have a drink.

'No, thanks. Your office tea's practically as good as a drink.' She smiled at the departing secretary, then thanked Tom for seeing her at once.

'In all the years we've known each other you've never before asked to see me urgently. And you sounded worried. What is it, love?'

She noticed that his Lancashire accent was well to the fore, as it usually was when he wanted to be particularly kind. He was the son of a once-famous music hall comedian and his personality, like his office, retained the aura of a long-vanished theatrical world – which did not prevent him from being a shrewd, and even hard, businessman.

'Oh, it's probably a lot of nonsense,' she said. 'Just me staging a panic. But first, have you any way of getting in touch with Miles?'

'I only know he's gone abroad. He rang me up to say so, on Sunday. For once, I made a point of asking where he'd be – because of the film – but he said he didn't know. He finally said he'd try to ring me, next Sunday.'

'We'll have to decide something before then – by Friday night, actually. But you'll probably say, do nothing at all.' She took the letter from her bag and handed it over, determinedly smiling. 'You'll see what rubbish it is. It's just that – with Miles away –'

'Drink your tea, love,' said Tom.

'You'll find it difficult to read.'

She watched him while he read. His pudgy features were not expressive but it was only a few seconds before he said, 'Oh, my God,' in a tone which left her in no doubt that he was taking the letter seriously. He then read on in silence and it seemed to her that he took an interminable time. Even when he raised his eyes to hers, he did not at once speak. But the pudgy features were now expressive enough. It was as if the mask of comedy was attempting to be the mask of tragedy. At last he said, 'Miles, of all people.'

'But it's not true. Surely you don't believe –'

He said hastily, 'I only meant that it's fantastically awful that this should happen to Miles. God blast the lousy child.'

'*Is* he a child? What does he mean when he says that Miles knew how young he is? Miles told me he was eighteen.'

'I'll tell you all I know about that – and I think I got the truth out of the little bastard when he came here last week. He started rehearsals saying he was fifteen, and therefore didn't need a licence. Peter Hesper began to think he was younger and told him to bring a birth certificate – which he did, and it said he was *eighteen*, but it was his brother's birth certificate. The name on it was Douglas Digby, not Cyril Digby, but he bluffed Peter into believing that Douglas was really his name. Then the boy got frightened and told Miles the truth – I gather that was just before the show opened in London. He said he was going to be fifteen in a week's time, and then everything would be all right. And if a licence had to be got at the last minute, the show might have to be postponed. So in the end, Miles said he'd keep the secret.'

'Did the boy tell you this, or did Miles?'

'I got it out of the boy first and then Miles confirmed it. I told him he was a fool to have involved himself in a conspiracy with the ghastly kid, but he said Cyril was in tears and in a state of nerves because Peter had been bullying him, and if there'd been any more trouble the boy wouldn't have been able to open at all. And what did it matter if he played for just one week without a licence? Anyway, there was no point in fussing about it as the damn play was now off. So that was that.'

'Then Cyril's really fifteen?'

'Search me. He may still be lying. He could pass for ten or eleven. And one thing's ominous. I told him I wouldn't even have his name on my books unless he brought me his own, genuine birth certificate. That was ten days ago and he still hasn't brought it. So he's probably younger than fifteen.'

'I wonder if Cyril confessed about the birth certificate that day they rehearsed at the flat. Afterwards, when I told Miles to get his mind off Cyril's troubles, he said, "You don't know the half of them."'

Tom looked suddenly relieved. 'Then you were in the flat?'

'Only as Cyril was leaving – in tears, incidentally, which would fit with his just having confessed to Miles.'

'Try to remember anything either of them said.'

Only odd snatches of conversation came back to her. 'Miles said Cyril had had a difficult morning, but everything would be all right – something like that. And Cyril said, when they were out in the hall, "1 swear I won't let you down." Incidentally, Miles's manner was fairly brusque. I was a bit surprised because you know how kind-hearted Miles is. But no doubt he was trying to buck Cyril up – he said afterwards, "The boy's a mass of self-pity." And he had, of course, been wonderfully kind to him up till then.'

'Quite abnormally kind.'

She looked at him indignantly. 'What's that supposed to mean?'

'I simply meant especially kind.'

But she didn't believe him. Nothing he had said, since his utter dismay on reading the letter, had made her feel he had complete faith in Miles. She said now, 'I'd like the truth, Tom. If you've any doubts at all . . .'

He was silent too long for her liking. Then he said:

'Jill, if anyone told me that Miles had done something dishonest, mean, or even been spiteful, I'd stake my reputation it wasn't true. But as regards this accusation – oh, for God's sake don't think I believe Miles is guilty but we can help him best by facing the fact that he *conceivably* is.'

'I shan't,' said Jill. 'But I've already faced the fact that Cyril might have, well, misconstrued something.'

'I doubt that. Cyril's no innocent. Either the accusation's true, or the letter's such a clever fraud that I can't believe the boys capable of having invented it. Perhaps the brother is, but even that's not easy to accept.'

'You find it easier to accept Miles's guilt,' said Jill,

coldly. 'How strange. I felt so sure you'd be a tower of strength.'

'Well, damn it, so I will – anyway, I'll do my best to be, and whether Miles is guilty or innocent. And I swear I'm not taking it for granted he's guilty. It's just that . . . Listen, love. Even my perfectly normal clients are pretty unpredictable as regards anything to do with sex, but when it comes to my homosexuals – ! About a fifth of my male clients are homosexual, including my four most important ones, of whom Miles is the most important. The general average of decency – in matters that affect me – is just about the same as with my normal clients. Of my four stars, two are pleasant, reasonable chaps, one's a right bastard, and Miles is just about the kindest, most likeable man I've ever met. But I don't know what makes *any* of them tick. I just don't understand homosexuality. I don't condemn it. I merely find it beyond my comprehension, and simply accept the fact that a fifth of the men who enable me to earn a living have feelings utterly alien to my own. And I also accept that I never know what they'll be up to next. That's why, with all my respect, admiration and affection for Miles, I can't feel one hundred percent certain he's innocent. Incidentally, this is not the first blackmailing letter I've read sitting at this desk. And, in every case but one, my client was guilty of what he was accused.'

'Were you able to help them?'

'Only to the extent of getting them the best legal advice – which was to pay up. Even the man who was innocent.'

'But that's fantastic. Surely if an innocent man goes to the police –'

'He was innocent of what his blackmailer accused him, but he was a homosexual. If he'd gone to the police, too much would have come out. There are limits to what the police will turn a blind eye on.'

'But surely the law's going to be changed –'

'It'll be more severe, not less, as regards what Miles is accused of,' said Tom grimly. 'I don't think you've quite taken it in, Jill. He could possibly survive an ordinary homosexual scandal, but not this, not an offence against a child. Anyway, he might get a heavy jail sentence.'

'But he's *innocent*, Tom.'

'You go on believing that, love – and I'll do my level best to. And I do find it hard to think that he could have been attracted by that horrid lad. Hardly Miles's type, would you say?'

'I don't know much about that, Tom.' She felt vaguely ashamed to admit it. 'Miles has become more and more reticent.'

'Do you know who's with him now? I take it someone is?'

'I imagine so. But he didn't give me the slightest hint – just told me, late on Saturday night, that he was going, and went on Sunday.'

Tom was looking at her closely. 'You're an odd couple. I know half a dozen married homosexuals – though a couple of them are bisexual; their wives just wait their turn, more or less philosophically. The other wives are motherly,

250

or plain cynical and having a good time on their own. But you and Miles . . . I've always felt you're merely devoted friends. Not that there's anything mere about devoted friendship.'

'It's been more than that, Tom. It's been love. There can be love without any sexual feeling.'

'Between a man and a woman? Well, different people mean different things by love. Anyway, I can take it you'll stand by him now, whatever happens?'

She hesitated only a couple of seconds before saying, 'Of course.' But in those seconds she knew how fully she had accepted that her life with Miles was over. *Could* she stand by him now?

Tom had noticed the hesitation. 'Funny. I didn't think you'd have any doubts.'

'I haven't. Of course I haven't. Of course I must stand by him.'

'Must? Listen, Jill, this is important. Even if you're not as sure of his innocence as you say you are –'

'But I am. It's got nothing to do with that.'

'What hasn't?'

'Don't fire questions at me. I've told you I'll stand by him and I will. Just leave it at that.'

'Like hell I will,' said Tom. 'Before I get legal advice I need to be dead sure of your attitude. It's one of the first things I shall be asked. And you're holding out on me about something. Now come on, love.'

It was a relief to tell him. And as she did so, his whole manner changed. She found he was offering her all the understanding and reassurance she had counted on getting from him about Miles.

She told him the bare facts and he asked for little elaboration though, whenever she paused, he helped her on with some sympathetic question. At last she concluded, 'Well, there it is. I promised Geoffrey – only last night – but he won't, surely, hold me to that now.'

'He ought to,' said Tom. 'He ought to drag you out of this mess before you're completely involved. Of course as Miles's agent I ought to put his interests first and work up your loyalty. But you're a normal woman, Jill. Anyway, you were once. Since you married you've been living in a state of suspended animation. Get out, love. And I bet you Miles will say the same – it's odd I can feel so sure of that when I can't feel dead sure he's innocent.'

She said with deliberation, 'If Geoffrey will agree, I shan't let Miles know I've given a thought to another man. Not until this horrible thing blows over.'

'If it ever does. As I see it, Miles will either pay up and go on paying, or else he'll fight and probably get involved in some disastrous case. Anyway, I'll talk to my solicitor tomorrow. And perhaps your boy friend can give some helpful advice. You did say he was a barrister?'

She nodded assent. 'Funny you didn't meet him that night at the Civic Reception.'

'I didn't go to it, remember? I drove back to London as soon as the curtain came down on the play. Even then Miles was a bit obsessed by that boy.'

'Blast you, Tom.'

'All right, all right. But he was. When will you see Thornton?'

'Tonight, God help me. The girls will be expecting me now.'

'You'll keep this from them?'

'Of course. But I must show Geoffrey the letter.' She held out her hand for it.

'I'll need to copy it for my solicitor. Don't worry, I'll leave out anything that might identify Miles. You'd better have a drink, love – you've got a difficult evening ahead of you. Just help yourself.'

Well, as it was unlikely that any stimulant would be pressed on her at the Thorntons' . . . She said, 'Thanks, Tom,' and from his drinks table looked back at him and thought how unexpected his reactions had been. He had increased, not calmed, her fears. And though she knew he would do everything in his power to help, she felt he was basically unsympathetic towards Miles's homosexuality. She was equally surprised by the warmth of his sympathy with her, personally. Up to now she had taken it for granted that he considered her as simply an adjunct to Miles.

He finished copying the letter, then looked up and smiled. 'No use telling you not to worry, but you might try counting your blessings. You've quite a distinguished man who wants to marry you, and a husband who will, almost certainly, put your interests before his own.'

'I can't let him.'

'That'll depend on how much you're in love – and on Geoffrey Thornton, of course.'

'Tom – oh, perhaps you can't say until you've spoken to the solicitor, but is there anything we ought to *do*? Go to that pub, try to spot who's waiting for Miles? Perhaps go to Cyril, try to reason with him?'

'We can do nothing until we've talked to Miles – and please heaven he does telephone me at the weekend. Then he must come home – unless . . .'

'Unless what?'

'If he's guilty, he might do well to stay where he is.'

'What, for the rest of his life?'

'God, I don't know. We're trying to work in the dark. Finish your drink, love, and let me clear you out. I've all my letters to sign.'

He saw her through the outer office and to the staircase, promising to ring her next day, 'Probably about noon.'

'I'll wait in till you ring. Bless you, Tom, dear.'

Hurrying out into the late afternoon sunlight, she found the narrow street congested with traffic; no hope of getting a taxi. This extraordinary, stirred-with-a-stick neighbourhood; she had known it well in her impoverished youth, often shopped in Berwick Market. But since then the atmosphere had become even more raffish: sinister, really. Dimly she remembered that Cyril, very suitably, lived in Soho. How did she know that? Presumably Miles had told her, in the days when he talked so much of Cyril. It almost *had* amounted to an obsession. Oh, God, she was as bad as Tom.

She got a taxi in Shaftesbury Avenue and sank into it with relief. But she was still thinking of Miles's obsessive interest and this now awoke a memory that shook her. That first night at the hotel in Spa Street when, before falling asleep, she had wondered why Miles – up by moonlit Queen's Crescent – had been in need of reassurance. It had flickered through her mind that he was sometimes solicitous, even apologetic, before starting an affair. Could it be that? She had pushed the idea away from her, which hadn't been difficult, seeing that he had been so fully occupied with the play and there was no one connected with it who could conceivably interest him. But suppose, even then . . . ? Again she pushed the idea away. But this time with incomplete success.

As usual, both girls welcomed her at the door of the Westminster house. She tried to behave normally but within a very few minutes they were asking her what was wrong. Possibly she'd given herself away by her disappointment on hearing their father was not yet back. 'It's just that I'm tired,' she said feebly. 'Could I lie down for a few minutes?' – anything to get away from them until she had talked to Geoffrey.

They escorted her to the divan in their sitting room, then left her alone. But soon Robin came back and said, 'I've brought you a drink. We felt you needed one.'

Jill found herself offered a tumbler full of neat brandy. 'Oh, darling Robin,' she said, laughing weakly. 'How *noble* of you, feeling as you do.'

'It's probably a silly way to feel. Anyway, Kit and I were saying only this morning that you'll hardly fancy having freakish step-daughters, so we think we ought to learn to

255

drink – well, in just a small way. It's weak-minded to be afraid of becoming alcoholics. See, I'll take a little sip of brandy.'

'No!' said Jill, hastily.

But Robin had already taken her sip. 'Gosh, isn't it filthy? I can't see myself becoming a brandy drunkard.'

Jill, too, disliked brandy but she made herself swallow a mouthful. Then she set the glass down.

'Oh, I'm sure you need more than that,' said Robin.

Mercifully, Kit then returned, bringing her father with her, and both girls tactfully slid out of the room. Jill said, 'Dear Robin not only brought a drink, she took a sip of it herself, to encourage me. I feel she was risking hell-fire for me.'

'Good God!' said Geoffrey, investigating the contents of the tumbler. 'I'd no idea she was so naive about drink. I'll have to teach her. Now, sweetheart, what's the trouble?'

He had never before called her sweetheart and it brought tears to her eyes. He sat down on the divan and took her in his arms, holding her silently for a moment. Then, almost brusquely, he said, 'Now out with it, Jill. Has it to do with Miles?'

'Yes, but it's nothing we could have expected.' She took the letter from her bag and began explaining, describing Cyril's visit to the flat, and rushing on to her interview with Tom.

'Just let me read the letter quietly,' said Geoffrey, putting on his spectacles.

It was the first time she had seen him wear them. They

256

changed him considerably, made him look older, more severe. But his face, in repose, was always a little severe – or did she only mean controlled? Perhaps it was a typical legal face. She found herself contrasting the letter's effect oh him with its effect on Tom – who had shown dismay before he had read half a dozen lines. Geoffrey, for all the emotion he displayed, might have been studying a brief.

Even when he looked up she could not judge his reactions. He merely said, 'There are several words I haven't made out but the gist's clear enough. One wonders if the boy's a very amateur blackmailer or diabolically clever.'

'It's all lies, Geoffrey. Of course it is.'

'It's certainly hard to believe Miles would assault the boy *after* hearing how young he was – and in a flat to which you were liable to return at any moment. You gave me some pretty incoherent information about that a moment ago. Give it to me again, slowly.'

As she did so, it seemed to her that every word told against Miles – far more so than when she had told Tom, because Geoffrey asked searching questions and unearthed facts she had not before remembered, none of them reassuring. He made no comment and even when she finally said, 'Oh, I know you can't be sure but please tell me what you think,' he merely said he hadn't the right to think anything. 'Nothing you've told me proves anything. And remember, I don't know Miles well – and Cyril scarcely at all. Kit, I believe, rather liked him. It will be interesting to see what she makes of this letter.'

257

'You can't mean you'll tell the girls –'

He cut her short and with a hint of impatience. 'Of course I must tell them. They're on tenterhooks to know what's wrong with you. And, my dearest Jill, you must get it into your head that I don't shelter them from this kind of thing. They'd take it as an insult. Incidentally, it's probable that Kit knows more about this type of offence than I do. When she studied homosexuality on Julian's account she took in some side lines. Now try to relax, while I talk to the girls. There's no need for you to see them yet.'

As he got up, she said urgently, 'There's one thing I want to know at once. I promised you I'd leave Miles, but you won't hold me to that now? Surely I must stand by him?'

He barely hesitated. 'Yes, I see that. If you walked out on him now . . . Don't worry. I shan't ask that of you.'

She said, 'Thank you, darling.' But as the door closed behind him she knew that, though she had asked the question in good faith to Miles, Geoffrey's answer had not come as a relief. It had filled her with dismay.

✄ 15 ✄

Love Letter

She woke early in the flat next day after what she reckoned
must be around three hours' sleep. She had certainly been
still awake when Big Ben struck four. She had a bath and
dressed; then made strong coffee, carried it into the sitting
room, and settled down to review the situation. She had
reviewed it again and again during the night but had a
faint hope that by daylight – and the room was flooded
with sunlight – she might feel more optimistic. Most of all,
she longed to get a more hopeful slant on the previous
evening.

Geoffrey had returned from talking to the girls to say
Kit was sure Miles was guiltless. 'And it wasn't only an
instinctive reaction. She says Cyril spoke of Miles with such
admiration, that night of your party. And when she and
Robin went to tea at the theatre Cyril was there and
Miles's behaviour to him didn't fit with anything but

259

normal kindness. Robin's not as definite as Kit but says she can't imagine it. Well, God knows I can't do that. Anyway, the girls think I should take you out to dinner. They quite understand you'd find it difficult to discuss the matter with them.'

His manner had been kindness itself and he had been kind throughout the evening. He had taken her to a quiet restaurant where their conversation could not be overheard. He had let her talk on and on – God, how she must have repeated herself. He had said, again and again, that he would do everything in his power to help. He, like Tom, would get expert advice in the morning. Never having been briefed in any case involving blackmail, he did not feel particularly knowledgeable. He had been patient, gentle, cheerful, without being annoyingly so. But he had not told her that, sooner or later, whether Miles was guilty or innocent, whether Miles paid blackmail or ended up in jail, she *must* leave him. Not once was she made to feel that her divorce, and subsequent marriage to Geoffrey, were still taken for granted.

And while they talked it occurred to her that, if the Digby brothers accused Miles to the police, the resultant case would create a far worse scandal than a divorce. She had worried because even a divorce might damage Miles's career and also affect Geoffrey's. But a divorce would be as nothing compared with a prosecution. Would Geoffrey's constituency stand for his marrying a woman who had been connected with anything so spectacularly unsavoury? Was he thinking about that and not merely agreeing she should stand by Miles because it was the decent thing to do?

This fear had been the worst bogey of her night. Now, sitting drinking cup after cup of coffee in the bright morning, she tried to vanquish it but without success. Of course Geoffrey must be thinking along such lines – and who could blame him, when he had only so recently begun a new life after the long misery of his marriage? And she now saw that it was her duty to stand by Miles not only for his sake but also for Geoffrey's. She ought to make it clear that she must now stay with Miles for good. Even if he paid blackmail he would never be safe. And if he went to jail she must wait for him and, if necessary, clear out of England with him. It was up to *her* to decide all this, and take the onus off Geoffrey. But she couldn't, she couldn't –

The post came, bringing only some bills. The morning papers came. Well, one could at least try to read them. One could not go on and on thinking; but one did.

Around ten-thirty Geoffrey telephoned to say he was consulting someone at eleven and would afterwards come straight to the flat. He sounded brisk and unaffectionate. Well, what else could she expect as he was telephoning from his office – no, barristers' offices were called 'chambers', weren't they? How ignorant she was about his work, both at the Bar and in the House of Commons. He'd said it didn't matter, but it did. From every point of view she ought to clear out of his life.

She went back to the morning papers. An article on the

South of France made her wonder if Miles was there. She hoped he might be having a last few days of happiness. She wished him that even if . . . God, how could she suspect him? She had always thought him the best man she had ever known.

She counted on hearing from Tom by noon. He did not come through until twelve-thirty and then he had nothing helpful to say. His solicitor shared his gloomy view that Miles might simply have to pay up – 'And be grateful that Cyril's talking in terms of hundreds, not thousands. Though he may enlarge his demands once he's tasted blood. But nothing can be decided until we can contact Miles. Well, keep cheerful, love.'

She had barely hung up before Geoffrey arrived. He kissed her, but it was a brief kiss. And he had received much the same advice as Tom had. But his own attitude was less defeatist – 'Miles may insist on fighting, whatever the cost. I believe I would.'

'You mean if you were innocent.'

'Which I've begun to feel Miles must be. Kit's views impressed me and she was even more determined this morning. If she's right, Cyril would almost certainly crumple in the witness box. But Miles's homosexuality would come out. That's the snag.'

She forced herself to say, 'Geoffrey, I think you should now bow out of this whole horrible business. You must consider your career. I was a bad enough hazard when I just had a homosexual husband but now –'

He said with judicial calmness, 'My dear, aren't you

piling things on? Perhaps it's because, as a woman, you're particularly outraged at what may – and *only* may – have been a crime against a child. You should remember that for a considerable period Miles thought Cyril was eighteen. Psychologically, at least, that's some excuse.'

She looked at him wonderingly. 'How kind you are towards Miles; even though, as a normal man, you probably have an abhorrence of homosexuals. Tom Albion obviously has.'

'That may be because they've caused him a lot of worry – as well as earned him a lot of money. And his background and education may have something to do with it. I remember talking to him at your party. Am I right in taking it he didn't go to a public school?'

She smiled. 'Tom? Good heavens, no.'

'Few men who did are completely lacking in . . . not so much understanding as acceptance of homosexuality. I consider myself fully male but, at school, I had friends who weren't and I even felt attracted by them; but it was an idyllic attraction, not physical. I've remained friendly with a couple of them and highly distinguished men they are. So's Miles. And I should be ashamed of myself if I felt revulsion for him, or felt that I was better than he is. Though I'll admit I should be shocked if he assaulted Cyril, both on the score of morals and sheer bad taste.'

'He didn't. Of course he didn't.'

'Only you're not sure, my love. You're shattered by doubt, which must be agony for you. Well, remember that he's entitled to the benefit of your doubts.'

'I oughtn't to doubt him, knowing him as I do. It's just that . . . I no longer *feel* I know him. Something there used to be between us is gone. I think it went when I fell in love with you. But I must be loyal to him, Geoffrey.'

'Of course you must, for the present. But not for ever. Now I must go.'

He took her in his arms but held her for only a moment, then said he was sorry he couldn't stay with her. 'I've an appointment I haven't been able to cancel. But I can be home by five. Will you be there by then? And try not to mind talking to the girls. Remember they're not shocked, just eager to help.'

'I shan't mind talking to them now.'

Coming back from seeing him out she momentarily felt there was nothing she would now mind, so great was her relief at those four words, 'But not for ever.' She repeated them to herself again and again. Perhaps she ought not to let them prove true – for his sake as well as Miles's. Perhaps she would be strong enough not to. But he had said them. She lay down on the sofa and closed her eyes. 'But not for ever.' Still clinging to the words, she drifted into sleep.

She was awakened by the telephone. On her way to answer it she caught sight of the clock and realized she had slept nearly three hours. She felt dazed, and apprehensive of more trouble, but the voice that spoke to her was cheerful and loving, if a trifle shaky.

'Jill, darling, this is Kit. Could you come here rather quickly? And could you let yourself in? I've put the key under the mat. Robin's taken Mary to buy a coat – Mary's

264

nervous of London shops – so I'm on my own. And I'll be in bed.'

'Kit! Are you ill?'

'Well, I just may be suffering from deferred shock. I think you can have it without knowing – and I did feel a bit groggy when I got back. Anyway, I'm going to bed with two hot-water bottles and I've drunk some disgustingly sweet tea – that's how you treat shock. And I do particularly want to see you. So if you could manage –'

'I'll come instantly. But oughtn't I to get a doctor?'

'Oh, no, no, no. That would be madly embarrassing. And I'm sure I'm all right, except that I suddenly feel sick. So I'll hang up if you don't mind.'

'Right, darling. I'll simply rush to you.'

She was lucky enough to get a taxi that had just brought someone, and was at the Westminster house in less than ten minutes. She found the key, opened the door and dashed upstairs. Half way up she heard Kit calling, 'Is that you, Jill? I'm fine now.'

Jill, entering the bedroom full tilt, thought she had never seen the child look so well, though the bright cheeks might indicate feverishness. She was sitting up in bed wearing a fetching Shetland bed jacket trimmed with swansdown.

'That sickness was a false alarm,' she assured Jill. 'Perhaps it was because I so hate sweet tea.'

'You're a bit flushed, Kit.'

'Oh, that's just heat. I wonder if I got the treatment wrong? It can't be good for a shocked person to be so hot.'

'Darling, what shocked you?'

Kit, leaning back on her pillows, said pedantically, 'Shock isn't due to being shocked in the ordinary sense of the word. Mentally, nothing shocks me; I should be ashamed if it did. A *state* of shock, physical shock, comes from being in an accident, and I *think* great excitement or severe nervous strain can cause it too. Not that I've been conscious of strain; I've really had a very jolly afternoon. But I *was* excited.'

'What about, Kit? Please tell me quickly.'

'I've been to see Cyril.'

'Oh, *Kit!*'

'Well, nobody told me not to. I knew where he lived in Soho because we drove him home after your party. Jill, you wouldn't believe the squalor. He and his brother live in just one room of an old house in a sort of court – I mean, it's a dead end. A horrible place, looks as if it's full of brothels – well, eighteenth-century brothels; I should think modern brothels would have to be smarter. There were masses of old cardboard boxes and broken crates, and rotting vegetables which smelt awful. And the house – such a shame, fine panelling in the hall, all hacked about and scribbled on, not that I'd time to read the graffiti – well, the smell there was mainly lavatories. It was so awful that I almost turned tail – filth's more upsetting than danger, don't you think? Though I'll admit I got more scared than was pleasant – oh, not of Cyril, I knew I could manage him with one hand, but I thought the brother might be there with razor blades and what not. I only thought of razor blades when I was on my way upstairs.

266

A very haggish woman told me where the Digbys lived.'

'Oh, God, Kit! *Was* the brother there?'

'He was not. He's in jail because he did slash someone with a razor blade, in a fight yesterday. And I should think he'd get a long sentence unless they send him back to Borstal. And there was poor Cyril, not knowing which way to turn and his face all puffed with crying, and he began again as soon as I started work on him. I almost frightened him to death. You see, I took a gun.'

'A real gun?'

'Well, perhaps it's too small to be called one. I must investigate firearms. It was in a cabinet in our great-grandmother's house. After she died, Father said we could take anything we liked, but I'm not sure he knew I picked the gun – if it is one. It's tiny and beautifully inlaid.'

'Is it loaded?'

'I've no idea. I didn't try to find out in case it went off. It's in my coat pocket, if you'd care to look. Taking it was melodramatic but I thought it might frighten the brother off. Of course I didn't have to frighten Cyril off – the mere mention of a gun made him go weak at the knees, though I think he felt even worse when I said the letter might be shown to the police. He'd hardly be *persona grata* with them seeing that his brother's been a criminal for years. And the poor child really is very sorry. He's hoping Mr Quentin need never know about the letter. It was the brother who made him write it, of course.'

'Then it's all lies?'

Kit hesitated and then spoke thoughtfully. 'Well, it's

only fair to say that it wasn't quite lies to Cyril when he wrote it. His brother made him believe that Mr Quentin wouldn't have been so kind without, well, some ulterior motive. Cyril said, "Doug said he *must* have been after me. And he did put his arm round me." Cyril got worked up into believing things happened that never did – in fact, he couldn't have written that letter if he hadn't pretended to himself that it was true. He said, "It was like being in a play, it was *sort* of real – just for a while." He has a lot of imagination, Jill. And strange as it may seem, I still like him – which is just as well because I'll probably have him round my neck for ages. I mean, when you smash anyone down as I smashed Cyril today, you have to rehabilitate them. Anyway, he's coming to tea tomorrow. You could come too.'

'No,' said Jill, chokingly. 'I never want to see him again.'

'Jill, what's the matter? Surely you're pleased?'

'Of course. It's just that –' But she couldn't possibly explain. And somehow, somehow she must get out of the house.

'Jill, what *is* it? Oh, goodness, are *you* suffering from shock now?'

Jill managed a smile. 'No, I couldn't be better. But – darling, how soon will Robin be back?'

'Any minute now. Jill –'

'Then will you be all right on your own till then? I have to . . . there's something I must do.'

'But what, Jill? Oh, do you want to dash to Mr Albion and warn him it's to be a secret from Mr Quentin?'

'Yes,' said Jill. Anything to get away.

'Well, there's no need – because I rang Mr Albion before I rang you; I knew from Father that Mr Quentin might be telephoning soon. So you don't have to go. Father will be home soon and we'll all have a marvellous evening. Can't you take it in, Jill? Everything's all right.'

'No,' said Jill, her control snapping. 'And it'll never be all right. Never! Never!'

She ran from the room. And Kit, leaping out of bed, came after her begging her not to go.

At the back of Jill's mind a still sane woman said, 'Don't fall down the stairs or you'll never get out of the house.'

From above came Kit's wail, 'Jill, please! You mustn't rush out into the street in a state of shock.'

'Leave me alone!' Jill shouted up. 'Don't come after me! Don't any of you come after me! Tell your father not to!'

She was in the hall now and, in another second, through the front door. She slammed it behind her and raced along the quiet street. When she reached the end of it she turned, half expecting to see a nightgowned figure coming after her. But Kit, now standing at the front door, did not attempt to follow.

The still sane woman now became dominant. 'It's no use running. There's nowhere to run to. But you'll be slightly better off in the flat. You can take the telephone off and refuse to open the door. They can't drag you out by force. And by tomorrow you may have the strength of mind to break things off with decency.' She hailed, successfully, a cruising taxi.

Already she was ashamed of herself. Never before had she so lost control. How could she have treated Kit so badly – and when the child had been through such an experience? She should have been thanked, most lovingly, for accomplishing a miracle. She could hardly be blamed because she had also plunged one into an abyss of guilt from which one could never climb. But one could at least force oneself to behave like a civilized human being.

No, she wouldn't take the receiver off the telephone. When Geoffrey rang up she would simply say she didn't feel well enough to see him. And then she would write and tell him that she had changed her mind and now wished to remain with Miles. That shouldn't be hard to write convincingly, as it was the truth.

And after all, Miles would never know of her guilt, her utter lack of loyalty. To have believed Cyril's letter! Perhaps she had wanted to believe it. Yes, that was it. A Miles less worth caring for set her free to care for Geoffrey – as she would never now be free.

She paid the taxi off, tipped the driver generously, smiled at the hall porter and said good evening to a fellow tenant with whom she shared the lift. From now on, one *behaved*.

The flat was surprisingly chilly; she saw that the french windows to the balcony had blown wide open. On her way to close them she noticed a long envelope leaning against the telephone. It was addressed simply to 'Jill.' Surely the handwriting was Miles's? And who else could have got into the flat and put the letter there? He must be back.

She was suddenly frightened. The wide-open windows
. . . and why should he leave a letter for her? He sometimes
scribbled messages on the telephone pad if he came in
when she was out but, judging by the weight, this was a
long letter. There were some pencilled words on the back
of the envelope but she was too sickly dizzy to read them.
Then she steadied herself. The entrance to the flats was
almost under the balcony. There had been no signs of any
disturbance, the hall porter had smiled at her – and Miles
was the last man to leave her a legacy of suicide. Her vision
cleared and she read the pencilled words. 'Just back.
Meant to put this through the letter box but as the hall
porter told me you've just gone off in a taxi I've been in
and grabbed a few things I needed.'

She sat down and tore open the envelope. The letter
had been written in Venice, the previous day. It read:

My dearest Jill,

It's strange how seldom I've written to you – no, not
strange really, considering we've so seldom been apart
except for those periods when I've felt unable to write.
This, by the way, isn't one of those times. I am quite
alone.

I'd better start by saying I have known about you and
Geoffrey almost since you first met. Oh, I don't mean
you both showed signs of falling in love on sight. And I
didn't at first know what it was I knew. Perhaps it was
simply that seeing you with him and the girls, even that
very first time in the hotel lounge, gave me a pang. I

271

suddenly saw you as you might have been as a normally married woman with charming children – though you'd have had to make a very early start to be Robin's mother. Later that evening we climbed innumerable steps to look at a very beautiful terrace and we talked – I wonder if you remember – about our marriage. That was somehow connected with having seen you with the Thorntons. I had a feeling of guilt.

During the week I wasn't too preoccupied with the play to notice Geoffrey's growing admiration. And though I can't say you showed signs of being in love – I doubt if you knew you were – when you were with the Thorntons you blossomed. Back in London I was more and more sure. I wasn't playing at detectives – indeed, I think I was trying *not* to be sure and anyway I was busy with the play, all the changes and poor Cyril's woes (remind me to tell you about those; he'd been using his brother's birth certificate). But – well, I was dead sure after you went with Geoffrey to his country house. You gave nothing away in words but you looked . . . as you always should have looked.

Will you believe me if I say I was glad? All right, don't. But I did tell myself I ought to be and I honestly believe I would have been, if it had happened earlier. When we married I took it for granted that you'd eventually have affairs – you'd been, from what you told me, a fairly sexy girl and I didn't expect you to turn into a nun. But you did, and damn near turned me into a monk. My occasional flings were more of a duty than a pleasure.

272

Every now and then I'd tell myself, 'Good God, you can't bow out of sex at your age.' And then I'd dash off with some usually embarrassing companion – and find myself missing you, and also worrying in case you minded. But don't feel responsible for any of this. The truth is that for me sex isn't very attractive without love. I've never loved anyone but Alan and you. With Alan, love and sex were a complete whole. With you, love has been the whole.

Well, as I was saying, I would have been glad for you if it had happened in our early days. And though I'd become a bit possessive over the years, I knew I'd no right to be. Also I thought that after a riotous affair with Geoffrey you'd come back to me as I've always come back to you. But you didn't seem to be starting an affair and I wondered if something in you (I suppose I mean what you felt for me) was resisting Geoffrey – so I decided to put up some counter attractions, such as getting a car, taking a country house, a Continental holiday. I even, that night you mentioned the Austrian waiter, invited you to reverse that very sensible decision you made all those years ago. How well I remember you sitting in that meadow, twiddling a very queer flower I'd picked for you. I afterwards learned that its name was a Wild Man – suitable flower for me as regards its queerness but God knows I never was wild (though in German the Wilde has an 'e,' which links nicely with Oscar).

Incidentally, don't imagine things would have worked

out better if you'd decided otherwise. My suggestion was
made from the most loving desire for your happiness,
but as a lover of women (off-stage) I'd probably have
been embarrassing if not farcical and you might have
turned agin me. As for children, I fancy it's pretty hellish
to have a homosexual father.

So – where was I? Ah, yes, thinking I might compete
with Geoffrey. And then – it was the night the play
ended, when we came back to the flat and you told me
he'd been there – I realized I was behaving most
selfishly. I ought to *encourage* you to leap over the wall of
your self-erected nunnery, not confuse you by suggesting
we should go abroad together – those travel brochures
I'd made you get looked at me accusingly. And my best
way of encouraging you was to clear out of England and
let you construe this as you rightly have in the past. I
thought that would help you to throw off your inhibitions
and, when I came back, I'd come out into the open and
give you my blessing.

The extraordinary thing is that it never once entered
my head that you and Geoffrey wanted to marry. No
doubt it should have but it simply didn't and I doubt if
it ever would have but for – prepare for a dramatic
encounter! Me, sitting in St Mark's Square wondering
what you were up to. A god-like youth comes strolling
towards me, smiling. Who is it? Yes – no – yes! None
other than the lordly Julian Thornton!

My, I wouldn't care to be that boy's father – nor
would I fancy any other relationship with him. Actually

he's not queer – yet. We discussed this. I gather he's sitting on the fence, *comme ci, comme ça,* depending on how his feelings and the main chance sway him. A cool, calculating lad – though some of it's put on, and I ended up by liking him. And I shall be eternally grateful to him for his frankness about you and his father. It seems that the whole Thornton family is bursting to acquire you for keeps. Julian, blast his impertinence, thinks you 'eminently suitable.' And so you are, my dear, and I can't think why I didn't see it before – especially when I did, in a way, see it that first day in the hotel lounge.

Of course that chance meeting with Julian only short-circuited things. Sooner or later, Geoffrey would have *insisted* on your leaving me – as I do, now. No arguments, love, and no more inhibitions, soul-searchings or whatever it is that has been holding you back. It's all settled. By the time you read this I shall have posted a letter to Geoffrey asking him to meet me and fix everything up. He'll know the best way. I imagine 'wilful refusal to consummate the marriage' (on my part, of course) will be all right. Nowadays such cases seem only to rate a few lines in the papers – though whether this is the law, or just decency on the part of the newspapers I don't know. Anyway, if I do get unwelcome publicity I bloody well don't care. There are times when I feel that those of us who have a little celebrity ought to stand up and be counted. I'm not one of those queers who think that medals should be struck for us but I do think we might be taken for granted, as if we'd simply been born with club feet or extra long ears or something. The fact that some of us like having club-footed long ears – and don't consider them disfiguring – is neither here nor there.

This isn't a farewell letter – I shall be in touch with you as soon as I've talked to Geoffrey. And we'll meet and go on meeting. Those Thorntons are going to find they've not only gained a wife and stepmother but also landed themselves with her devoted hanger-on. And one tiny, sordid detail. During the past ten years you've devoted your entire life to helping me make a considerable amount of money. Some of that, from every conceivable point of view, belongs to you and you will, my girl, accept it.

That's almost all – and it had better be, or I shall be smitten with writer's cramp before I can write to Geoffrey. But there's one last thing I want to say and it's more difficult than the whole of the rest of this letter, because I'm so terrified you'll misunderstand me. Please don't. I force myself to say it because it's my best hope of setting you quite free. Well, here goes. It's *just* conceivable that being deprived of you may enable me to find someone for whom I can feel just a little of what I felt for Alan. Loving you – so genuinely loving you – has meant that I've had no genuine love to spare for anyone else. So I've only had meaningless affairs. Perhaps it's too late for anything else but one never knows. This does *not* mean that our marriage was a mistake and I'm not going to pretend that I wouldn't have liked it to go on for ever. Losing you will be like losing a limb – oh, worse than that. Still, compensation isn't utterly out of the question. Tell yourself that – but at the same time tell yourself that I am your most truly loving

MILES

P.S. No use trying to find me. I shall remain elusive until I've talked to Geoffrey. By the way, I like him very much. And I adore the girls.

She folded the letter and put it back in its envelope. Soon she would read it again but, for the moment, she just wanted to think about Miles. She imagined him writing, probably in a hotel bedroom, with the sounds of Venice coming up to him. Page after page of neat, legible writing . . . she had often heard him say he wrote a schoolboy hand and she knew he believed that homosexuality was largely due to continued adolescence. But she found nothing immature in the contents of the letter.

She felt closer to him now than she had felt for weeks . . . perhaps closer than she had ever felt. It was as if a veil, a veil of reticence between them, had lifted. She knew him now not so much with her mind as with her heart – to which, without conscious volition, she had clasped the letter as if for comfort. Realizing this, she put the letter down. It had no talismanic quality to help her now. Nothing had. She must just sit back and let the waves of regret wash over her.

In the taxi, coming back from Westminster, she had

decided to stay with him because it seemed her best way of making up for her traitorous disloyalty. She had told herself that she wished it, but she had also thought of it as a penance. Now, if he could suddenly come into the flat with the past weeks blotted out, how gladly would she resume their life together, their easy companionship, their trust in each other's affection. How utterly she had betrayed that trust. It seemed to her now that not only should she have disbelieved Cyril's accusation; she ought also to have known she would still care for Miles if the accusation were true. Sex was a besieging force, outside the essential self. It could drive out decency and reason. Whatever Miles had done, the essential Miles would have remained the same. But Miles hadn't done anything. It was *her* decency and reason which had been driven out. Well, perhaps no wonder, seeing that she had for ten years lived, as Tom said, in a state of suspended animation. That rendered one vulnerable.

She had also lived in a state of great comfort, even luxury. Food, warmth, clothes and, above all, absence of anxiety . . . compared with the hell of her early years, life with Miles had been pretty like heaven. And as sex had brought her little but misery she had barely felt the lack of it. But it had been there all the time, tunneling, undermining – and sometimes coming to the surface surely? Had there not been days when she had scanned the face of almost every man she met – scanned even the faces of strangers – wondering, seeking? But the seeking had been swiftly repressed; always she had reminded herself of past misery, concentrated on present contentment. The state of suspended animation had been self-induced.

That day she had first met Geoffrey . . . she saw herself strolling along Spa Street, in the afternoon sunshine, remembering her youthful self. She had been fully conscious then of the lack in her life. Perhaps her need had somehow materialized Geoffrey, brought about everything that had happened since. But now she could not feel even a flicker of desire for him. There had been more than desire when they sat here together in silence. Was that all gone too? Perhaps something would creep back, when she let it. But for the moment she only wanted to wrap the years with Miles round her, especially those womb-like years in the old Islington house. But even the months in this flat now seemed valuable.

Where was Miles now? If only she could reach him! Oh, she wouldn't try to persuade him, it wouldn't work. But she would be thankful just to be with him for an hour or two. Well, she could be, perhaps even tomorrow. But by then their life together would be a thing of the past. She wanted to prolong it . . . just a little longer.

The doorbell rang. She ignored it. There was nothing to prove she was in. It rang again. Then the flap of the letter box was pushed in and Kit's voice came through.

'Jill, darling, are you there? Oh, you *are* – I can see a bit of you through the sitting-room door. *Please* let us in.'

Then Robin spoke. 'Jill, dear, Kit's terribly worried in case something she said upset you. Do let us come in – for just a moment. Father, you speak to her.'

Geoffrey said, 'At least let us know you're not ill.'

'But she is, Father,' said Kit. 'She must be.'

Well, one must behave. One must not alarm people. But the voices had dispersed the last lingering warmth of the years with Miles. And as she called out that she was coming she thought of herself as plunging into cold water. But one could get used to cold water, find it stimulating. And the great Thornton take-over bid would soon be a completed operation.

She flung the door open with resentment – and found herself gasping, 'Oh, my darlings, how could I worry you so? I'm perfectly all right, everything's all right. And I love you all.'